THE
WEDDING
GUEST

BOOKS BY KATHRYN CROFT

THE
WEDDING
GUEST

Kathryn Croft

bookouture

Published by Bookouture in 2023

An imprint of Storyfire Ltd.
Carmelite House
50 Victoria Embankment
London EC4Y 0DZ

www.bookouture.com

ISBN: 978-1-83790-685-7
eBook ISBN: 978-1-83790-684-0

For Pamela Garland
Always remembered
x

ONE

NOW

I stand on the balcony of our villa, watching the turquoise sea gently caress the shimmering white sand, and for the first time I let myself believe that I might be free. It is my past that holds me captive. And no matter how much time passes, it hovers by my side like a shadow I can't detach from. But today, I will allow myself to exhale. Today is the beginning.

'Don't you look lovely, Emily!'

Jeremy's mother Pam is leaning against the doorway, smiling, and I wonder how long she's been standing there. I had been mesmerised by the waves and lost myself for a moment, so I failed to hear her approach.

Does this mean I've finally stopped looking over my shoulder?

'That dress is just beautiful.' Pam offers a nod of approval as she walks towards me. 'Stunning.'

It's understated. A long slip dress that skims my body rather than clinging to it. And it's not white, but ivory. In my hair is a simple light pink peony. I've never been married before, but I couldn't bear the thought of wearing white. It's meant to represent innocence and purity. Neither of these are words I can apply to myself. But as well as this, I don't like being on show. All eyes on me, studying me. If people look too hard, or for too long, then what might they see?

Pam places her hands on my arms. Despite her kindness, I almost flinch. 'You've made Jeremy so happy,' she says. 'And Lexi, too, of course. I never thought I'd see either of them smile again after...' She trails off, letting go of my arms, and I'm glad she doesn't summon ghosts to haunt this day. Not when this morning I'm determined to keep darkness at bay. For all of us.

'Well, I feel so blessed to have found them,' I say. And I mean every word. There isn't a passing second when I'm not filled with gratitude for Jeremy and his ten-year-old daughter Lexi coming into my life. Saving me. 'You look lovely too, by the way.' I'm not just humouring her; Pam has an innate sense of style.

'Oh, this.' Pam gestures to the pale orange sundress she's wearing. The straps show off her thin, lightly tanned arms; she's been here in Kefalonia for a week already so has caught the sun. 'It's not what I would have chosen for a wedding, of course, but it's so hot here, isn't it? Comfort first.' She smiles. 'I'm sorry your mum couldn't be here to see this day. She'd be so proud of you.'

The lump in my throat threatens to choke me, yet somehow I manage a thank you. 'I have *you*, though, don't I? I have everything I could possibly want right here.'

'Oh, Emily... you'll have me in tears in a minute.' She takes my arm. 'But I meant what I said. You've been so good for my son and granddaughter. After everything they went through... I'd hate to—'

'There you are.' Jeremy's voice fills the room, causing Pam and me to turn towards the door. 'Come on, Mum, it's time to take your seat.'

The sight of him in his tuxedo, his face freshly shaved, stops my breath.

Pam rushes to him. 'No,' she says, ushering him away. 'Out!

You can't be in here. You're not supposed to see the bride yet. It's bad luck, Jeremy! Don't look at Emily.'

I'm not superstitious, but a knot forms in my stomach. I don't believe in perfection, but I need this day to go smoothly.

Jeremy laughs and stays where he is. 'Oh, Mum – that's all nonsense. Do you know how many mirrors I've broken in my life?'

I'm relieved he doesn't add what we he and I both must be thinking: he didn't see Tia on their wedding day, yet look how that turned out.

No ghosts. Not today.

'It's tradition,' Pam insists. 'Now, go! You'll ruin everything.' She flaps her arms, but again Jeremy ignores her attempt to coax him out of the room.

'Mum, I need to talk to Emily,' he insists. 'Just for a second. Anyway, I've seen her now.' Jeremy looks at me and smiles, his whole face brightening. 'Wow.'

'Oh dear,' Pam mutters, rolling her eyes as she makes her way out. 'What are you two like? Don't say I didn't warn you.' She pulls the door shut behind her.

When we're alone, Jeremy takes my hand and leads me to the end of the bed, easing me down so we're both sitting. 'I had to see you before,' he says. 'I don't believe any of that crazy superstitious stuff, do you?' He kisses my forehead.

'No.' I wrap my arms around him, breathe in the scent of his shower gel.

But who knows? There are so many things we can't under-stand in this universe.

'Good,' Jeremy says. 'Because nothing can ruin this day. Even if a tsunami came along, I wouldn't care. It's only the three of us that matter. I mean, I'd prefer it if we got to say our vows first, of course. But then after that, we're ready for anything, right?'

I nod. 'Nothing or no one else matters. Just us.' It's a mantra

I've been repeating silently for months now. I take his hand, noticing how smooth and cool his skin feels. 'What did you need to talk to me about?'

'Oh, yeah. I just wanted to tell you that... I love you. And nothing could ever change that. Eyes wide open, yeah?'

Eyes wide open. It's what we've been saying to each other since we got together. Everything is laid out on the table. No skeletons. No lies. So that we both go into this with full knowledge of each other.

Yet I am lying to the man I'm about to marry.

I am not the woman he thinks I am.

'Eyes wide open,' I repeat. I let go of his hand. 'You'd better go before people start thinking we're having second thoughts.' I laugh to mask my nerves.

It's not a large congregation gathered out there on the beach. Some work friends of Jeremy's who could make it out to Kefalonia. Jeremy's mother. His best friend Stuart, who lives in New Zealand. We wanted it this way: small and intimate. No fuss. The only person here for me is Sue, the head teacher from the school I teach at. Over the years I've deliberately kept my circle of acquaintances small; the fewer people I have in my life, the better. It's hard to mask who you are when someone is regularly in your life, more difficult to hide in the shadows. I don't know how I've managed to do it with Jeremy, but he and Lexi are about all I can manage. All I *want* to manage.

He kisses my cheek then leaves, waving from the door before he closes it behind him.

In the bathroom, I check my make-up once more, and smooth down my dress. I'm ready now.

As I close our bedroom door, I smile to myself. The next time I walk into this villa, Emily Thomas will be gone. And I will be someone new, a phoenix rising from the ashes.

Downstairs in the living room, Lexi is waiting for me. The light pink dress she wears is the exact shade of the flower in my hair, and matches the small bouquet of roses and peonies she's holding. Pam sits beside her, smoothing out her dress, and both of them spring up when they see me.

'Oh, Emily, you look so nice,' Lexi says, her smile stretching across her face. 'Daddy will be super happy when he sees you.'

'He already has,' Pam says.

'Isn't that supposed to be bad luck?' Lexi asks.

'Only if you're superstitious,' I counter, glancing at Pam.

My soon-to-be mother-in-law smiles as she hands me my bouquet – a slightly larger version of Lexi's. 'Are you nervous?' she asks.

I smile at her. 'Does it show?'

She laughs. 'Not really. You'll be fine.'

'We've been learning about superstitions at school,' Lexi says, smiling. 'Did you know you should never walk under a ladder? Well, some people think that, anyway. I don't. Or maybe I do. I don't know. Is it all true, Emily?'

I take her hand. 'No, I don't believe so. But no harm in avoiding ladders, is there? Just in case.'

'Or black cats. Or pavement cracks.'

I smile. 'Are you ready to walk with me down the aisle and give me away to your dad?'

Lexi smiles. 'Deal!'

And once again I am left wondering how I got so lucky.

Our villa is right on the beachfront, and the wedding pillars, adorned with green foliage, roses and peonies, have been set up only a few metres away. Behind them, the sea stretches to infinity in a beautiful backdrop. I take off my shoes so I can feel the soft golden sand under my feet, and Lexi giggles as she does the same and slides off her silver ballerina pumps.

I take her hand and we cross the beach, Lexi's chatter floating around me, fuelling me with warmth that's stronger than the sun beating down on us. She squeezes my hand, and it shows me that she and her father do need me; it's not just the other way around.

Up ahead there are three rows of chairs, all of them covered with white lace. There are too many for the number of guests we've invited, and several seats remain empty. Still, it's perfect. Jeremy stands under the flower arch, and even though his eyes are fixed on me, he doesn't forget to smile at Lexi. He looks blissful and content as Stuart, his best man, leans in and shares something that makes them both chuckle. Even the registrar joins in the joke.

'Somewhere Over the Rainbow' by Israel Kamakawiwo'ole starts to play, as Lexi and I, still holding hands, make our way towards the flower arch.

'You made it,' Jeremy whispers, leaning in, and I giggle as his lips tickle my ear.

'Nothing better to do,' I say, smiling.

We deliver our vows as the sun toasts our skin and the waves roll against the shore. Neither of us wanted a protracted ceremony. Instead, we planned it to be short and powerful, eyes not upon us for any longer than necessary. At least that's what *my* aim was. I think Jeremy's was just to marry me as quickly as possible in case I changed my mind.

Everything is perfect. The past is now behind me.

Then, just as the registrar finishes speaking, and Jeremy and I kiss for the first time as husband and wife, I turn to the congregation and see the face of a ghost. Someone I was hoping never to lay eyes on again.

Impossible. I'm just conjuring him up because this is the one day I don't want to acknowledge his existence.

Christian Holmes. He's standing behind the last row of chairs, his hands in his pockets, staring at me. He is out of place in this picture of my life. And in his khaki utility shorts and navy T-shirt, he looks it.

My past catching up with me.

Slowly Christian smiles, but there is no warmth in his gesture. I close my eyes, praying that when I open them he will have disappeared. It wouldn't be the first time my mind has created illusions. Brought on by trauma, I've read. It's been stressful planning this wedding, so perhaps it's anxiety gripping hold of me. But when I open my eyes, Christian is still there. And now he's walking towards me and Jeremy, with too much purpose in his stride. My legs won't support my body for much longer. Almost subconsciously, I let go of Jeremy's hand. I'm moments away from throwing up, all over this expensive ivory wedding gown and the shimmering carpet of sand I'm standing on.

Jeremy frowns as he watches our uninvited guest head towards us. 'Hi, can we help you?' He holds out his hand. He must assume that Christian is one of the locals; with his casual clothes, it would be a reasonable assumption.

'Congratulations,' Christian says, taking Jeremy's hand. His voice causes my stomach to tighten, and a fiery heat flares beneath my cheeks. 'I'm Christian,' he continues. 'A very good friend of Emily's.'

My legs begin to buckle.

This can't be happening. Not now. Not here.

Jeremy glances at me as he shakes Christian's hand. 'Oh, Emily never said you were coming. Sorry, you missed the ceremony.' He turns to me, a question paused on his lips.

'I didn't know...' I manage to say. I turn to Christian and force myself to play along with whatever he's doing. 'You... you never said you could make it.'

'Oh, didn't I? Sorry, Em. I thought I'd RSVPed. My fault. I hope it's okay that I'm here?' He directs his question at Jeremy.

'Of course,' Jeremy says. 'The ceremony wasn't that long, to be honest. Neither of us like to be the centre of attention, if you know what I mean.'

Christian chuckles. 'Yep, I sure do. Don't worry, I saw the part that counts.' He nods. 'Just beautiful.' To Jeremy these words must seem perfectly innocent; only I know they're infused with menace.

'Well, you'll stay for the wedding breakfast of course?' Jeremy asks. 'It's more of a wedding buffet, here on the beach.'

My instinct screams at me to run, to grab Jeremy and Lexi and get as far away from this island as possible. But drawing attention to myself, or to Christian, would be the worst thing I could do.

Keep playing along. You don't have a choice.

'Oh yeah, I'll definitely be staying,' Christian says. 'I want to meet all of Emily's lovely friends. We go back a long way, don't we, Emily, and I've got lots of stories to share.'

'Well, it's only a small gathering,' Jeremy says, glancing at me. 'A lot of friends couldn't make it out here. But you're more than welcome to join the celebration, isn't he, Em?'

I nod, frozen, wondering if I'll ever be able to move again. 'Of course.'

'So, how do you two know each other?' Jeremy asks.

I'm not sure which one of us he's asking but I need to take control of this situation before Christian rips my world to shreds. 'University,' I say. 'I've learnt to stick to as much of the truth as possible when lying.

'Yep, that's right,' Christian agrees. 'We go *way* back.'

Jeremy nods. 'Oh. Sorry. I'm not sure Emily's mentioned—'

'I must have,' I interrupt. 'Maybe you just forgot?'

'Yeah,' Jeremy agrees. 'That does sound like something I'd do. Well, I'd better mingle. I'll leave you two to catch up.' He kisses my cheek before walking off, but not before I've caught the questioning look on his face.

Before he's even out of earshot, Christian grabs my arm. 'Well, don't you look beautiful? You've hardly changed since the last time I saw you. I watched you, Emily. Walking down the aisle. As if you didn't have a trouble in the world. A beautiful bride on her wedding day. In this... picture-perfect place. You certainly landed on your feet, didn't you?'

I glance around, relieved that no one is paying much attention to us. 'What are you doing here?' I hiss. 'You can't be here. Just go.'

'Did you think I wouldn't come back for you? Have you honestly believed that all these years?'

The truth is that I've always suspected Christian would resurface. I've been planning for it. The suitcase under my bed has been packed for years, ready for when the time came. I just didn't expect it to be here on this tranquil island, on my wedding day. Maybe I'd fooled myself into believing it might never come after all. I should never have let my guard down.

'Why now? Why here?' I demand. 'You don't have to do this.'

'Because, Emily, it's time you faced the consequences of your actions.' He gestures around him and holds up his hands. 'Do all these lovely people know what you did, Emily?' he shouts. His voice echoes across the beach. 'Don't you think it's time you told the truth?'

TWO

BEFORE

Emily is a fish out of water in this place. Not only is it huge, but everyone appears so confident. Even the other first-year students, who are as new to university life as she is. They've slotted into place, as if they've lived this life before, while she swims out of her depth.

At least she's far from home. Anything is better than being a virtual prisoner while her mum bleats on about how terrible the world outside their four walls is. How dreadful things can happen to you just by stepping foot outside. Living in the real world.

Emily just wants to be free, and the University of West London in Ealing is the first step in that direction.

She's read all about how you should fake it until you make it, and has learnt that she should hold her head up high, put on an outward show of confidence to boost her internal deficit. But right now, she's not sure it's working. Her mother's influence is too strong. She's had years of following directions and rules for how she should live her life. She refuses to live like that any more.

Emily is conscious of the squeak of her trainers on the shiny wooden floor as she walks through the maze of corridors, searching for the lecture hall she's meant to be in. She clutches books and folders she can't squeeze into her bag defensively to her chest like armour. She should probably get a bigger bag, but she's saving every penny she can to see her through the year. She won't ask her mum for a penny. If she's going to do this whole independent thing then she's doing it properly. Whatever sacrifices she has to make. And there's no way she'll risk ending up back at home.

She doesn't notice him until it's too late and she careers into another student, the impact causing her books to thud to the floor, landing in a pile at her feet.

'Hey,' he says. 'Watch out.'

Leaning down to grab her books, she looks up and offers an apologetic smile. 'Sorry. I just—'

'Don't worry about it,' he says. And then he's gone, strolling off down the corridor. A guy who knows exactly where he's going.

Emily gives the incident no more thought until she sees him again a few weeks later. When she does spot him in the university bookshop, it's as if fate has drawn them together, everything in her life conspiring to bring about this moment.

Emily has no social life here, so she's thrown herself into her studies, and has saved up enough to buy the books she needs for the next semester. Her phone rings – it's her mother again. She's already left Emily three messages this morning, instructing her to call so she knows Emily's still alive. 'I'm only your mother,' she adds, laying on the guilt. It's overkill. Smothering. Emily can't breathe when she thinks about what it's like being at home. She'll have to go back at Christmas; there's no way to avoid it.

'Knocked into anyone lately?' he says as she's searching the shelves for a book she needs on postmodernism.

It takes Emily a moment to place the student with light brown hair flopping across his face, and green eyes. 'Oh, yeah, um. No. I'm not usually that—'

He laughs. 'I'm just messing with you. Don't take things so seriously.'

'I'm not, sorry, I just...'

He smiles. 'And never apologise when you haven't done anything wrong.' He holds out his hand. 'I'm Christian. Second year of uni but I've just changed degrees. Doing business now instead of law. It wasn't really my thing.'

A frisson of excitement runs through Emily when she shakes his hand. At least that's what she thinks it is. She's never felt anything quite like it. 'Emily. Literature and philosophy. First year.' It's weird introducing themselves in this way, as though what they're studying defines them. She supposes it does, in many ways.

Christian raises his eyebrows. 'I'm impressed. That must be some mind you've got in that head of yours.'

Her cheeks flood with heat and she turns back to the book-shelf, hoping he doesn't notice how beetroot-red she must be.

'It can be hard,' he says. 'Getting used to this place. Don't worry, by Christmas you'll know how the land lies.'

Indignation swells inside her. 'I didn't say I was finding it difficult!' As soon as she's said it she regrets being so defensive. 'I'm sorry, I—'

Christian laughs. 'Uh-uh. What did I just say? Never apologise when you haven't done anything wrong.'

She smiles, and for the first time since she came to this place, she feels her shoulders drop, her body becoming less rigid. 'You're right,' she says. 'I take back both my apologies.' She holds up the books she's carrying. 'I'd better go and pay for these,' she explains.

'Yep. They don't take kindly to shoplifting around here. Might even get you thrown off your course. Bye, then, Emily.' He's smiling as he walks away, his hands in his pockets.

After she's paid and left the bookshop, Christian catches up with her in the corridor. 'Wait up,' he calls, and she spins around, assuming she's forgotten something. He smiles. 'Do you have plans tonight?' He doesn't wait for an answer. 'A few of us are heading to Freddie's Bar if you're interested? Should be a good night.'

'I, um—'

'Great. Give me your mobile.' He holds out his hand.

'What? Why?'

'So I can give you my number, of course.' He laughs, taking the phone as she hands it to him. 'And now I've got yours,' he says, calling his phone. 'So, no excuses about not coming tonight. No pressure, though. Totally up to you. Come. Don't come. Whichever.'

Emily rarely goes out in the evening so she's already made up her mind that she will. Christian seems fun. And she's not scoring well on the making friends scale. She needs to embrace student life, and make the most of being away from home, instead of sitting in her room every evening while life carries on around her. Her two flatmates are always inviting her out, and not once has she said yes.

She imagines her mother's eyes widening in horror at the thought of Emily being out in the evening, the crinkles in her face as she tries to force Emily to believe that it's too dangerous going out at night.

'I'll see you there,' she says, and she watches Christian walk away, her stomach flipping when he turns around to smile at her.

Once he's disappeared around the corner, Emily realises that she didn't get a receipt for her books. Her mother's words ring in her head: *Always get a receipt. You never know when you'll have to return something. It will cause you nothing but trouble to not have that little bit of paper.* She almost doesn't go back – defying her mother in this tiny way is tempting.

But she doesn't listen to the voice encouraging her to break free, and she heads back to the bookshop, annoyed with herself for giving in.

'I'm sorry, I forgot to get a receipt for these.' She holds up the books.

The girl at the till sighs.

'You know, just in case I need to bring them back. Sorry.' Emily recalls what Christian just said and instantly regrets apologising again.

I made a mistake and forgot my receipt. There's no harm done.

'I think I chucked it,' the girl says, rummaging through the bin.

She shouldn't have bothered coming back for the receipt. It's wasting her time, and she feels bad for putting the girl out.

'Do you know that student you were chatting to?' the girl asks as she hands Emily her receipt. The print on it is so faded that Emily can barely read it.

'Not really. We just met. Why?'

The girl's eyes narrow as she studies Emily. 'No reason. Is that everything you need?'

Emily has been assigned a student flatshare on the other side of Ealing with two other girls. She would have preferred to be closer to the university, but it's a block of ten flats on a busy road that feels safe to her. There's a video entrance system, and a security chain on their front door. Still, Emily would never bring her mum here. It's the complete contrast of Shere, the sleepy Surrey village Emily's lived in her whole life until now.

Although the bathroom, kitchen and living room are

communal, they each have their own rooms, and Emily loves that she can close the door on everything if she wishes, while also never having to feel isolated. And here, she is far away from her mother's brainwashing.

Kirsty and Erin, her flatmates, seem pleasant enough. Different to her, but kind and accepting of their differences. Kirsty is out most nights; growing up in west London means she has a local network of friends. And Erin seems to be inseparable from her boyfriend, Andre. They met in school, she'd told Emily. 'Love's young dream, like Romeo and Juliet.' Emily hadn't wanted to point out how that fictional relationship had turned out. It's clear that there's not much room for anyone else in Erin's and Andre's lives. He's at the flat so much that he may as well move in officially. Still, Emily's too grateful to be away from home to mind anything her flatmates do.

'You look... different,' Erin says, wandering past Emily's room this evening.

Flustered at not having found the right shoes to wear tonight, Emily sits down on her bed.

'I meant that in a good way.' Erin walks in and stands by her door. 'Nice top. Going somewhere special?'

'Just the student bar. For a drink.' Emily doesn't add that she dipped into her savings to buy the black blouse she's wearing. It was the closest thing she could find to an evening top without feeling uncomfortable and overdressed.

'Oh... good. I was beginning to worry about you.'

Emily frowns. 'Why?'

Erin joins her on the edge of the bed. 'You just don't seem to get out much. All you do is study. And there's Kirsty out every night. And me always with Andre. I'm just glad you're actually going somewhere. No offence.'

Emily assures her there's none taken. 'Do you think this skirt is okay?' As soon as she says it she feels vulnerable. Now Erin will know how pathetic she is.

'You look great,' Erin assures her, flicking a strand of dark blonde hair from her face. 'But you need some make-up. And maybe wear your hair down for a change.' Erin studies her. 'You have lovely waves, you shouldn't tie it up all the time.'

Emily looks away. 'I think I'll just keep it up.' She needs to feel comfortable, above all else.

Erin shrugs. 'What shoes, then?'

'Um... trainers?'

'Nope. You can borrow my knee-high boots – the heel isn't too high and they'll look great with that skirt. And don't wear tights. You won't need them. It's not freezing yet.'

Ten minutes later, Erin has applied some make-up to her eyes and lips, and Emily is ready to leave. On the way out, she pauses to study herself in the mirror, surprised to find that she likes what she sees. 'I'm still me,' she whispers.

'I hope he's worth it,' Erin says, watching Emily from her bedroom doorway.

Emily blushes. 'No, it's not like that.'

'Whatever you say!' She turns away and closes her door.

The doubts set in while Emily waits at the bus stop. Her mother's voice ringing in her ears drowns out the heavy thrum of car exhausts: *So many young women get attacked or killed on their way home from nights out. London is a crime hotspot. People spike drinks, and you won't even realise until it's too late.*

She freezes when the bus pulls up. What does she think she's doing? She doesn't have to prove anything. She can go home and make some dinner and get on with her coursework. She's got that essay to write on how Plato's *Republic* is about justice. The sooner she starts working on the plan, the better.

Her phone pings with a text, and for a second she considers ignoring it. But her mum will be waiting for an answer. She'll freak out if she doesn't get a reply soon, and Emily will never hear the end of it. At least she doesn't have to worry about her mother turning up on her doorstep. She would never dare venture this far from home.

But when she pulls her phone from her bag, it's not her mum – it's Christian.

Hope you're still coming. No pressure of course!

Emily smiles. 'Wait!' she shouts, as the bus door hisses closed. But it's too late; the driver ignores her and pulls away.

It takes her forty minutes to walk to the student bar near the university, and despite the chilly November air, a layer of sweat coats her body, soaking through her top. Her hair is damp. Straggly, not nice waves like Erin had said. She should turn back, go home to her warm bed and start working on that essay plan.

She turns to leave, her mother's voice once again echoing through her head. The negativity. The warnings of doom. But her mother is wrong – life isn't all awful. Emily has to believe that. 'I'm going to the bar,' she says aloud. 'I don't care what a mess I look.'

Freddie's Bar is packed with students, none of whom are paying any attention to personal space. Emily's stomach clenches; she's so far out of her comfort zone that she may as well be on a different planet. She fights her way to the bar to get a drink to help her blend in. Nobody knows her; here she can be whoever she wants to be.

Having no idea what to order, she scans the room and sees most students holding pints of beer. She orders one, cringing as the bartender raises his eyebrows before reaching for a glass. She's wearing her naivety like a coat, and she has no idea how to hide it. Fitting in is going to be harder than she's imagined.

With her drink in her hand, Emily scans the room for Christian. Judging from his text message, he must be in here somewhere. After a minute, when there's no sign of him, she pulls out her phone and types a message.

Just got here. Where are you?

As soon as she's sent it, she's plagued with doubt. Is it too forward? It's not as if she was the only one he'd invited here. Christian had made it clear that a group of them were meeting up, so why is she entertaining thoughts that it's anything more than that?

She's making her way to the toilets when she spots him at the end of the corridor, wearing a navy blue hoodie and jeans. She's about to call out to him when she notices he's standing with a girl, leaning so close to her that it looks as if they're about to kiss. The girl looks a couple of years older than Emily, and her black curly hair is scraped tightly into a bun on top of her head. She's wearing a mid-length fur coat, which Emily hopes isn't real. She can't abide animal cruelty.

Only when she gets closer does Emily realise they're having an argument. Fur-coat girl jabs her finger towards Christian's face, and in response he shakes his head and pushes her hand away before disappearing into the men's toilets.

Unsure what to do, Emily makes her way towards the girl and asks if she's okay. But all she gets in response is a glare as the girl brushes past her and makes her way back to the bar.

Her mother was right. Why did she bother coming here? Emily abandons her beer glass on a table already crowded with drinks and leaves the bar.

And against all her mother's warnings, she begins the walk home through dark, deserted streets.

THREE

NOW

I stare at Christian as he utters words no part of me wants to hear. *Do all these lovely people know what you did?*

Shock renders me numb, unable to speak, and I feel the heavy gaze of questioning eyes on me. Everything falls silent, other than the waves gently rolling up to the shore.

I focus on Lexi, who clings to Jeremy's arm, frowning.

Pam is the first to break the silence, standing up and coming towards Christian. 'Who are you?' she demands.

Finally, fear kickstarts me into action. 'Very funny' I say, taking Christian's arm and leading him away from the wedding guests. 'Nothing to worry about. This is an old friend of mine. Always playing practical jokes.'

'Sorry, everyone.' Christian turns back to explain. He holds up his hands. 'Emily and I always used to joke that if either of us got married, the other would stand up and say they know of a reason why the bride and groom shouldn't get married. You know, like you always see in films. Just a bad joke, I'm afraid.'

I force myself to throw my head back and laugh; a consummate actress. And slowly, far too slowly, others begin to chuckle too, until eventually the chatter Christian had interrupted resumes.

'What the hell are you doing?' I demand, when we're out of earshot.

'Wow, Emily. Do you think you should be talking to me like that? I'm just giving you a little taste of what's possible. How did that feel?'

I study Christian. He's hardly changed: green eyes still so piercing it feels as though they're penetrating my mind, and light brown hair long enough to fall across his forehead. I used to love the way it did that, so that he'd have to constantly flick it from his eyes. Now it only makes me shudder.

'How did you find me?'

'Oh, Emily. You can't run these days. Don't you know that? I've known where you were for a while. I know everything about your life, Emily.' He points to Lexi. 'That sweet little ten-year-old girl over there who you've just become a mother to – she was your student wasn't she? A few years ago. And that's how you met your wonderful husband over there. A pilot, isn't he? Done well for himself, despite having a failed marriage behind him. Let's hope this one lasts longer.'

'That wasn't his fault,' I hiss. 'We all make mistakes. Choose the wrong people. Better to find out late than never.' I'm taking a huge risk saying this, when all Christian has to do is open his mouth and send the life I've built crashing down around me.

He raises his hand and lifts my chin. 'I wonder what your in-laws would think if they knew about you.' He glances at Pam, who is talking animatedly to Jeremy's friend. Stuart glances over at me, but quickly turns his attention back to Pam.

'Just tell me what you want.' I try to keep my voice level, despite never feeling so afraid before.

He raises his eyebrows. 'Oh, that's easy. I want my life back, Emily. You stole it from me.' He stares at me with eyes I don't recognise. 'And that means—'

'Everything okay here?'

I'm so relieved to hear Jeremy's voice that I instinctively reach for him, grabbing hold of his arm, trying not to clutch too tightly. 'We're just catching up,' I say, forcing a smile.

Christian nods. 'Yep, it's been a few years. What is it? Fifteen? We lost touch and I haven't heard from Emily in all that time.' He turns to Jeremy. 'That's why I hope you don't mind that she's agreed to have a quick drink with me this evening. I know it's your wedding day, but I fly home early tomorrow.'

Jeremy frowns. 'Um... well...' He glances at me, and I can see he doesn't want me to go. But Jeremy would never try to control me in any way. That's part of what I love about him.

'Maybe just for an hour,' I say, when he doesn't answer. 'We can't be up late anyway, can we?'

This seems to convince Jeremy. 'Okay.' He looks at Christian. 'We've got an early flight home. I have a long-haul flight the day after so need to rest.'

'Ah, yes. Emily's just been telling me you're a pilot. She's so proud of you.'

Jeremy smiles, his brown eyes lighting up as they always do when he talks about his work. 'Yeah. Since I was a kid I wanted to fly planes. Can't believe I actually get to do it.'

Christian pats him on the back. 'And get paid for it. Living your best life, eh, Jeremy? Good for you.' He lifts the can of beer I've only just noticed him holding. I don't know how much he's already consumed, but even stone-cold sober, Christian is dangerous.

My new husband averts his eyes. He's not good at taking compliments. If only he knew that none of Christian's words are genuine. 'Thanks,' he says quietly.

I have no choice but to go along with Christian's plan; I can't risk him saying any more. 'We won't be out late,' I assure Jeremy.

'Certainly not,' Christian says. 'It is your wedding night, after all.'

Jeremy smiles. 'Well, we've got the rest of our lives together, haven't we, Em?' He turns to Christian. 'So, what is it you do?'

'I've been running a business in America,' he says. 'Now I've come back to sort a few things out. Tie up loose ends. Anyway, I won't bore you with all that. So how did you and Emily meet?'

Jeremy glances at me. It's always awkward telling this story, but we've got nothing to be ashamed of. 'Emily was Lexi's teacher a couple of years ago. But nothing happened at the time. It was only later we bumped into each other again.'

'Ah, romantic. I guess fate brought you together. Anyway, I have to shoot off now. Lovely wedding.' He shakes Jeremy's hand then turns to me, smiling. 'See you at seven, Emily. Don't be late!'

Jeremy and I watch him leave, and I prepare for a barrage of questions.

'He's confident,' Jeremy says.

An intense rush of heat rises through my body. 'Yeah.'

'Were you close, then?' he asks, searching my face.

'Kind of. We used to hang out. A bunch of us.' *Lies come back to haunt you, haven't you learnt that by now?* 'But it was such a long time ago.'

It's a relief when Lexi runs over, pulling at Jeremy's shirt sleeve. 'Dad, Emily, you have to come and see what Grandad's doing. It's hilarious!'

We follow Lexi, my legs feeling like concrete as I struggle to appear normal. As if everything is okay, and my wedding day hasn't just turned into a horrific nightmare.

The rest of the day passes in a blur. Christian's shadow looms over me, and I'm constantly on edge. Jumpy. Unable to focus on anything anyone says. It's almost a relief when our guests begin saying their goodbyes, heading off back to their hotels and villas to enjoy the rest of their time on this sun-drenched island. *Such a beautiful day. What a wonderful couple you are. We wish you a lifetime of happiness.* The comments ricochet off me; they don't belong in my mind.

Back at the villa, I spend some time with Lexi, letting her stories fill my head, pushing out the things I don't want in there. But each time I look away from her, I notice Jeremy watching me. The smile he offers whenever our eyes meet does nothing to mask the questions lying beneath the surface. He's confused about Christian, of course he is. And how can I answer any of Jeremy's questions?

'Are you okay?' Lexi asks. 'You're being a bit... quiet?'

We're sitting on deckchairs in the back garden, while Jeremy swims in the pool. Lexi's been in there with him, but now she seems tired. I take her hand. 'This has been the best day of my life,' I say. 'Because now we're a family. You, me and your dad. This is all I've wanted.' I don't add that it has been tainted by Christian turning up. Here to make sure I pay for what happened.

'You really love him, then,' Lexi says. 'Because Mum didn't, did she? She was... horrible to him.'

Still holding her hand, I shuffle closer. 'They just weren't right for each other, Lexi. But they both love you very much.'

She bites her lip. 'But it's okay, anyway, because he's got you now.'

Her words should fill me with comfort, and be the greatest gift I could receive, but instead I feel nauseous. I need to find out exactly what Christian wants, and then, somehow, I need to stop him.

. . .

He's late. I sit at a table outside the bar for twenty minutes before I begin to wonder if I've got the wrong time. It's strange to sit here, surrounded by fir trees in this tranquil place, where the warmth of the day still wraps itself around me, knowing that Christian is coming for me. There is no way he will have changed his mind and decided to leave me alone. Not now he's tracked me down.

The truth of it is that I will wait here until he decides to turn up, no matter what time that may be. And we both know it.

Jeremy messages me to ask how it's going. I know he wants to ask me how long I'll be, so that we can spend our wedding evening together – as it should be – but he respects me too much to make any demands.

And that only makes me feel worse.

It's ten to eight when Christian finally appears, dressed in the khaki utility shorts and navy T-shirt he was wearing earlier. Briefly, I wonder what he's been doing since this morning, before I realise the less I know about his life now, the better.

'Oh, am I late?' he says, sliding into a chair. 'Oops. Sorry.'

'No,' I say. 'You said eight, didn't you? That makes you early.' If he's going to play this sick game, then the best thing I can do is beat him at it.

He glares at me and folds his arms. 'Let me buy you a drink. For old times' sake.'

'No thanks.' I gesture to my glass of water. 'Already got one.'

'Water? On your wedding day.' He smiles. 'That doesn't bode well, does it?'

I don't care what he says; there's no way I will sit and drink alcohol with him. I lift my glass and take a sip, relishing the cold sting of ice on my tongue.

Christian stalks off to the bar. 'Suit yourself,' he mutters. 'Don't go anywhere, now.'

As I watch people strolling past, laughing and chatting, couples holding hands and smiling, I consider bolting. I could

disappear and make sure that nobody ever finds me. But it's a
fleeting thought, vanishing the second I try to add detail to it. I
could never leave Lexi like that. She's already been through so
much with her mother, and I'm supposed to be someone she can
trust. And Jeremy would be devastated. He's a good man; he
deserves for me to fight for the life we've built, no matter how
fragile the foundations.

'It's funny,' Christian says, when he comes back, sliding into
the seat and placing a pint of beer on the table. 'When I was
inside the bar, I thought you might have disappeared on me.'

*He knows me too well, still. Despite the ocean of time that's
spread between us.*

'What do you want, Christian?'

He holds up his hands. 'Woah, hold on. Slow it down a bit.
We've got a lot to catch up on, haven't we? Fifteen years.' He
narrows his eyes. 'And I've been counting every year. Marking
the anniversary.'

I stare at him, and it takes me a moment to find my voice.
'Where did you go? You disappeared. Even your family didn't
know where you were.'

'Because you changed everything. With your actions.
Everything you do has a ripple effect, surely you've learnt that?
How could I come back after what happened?'

I avoid his gaze. 'You don't have to do this. It's in the past.'

He slams his fist on the table. 'Don't you see, Emily?' He
looks up at the sky. It's shades of purple now, gradually darken-
ing. 'Do you remember what you said to me once? *We're like
two stars up there. Always together, no matter what.* How right
you were.'

'I'm married now. You just saw me. You didn't try and
stop it.'

He takes a slow sip of beer. 'I could have, couldn't I? It
would have been so easy. But the thing is – this way will hurt
you a lot more.'

I stand up, pushing my chair aside.

'I don't think you want to walk away, Emily. Not when you haven't heard what I want.'

Anger and fear course through my blood. I can't be back here again. I'm no longer that person. I've worked too hard to banish her. But I also know that I need to hear him out.

'You owe me, Emily. We both know that, don't we? And now it's time for you to pay up.'

Reluctantly I sit back down. 'Is it money you want? I have a bit saved, but not—'

'Don't *insult* me.' Christian leans in to me. He takes my wrist and grips it tightly. 'I don't want your money.'

I glance around but nobody's paying any attention to us. 'Then what?'

'You destroyed my life, Emily. And now I'm here to return the favour. I've lost fifteen years because of you.'

My mind scrambles to make sense of his words. 'You said you live in America. And you have a business there. You could just go back—'

'Wrong. I'm back in London now. It was time for me to come home.'

'But you must have made a life for yourself there. There must be people you care about. A girlfriend or wife? Children?'

Christian smiles. 'There's nothing tying me to the US. Here, though... well, that's a different matter. But my private life is none of your concern.'

But Christian turning up here like this is making it my business. 'You have parents. And a brother.'

'My mum died, Emily. And it shouldn't have been that way. She should have had years left. But her health deteriorated because you made sure I had to disappear.'

He waits for that to sink in, and I picture Audrey, how graceful and kind she was. Nothing like her son.

'I'm sorry. I really—'

'I don't want your sympathy. And as far as my dad and brother go – neither of them can look at me the same way after I disappeared. I've been back in the UK for months now, Emily, and it's clear that they don't trust me. Don't think I'm in my right mind. All because I had to disappear. They think I'm hiding things. That I can't be trusted. And that's because of you.' He lifts his glass and sips slowly. 'I can't tell them the truth, can I?' He leans in again.

'I'm sorry,' I repeat. 'I... I'm not that person you used to know. I've—'

'That's all well and good, but you've never actually paid for it, have you? And that's why I'm here.'

My breath catches in my throat, struggling to find its way out. 'I don't understand.'

Christian smiles. 'It's perfectly simple. You're going to do whatever I want, whenever I want it.'

My mouth hangs open. 'No... no, I won't.'

'Wrong, Emily. Unless you want the world to know what you did?'

'You can't prove—'

'That's where you're wrong. I have evidence. Very compelling it is too.'

Shock renders me mute. 'What evidence?'

'I think for now I'll keep that to myself. But look at me, Emily.' He reaches across the table and forces my chin up. 'I think you know I'm not lying.'

Again, I can find no words.

'Don't worry,' Christian continues. 'You won't have to sleep with me.' He smiles. 'Although, if I remember right, you never had any complaints.'

'This is insane. I'm not doing it.'

'But you don't have a choice, do you? Otherwise, you'll lose everything. Your new husband. Your stepdaughter. Your job. It's hardly fair that you're a teacher after what you did. Oh, and not to mention the other consequences. You know what I mean. I don't need to spell it out to you, do I?'

I lean forward and fold my arms across my stomach. Any moment now I will surely throw up. 'Please don't do this, Christian. If you ever loved—'

'Don't you dare talk about love,' he hisses. 'You stole years of my life, Emily, and now I'm taking them back.' He finishes his beer and slams the glass on the table. 'I know everything about your life, so there's nowhere to hide. I know your husband's schedule. There's plenty of time for us to have special evenings together. Oh, but you might need to think about childcare for your new daughter, otherwise it could cause a problem. We wouldn't want Lexi to have to come along with us, would we? It might confuse her a bit.'

'Don't talk about Lexi.' I can't bring myself to look at him. I stare at the scuffs on his white trainers. He was wearing white trainers that night too. I remember how dirty they got, and he'd only just bought them.

'How did you find me?' I ask. 'How could you have known I was getting married here?'

'It's amazing what you can find out about someone if you're willing to pay for it.' Christian rises and pushes his chair back. 'How about you take a bit of time to come to your senses. Have a good flight home, Emily. I'll be in touch.'

He disappears around the corner as fear grips me in a stranglehold. And if it wasn't for his empty glass of beer sitting abandoned on the table, I might be able to convince myself that he'd never been there at all.

FOUR

BEFORE

Two weeks pass before Emily sees him again. He'd sent her a flurry of texts that night after she'd left Freddie's Bar, first asking why she was a no-show, and then worrying about whether she was okay. She replied to only one, to end the outpouring of messages, assuring him she was fine.

She's not sure who that girl with the fur coat and pretty curls was, but whatever was going on with the two of them, she wants no part of it. She was foolish to believe he was interested in her. Quiet, naive Emily from a sleepy village in Surrey. Besides, her mother is probably right – relationships only end up causing pain. Emily's good at masking things, though, shutting them away and pretending they don't exist. She's had to be.

And now, when she's not expecting it, and has shoved him out of her mind, Christian is standing in the queue in the university café, talking on his phone. He doesn't notice her, and it would be easy to slip away unseen, but she's rooted to her spot in the queue. She's waited too long here to lose her place now.

Seeing him again stirs something within her. Is it fascination? She's drawn to him and can't explain why. She's liked guys before, but she's never felt a magnetic pull like this.

He ends his call and pays for his food, and she can't deny that she's disappointed when he takes his change and walks away without a glance back. He's got a girlfriend, she reminds herself. An attractive girl who wears real fur. Emily has decided it must have been, even though she has no evidence.

For the rest of the afternoon, her mind wanders to thoughts of him, when it should be focusing on the knowledge her lecturers are imparting. Scrambled images of Christian that offer her a mixture of pleasure and unease. Why is she even wasting her time thinking of him? *Because aside from my studies, there's nothing else. Just a controlling and overprotective mother, who I need to be free of.*

After her last lecture, Emily steps out into the cool November air and decides to walk home, even though it will take her the best part of an hour. All that waits for her at the flat is the call from her mother, and more studying.

A firm hand lands on her shoulder and she jumps.

'Sorry, didn't mean to scare you.'

It's him. The one person she's been trying to avoid. And now that he's standing right in front of her, she has no choice but to acknowledge him. 'It's okay,' she says.

He looks nice in his thick padded coat and beanie hat. 'So at least I see you're alive, then. You know, I was a bit worried when you messaged that you were at Freddie's and I couldn't find you. I looked everywhere. Didn't you get my messages?'

'Sorry about that. I had a... family emergency.' Inwardly she cringes. She's so careful about lies, especially when her mother can so easily sniff out deceit, like a dog trained to detect drugs.

Christian hesitates, as if he's about to probe her further about this so-called emergency. And what will she say? 'Hmm,' he says. 'I feel a bit like you stood me up.' He gives a nervous chuckle and shoves his hands in his pockets.

His words surprise her. She had been ready to defend herself with more fabrications. 'Really? But—'

'I know, I know. It's not like it was a *date* or anything. But... I *was* disappointed.'

Emily nods. 'Me too.' She's not sure why she says this. She would have liked to spend time with him, but it is fur-coat girl who bothers her more.

'You could make it up to me,' Christian says, smiling. 'Come for a drink tonight. Just you and me. Forget the student bar.'

'You mean like a date?'

Christian waits for a group of students to walk past them. 'Well, we don't have to label it, but yeah.'

'But what about your girlfriend?' Emily's cheeks burn.

Christian stares at her. 'What?'

She realises her mistake. 'Nothing. I'm just... guessing you must have one.' She shrugs. Tries to make it seem like a casual enquiry.

His eyes narrow. 'Now why would I be asking you out for a drink if I had a girlfriend?' He smiles. 'No. Been single for a while now. Happy that way.' He checks his phone. 'So, what do you reckon about that drink?'

The flat is silent when Emily gets home – just what she'd hoped for. She doesn't want Erin or Kirsty asking about where she's going and who with. It's too early for her to share anything about Christian, when she doesn't even know what's going on herself.

At six o'clock, her mobile rings. She'd forgotten about this scheduled call, and how her mum is never even a second late to call. 'Hi Mum,' she says, trying to muster enthusiasm. She doesn't want too many questions tonight – she needs her mum to believe that everything is normal. And that all she's doing is studying.

'You sound out of breath,' her mother comments in place of

a greeting. 'Are you okay? You're not ill, are you? Don't lie to me, Emily. What's going on?'

'I'm fine, Mum. I just ran to the kitchen to answer my phone. I left it in there. I was in the bathroom.'

There's a pause, and Emily's convinced her mum's trying to ascertain whether or not to believe the story Emily has spun. 'And where are your flatmates?' she asks. 'Out as usual, I suppose. I hope you don't go with them. Clubs and bars and that sort of thing. You know they're awful places, don't you? Full of people like—'

'No, Mum. I haven't been anywhere. Just lectures, work and home. That's it. Rinse and repeat. And my flatmates are still at uni. Late lectures,' Emily explains. She has no idea where Erin and Kirsty are, but feels a strong urge to defend the girls. 'How are you, Mum?'

'Well, I'd feel a lot better if you'd gone to a university closer to home. I'll never know what on earth possessed you to choose London of all places.'

'I didn't get a place in Surrey, remember? I tried.' This was a lie she'd had to tell. In truth, she'd only applied to London universities, completing and submitting her application at college during her lunch break. If she'd done it at home then her mother would have demanded to see it.

'I'm fine here, Mum,' Emily continues. 'I've even made some friends already.' *I've met a boy.* She pictures her mother's face if she were to tell her about Christian.

'Just be careful who you associate with, Emily,' her mother warns. 'I'm worried sick about you being in London. Did you hear about that nurse who got murdered on her way home from a night out with friends? She was only a bit older than you. It was a fifteen-minute walk from her house too. It wasn't even that late. This world is a terrible place, Emily. I pray for you every day. Every single day.'

Emily sighs. 'You don't have to worry about me, Mum. I'm

okay. I go to uni then home, then work in the clothes shop on Saturdays and that's it.'

Her mother tuts. 'I bet you get all sorts coming into that shop. And you're on menswear of all things! It's not appropriate, Emily. Did you speak to the manager about moving you to ladieswear or childrenswear?'

Emily's part-time job in Next has caused more hassle than it's probably worth, but she's determined to earn her own money while she's studying. 'I did speak to him but he can't move me.'

'You're lying, aren't you? Playing into the devil's hands.'

'Mum, stop!'

'You have to be careful. Did you hear about—'

'Mum, I have to go – I need to check through my assignment before I hand it in tomorrow.'

Her mother ignores her. 'Are you coming this Sunday?'

'I don't think—'

'I'm all on my own here, Emily. The least you can do is visit me at weekends.'

Emily sighs. They both know she will give in. 'I'll be there. But I really need to go now, Mum.'

'Suit yourself. See you on Sunday. Try and come early.'

The bar Christian has picked is far quieter than Freddie's was. Emily is shot with nerves as she pushes through the door, and she scans the room for him, praying he's already arrived. He's there at a table in the corner, dressed in jeans and a navy sweatshirt, tapping something into his phone. He's always wearing navy blue, she notices, but it suits him so she can understand why.

As if he can sense her, he looks up, then smiles and waves her over. 'You came.' He lifts his phone. 'I was just messaging you. You do realise you're seven minutes late?'

'Oh, I... sorry.'

'I'm just joking. Sorry. You'll get used to my sense of humour. As misplaced as it may be. Come and sit and I'll get you a drink. What'll you have?'

Emily has no idea what to ask for. She doesn't want a beer like she ordered at Freddie's. In fact, she doesn't even want to think about that night. 'Surprise me,' she tells him.

When Christian comes back with a vodka and orange for both of them, she tries her best to hide her disappointment and look appreciative, lifting the glass and immediately taking a sip. It's too strong and burns her throat, but she smiles anyway.

'I thought you'd like that,' Christian says.

Emily smiles in reply; the fewer lies she tells about herself, the better. She can't explain why but she likes Christian, despite his extreme confidence. Perhaps some of it will rub off on her.

'So, Emily Thomas. I want to know everything about you.' Christian folds his arms and leans on the table, watching her.

'How do you know my surname?'

'You told me. Remember?' He chuckles and takes a sip of his vodka.

Emily can't recall when she might have done this, but how else would he know it? 'I don't know *your* surname,' she says, blushing.

He laughs. 'I'm offended. I definitely told you. It's Holmes. Like Sherlock. Only, I'm not as clever as he was.'

Emily smiles. 'I think actually it was Watson who was the real mastermind.'

Christian smiles. 'You could be right there. So go on, then. Tell me all about Emily.'

Heat flushes across her cheeks again. 'What do you want to know?'

'How about I tell you what I already know about you?'

She raises her eyebrows. 'Well, it can't be much, given that we're virtual strangers.'

'I know you're nineteen, and you've come to uni straight from doing A levels.'

'Right you are, Dr Watson. What a mastermind!'

Christian leans back in his seat. 'Funny. And actually, I could have been wrong. I'm twenty-four.'

Emily's eyes widen. 'Really?' She would never have guessed that he was five years older than her.

'Yep. Had a few years travelling before I started uni last year. Good for the soul. Anyway, let me continue.' He winks. 'I know you don't realise how beautiful you are. You're extremely shy. You hate people looking at you – you just want to blend into the background. Observe without being seen.'

The burning in her cheeks intensifies. She can't look at him, despite being desperate to read his expression. How has he summed her up so perfectly? 'I'm not shy,' she says.

He reaches across the table for her hand. 'I think it's a good thing,' he assures her. 'I'm so sick of girls whose confidence is nothing more than arrogance. You're so... refreshing.'

She forces herself to look at Christian, and is pleased to see his smile doesn't seem patronising.

He leans forward. 'Do you think we're born with our personalities fully formed?' he asks. 'Or is it nurture that shapes us?'

'Can't it be both? But I'm leaning more towards the nurture argument.' Either way, Emily wonders if she's doomed.

'What makes you say that?'

She's at a crossroads now. A gap has opened up where she could tell him about her mother, but she's only just met him. *If I like him and want him in my life, he'll find out eventually. May as well get it over with and give him a get-out clause.*

'My mother isn't... like other mums.'

'Oh?'

'I just mean I'm probably the way I am because of her. As I've grown up, it's been drummed it into me that the world is a horrible place and that we should fear everything. *She* fears everything.'

'What? That sounds awful. What about your dad?'

'I don't see my dad. He left us when I was thirteen and went to live in another country. We don't even know where he went. Just that it was abroad. We never heard from him again. Not even on my birthdays.' Emily grabs her glass and takes a long sip. The vodka still burns her throat; she'll never get used to it. 'Mum thinks the world is self-destructing and we're all doomed.'

Christian frowns. 'That must be hard for you.'

'It is. Since my dad left, she's tried to keep me on a tight leash.'

'So, she's just overprotective?'

Emily should stop talking now. Quit while she's ahead. She's already said too much but there's still a chance to play this down. 'I'm not close to her any more,' she explains. 'She's just so different to me, and the older I've got, the more we've drifted.'

'I hope you don't blame yourself.' Christian walks around to her side of the table, sitting next to her and stroking her cheek. 'I read this book once about how our parents mess us up.'

'That sounds like a fun read,' Emily says, surprising herself by laughing.

'You're right. It was heavy. But it helped me put my own parents into perspective. Or my dad at least.' For a fleeting moment, his smile disappears.

'Do you want to talk about it?' Emily asks. She's much more comfortable hearing about someone else's issues than discussing her own.

'That's for another time,' Christian says, smiling once more. 'Enough about parents. All we need to know is that they fuck you up, right?' He laughs. 'Are you hungry? There's a pizza place round the corner, and I'll bet you've never tasted pizza like this in your life.'

Emily nods. 'Sounds good – I'm starving.' And she could do with something to soak up the vodka that's gone straight to her head. As clearly as if she were sitting next to her, Emily can hear her mother's words: *Nothing good can ever come of indulging in alcohol. We're not in control of ourselves when we drink.*

They're heading outside when Christian's phone rings. He looks at it and frowns, then turns away to answer it. 'Yeah. Okay. Right.' He ends the call and leads her out. 'I'm so sorry, Emily, but I have to go. Let's do pizza another night? Do you need me to walk you home?'

Taken aback, Emily shakes her head. 'No, I'm fine.'

He leans down to kiss her cheek. 'I'll text you.'

Emily watches him walk away.

She'd heard a girl's voice on the phone, she's sure of it. Fur-coat girl? Or someone else? Whoever it was, something just happened that made Christian disappear abruptly, with no explanation.

And one thing she knows for sure is that she doesn't like playing with fire.

FIVE

NOW

It's late afternoon when we arrive home from the airport. I spent most of the three and a half hour flight with my eyes shut, feigning sleep while I tried to work out how to deal with Christian. Yet somehow stepping into our home feels so normal, so far removed from the darkness he's cast over our wedding.

And when I close our front door, I also shut him out.

'Let's order pizza,' I suggest. 'Then we can open all our wedding cards and presents.'

'Can I help?' Lexi asks, already making her way upstairs to the spare room, where we've left them in a neat pile.

When she's gone, I pull Jeremy towards me and kiss him.

'Well, if this is what married life will be like, I could get used to it,' he says.

'I'm not making any promises,' I tease. 'Seriously though, do you feel okay about tying the knot again?'

'Absolutely.' He strokes my cheek. 'Especially if pizza for dinner becomes a regular thing.'

'You'd better call and order then,' I say. 'You know how long it takes.'

I head upstairs and unpack our cases. I've already filled the house with empty picture frames, ready for when our wedding photos come back from the photographer.

Thankfully, Christian had left before the photographer took the formal photos; I shudder at the thought that he could have been lurking in any of them.

He can only hurt me if I let him. And I refuse to do that.

As a treat for Lexi, we sit on the sofa with plates of pizza on our laps.

'Don't get used to this,' Jeremy warns.

Instead of rolling her eyes at him, Lexi nods. 'No problemo,' she says, taking a bite of pizza.

In between mouthfuls, Lexi gushes about how we're a proper family now. I knew she was happy for us, but it's only now dawning on me just how important this wedding has been for her. She beams at me. 'How cool that we've got the same surname!'

I turn to Jeremy and see that he, too, is smiling. This is all I need to get through whatever may happen.

What I don't expect is to come crashing back down to earth so abruptly with just one text message.

Don't think I've forgotten about you.

'When's Daddy coming back?'

I roll over in bed to see Lexi standing in the doorway, dressed in her lilac unicorn pyjamas. The sight of her is a welcome distraction from thoughts of Christian and what he's forcing me to do. For two days I've barely slept, and hardly a mouthful of food has passed my lips. He's yet to make further contact, but that only makes things worse.

All I can do is wait. Knowing that whatever is coming will not be pleasant.

'Oh, sweetheart,' I say to Lexi. 'It will only be a few days this time. He'll be back before we know it.' I pull myself up and glance at Jeremy's empty side of the bed. Neatly made, as he always leaves it before he has to fly.

Lexi ventures into the room. 'I just don't want to go to Mum's today,' she grumbles. 'There's nothing to do there. And she's always working. She practically ignores me. Even though I only go at weekends.' She sighs and plonks herself onto the bed.

For Lexi's sake, I slip into my regular role when it comes to defending Tia, though I know she puts herself before her daughter. That's why she was happy for Lexi to live with Jeremy, for him to be Lexi's main carer. 'Your mum works really hard,' I explain. 'It can't be easy for her, being on her own. And, hey, it's not for long, Lex. I promise I'll plan some fun things for us to do before school starts.' There are only three weeks left of the school holidays. Three short weeks for me to get Christian out of my life. I can't have him hanging around when school starts back. This needs to end quickly.

'Okay,' Lexi says, sighing. 'Can I have breakfast before we go, though?'

'How about French toast – your favourite?'

'Thanks, Emily.' She beams. 'I'm so glad you married Dad.'

'Me too,' I say.

My words catch in my throat.

Lexi's mother lives in Fulham, not too far from our house in Putney. My mind is distracted, and it takes a concerted effort to focus on the road, on getting my stepdaughter to her mother's house on time.

We pull into the road and I stare at the large white detached house. For all her faults, Tia works hard, and didn't take a single penny from Jeremy in the divorce. She even let him keep the house they owned together, not asking for a penny when he sold it. 'You just have main custody of Lexi,' she'd insisted. And he'd readily agreed, despite it being difficult with his flight schedules. Of course Pam stepped in to help, and before I came along Lexi spent more time with her grandmother than her own mother. It was a win–win situation for Jeremy, despite him knowing the underlying reason Tia wanted this arrangement.

'Ugh. Here I go,' Lexi mutters in the back of the car.

'Remember that your mum loves you, Lexi.' I find myself wanting to defend Tia; I saw first-hand my own mother's struggles with parenting.

I turn around and reach for Lexi's arm. 'Hey, Wednesday will be here before you know it. And I'll be right here waiting, okay?'

'It's not the weekend, I shouldn't have to be here now.'

'I know, but she didn't get to see you at the weekend because of the wedding. It's important that you spend time with her, Lex. You know that, don't you?'

She shrugs. 'Yeah, I suppose.' She pauses. 'Sometimes she's fun.' She turns to open the door, and I notice the glimmer of a tear on her cheek.

We walk down the path to the front door together, my arm protectively around her shoulder. It shouldn't be like this. Lexi should be racing off to be with her mum, not shuffling forward at a snail's pace.

Before we've reached the door, Tia opens it and stands with her arms folded, watching us. 'Bit late,' she says, before hugging Lexi. 'I've got a Zoom call in five which I can't be late for, otherwise I'd invite you in.' She looks me up and down. 'So, now you're the new Mrs Jordan?'

'Yes.'

'I have to say, I'm surprised you didn't keep your maiden name. I definitely had you down as a feminist.'

'It's about personal choice,' I say. I'm used to remarks like this from Tia. And instead of bothering me, it reassures me that she knows nothing about me. I would have loved to have kept my name, but I will never explain to Tia why I wanted to take Jeremy's.

'Just be careful, won't you?' Tia says.

'And what does that mean?'

Her eyes narrow as she stares at me. 'Nothing.' She ushers Lexi inside. 'You'll be here at nine sharp on Wednesday? I have to be somewhere mid-morning.'

'More like ten or eleven. Depending on traffic.' I refuse to let Tia control any aspect of my life.

Tia glares at me, closing the door before I've had a chance to ask her again what her warning to be careful meant.

Instead of going home I drive to my school in Barnes. My classroom displays from last year need to be taken down and replaced with new ones for my new Year 4 class. I walk through empty corridors; it's interesting how soulless schools can feel without the noise of children to fill them. And now, more than ever, I'm acutely aware of the ominous silence. There'll be someone in this building, I tell myself – there always is. William the caretaker can always be found onsite during the holidays.

But a blanket of apprehension surrounds me as I make my way to my classroom, and when my phone rings, blaring into the silence, my body jolts.

The unknown number on the screen convinces me it's Christian. Tentatively I answer. Better to know what he wants than avoid it. He's made it clear that I can't ignore him. Yet the thought of him fills me with fear, despite the years that have passed.

I'm not that person any more, I remind myself. I can deal with him now. Nothing he can say can hurt me now.

Oh, but it can, Emily, can't it? Because he knows the truth about what happened. The truth about you.

'Hello?' I say quietly. Even at barely more than a whisper,

my voice seems to echo through the corridor, loud enough for anyone to hear.

'Well, that's not much of a greeting, is it? How about some enthusiasm for the man you love?'

Bile rises in my throat. 'Don't do that.'

He snorts. 'Your life's hanging by a thread isn't it?' He chuckles. 'And I'm holding scissors. Snip!'

I don't speak; what can I reply when I'm at his mercy? I have to find a way to end this, because I know he won't stop until he's destroyed me. I stop walking and lean on a windowsill, staring out of the window to try and ground myself, to stop the panic rising even further. I focus on a magpie that's just flown into the playground. *One for sorrow.*

'So now that you've got childcare for your new daughter,' Christian continues, 'you'll be free to meet me tonight.'

He makes it sound so pleasant. Harmless. But every word fills me with terror. 'I can't. I—'

'Yes, you can. Your new hubby is away. Canada, right? So, there's nothing stopping you. Come to think of it, even if he was at home, waiting for his new bride to have dinner with him, you'd still have to find a way to see me, because you have no choice.'

There's no need to ask why he's doing this. I know his reasons. He could never let me go before, and now he's back to claim what he believes is rightfully his. 'Where?' I ask. 'What do you want from me?'

'Oh, Emily, please don't sound so... begrudging. You used to love spending time with me. Remember? We used to have fun, didn't we? Neither of us can deny that.'

A chill travels through my body, despite the sun streaming through the windows. This building is a furnace in the summer.

I'm not that person, and I won't let Christian take me back.

I want to scream at him, 'Just tell me,' but I know only too well that won't work.

'I'll pick you up at seven thirty. Just be ready.'

'I need to know where we're going.'

'It must feel awful having no control over anything. Now stop asking questions. And wear something nice.'

He's here at seven twenty-eight, parking on our drive as if he has every right to be there. My stomach twists into tight knots as I watch him.

I've chosen to defy him by staying in my jeans and oversized T-shirt. It's a small victory, but I'll pay for it later.

Since I got home from school all I've thought about is running away. Leaving a note explaining everything for Jeremy. Starting again somewhere else is something I've done before. But then I thought of the devastation it would cause him and Lexi. There has to be another way.

It's beginning to rain as I lock the door and traipse to Christian's car, his windscreen wipers screeching against the glass.

'I told you to wear something nice,' he says, as I open the door. 'You look awful.'

I shrug and get into the car. 'Didn't have time to change. Take it or leave it.'

He grabs my wrist and squeezes it until my skin burns. 'Let's just get one thing straight. You'll do as I say, Emily. I'm sure I've told you that already.' He lets go of my wrist and pulls at my T-shirt. 'That means if I tell you to take this off, then that's what you'll do.' He locks the doors.

I shudder. I'm at his mercy now, here in his car.

Without another word, he starts the car and reverses out of my drive. There's no point asking where we're going, so I turn away and try to focus on how I can stop him.

Only when I see signs for Ealing do I realise where he's taking me. Back to our past.

'What are you doing?' I ask, as we pass Acton station. 'Why are we here?'

He ignores my question. 'Have you been back here? Since you left?'

'No. I transferred to a different uni. And did my teacher training in Manchester. Far away from here.'

'I'd never been back until recently either,' he says. 'Couldn't bring myself to do it before.' He glances at me before focusing back on the road. 'I wanted to. But I just couldn't.'

'Why now, then? How is coming here with me going to help?'

'Because just knowing it will be hard for you is enough.'

There's no reply I can give – I won't let him know how sick I feel being in such proximity to Ealing. And such proximity to him. So I stay silent and wait to see what he has planned.

Within minutes, Christian has parked up, and he orders me to get out. I do as he says and stand by the car. I know where we're going, and I also know my body is fighting it. 'Please,' I say. 'Can we talk. I'm sorry for everything. I—'

He nods. 'I actually believe you are. But sometimes it's just too late for apologies.' He grabs my arm, pinching my skin with such force that I know I'll sustain bruising. And how will I explain that to Jeremy?

He drags me towards the university, so subtly that no one passing us would be able to tell I'm being forced against my will.

A young couple walk past us, holding hands, and I open my mouth to scream for help – then remember I can't.

We reach the steps leading up to the main door. 'Remember?' he says. 'This is where it all started.'

I stare at the huge building – the glass front of the ground floor and the square windows on the other floors are exactly as I recall. I've gone back in time and I don't know if I can deal with it. 'I wish I'd never met you.' My breathless words are barely audible.

Yet Christian hears me loud and clear. 'Not as much as I do.' He drags me towards the side of the building, where the entrance to the car park is.

There aren't many cars left; most lectures will be over by now. 'Why are we here?'

He ushers me to the steps leading to the library and pulls me down to sit. 'We're waiting for someone.'

Confusion clouds my brain. 'Who?'

'Someone else whose life you destroyed.'

'What? I don't—'

'And there she is.' He checks his phone. 'Right on time. Never a second's deviation. And I've been coming here for weeks now.' Christian sounds as if he's talking to himself. He stares at a woman coming out of the main block and heading across the car park.

She looks around my age, and wears a maxi skirt and V-neck blouse. Her skirt swishes around her ankles as she walks. Her dark, curly hair is tied in a bun. 'I don't know her,' I say, with a flush of relief. I don't know who I've been expecting.

Christian keeps his eyes on her. 'You really don't know who she is?'

'No.' But Christian's brought me here so she must be significant. 'Who is she?' I whisper, even though I don't want to know the answer.

'Look at her!' he demands. 'Look at her face! You must see it!'

And then I know.

'That's Ella. She works here. Has done for years. Not when we were here, of course. I wonder if she got a job here because of what happened? I don't believe in coincidences.'

'Why did you bring me? To torture me?' I can't let him know that it's worked.

'You never bothered to find out about her? Not once?'

My stomach cramps and I lean over.

'Thought not,' he hisses. 'I wonder what she'd do if she knew who you are? It would be devastating for you if someone were to tell her.' He raises his eyebrows. 'Keep that in mind, Emily.'

I stare at this woman as she climbs into a red Peugeot. She reverses out of her parking bay and drives right past us. She looks intent as she drives past us, yet somehow at peace.

But I know that can't be true.

SIX

BEFORE

Her eyes snap open and she turns to find Christian watching
her, smiling. She's seen a lot of him over the last few months.
He's under her skin, in a way nobody has been before. He
makes her laugh, helps her to be the person she's desperate to
be. *Fulfilling my potential.* That's how she thinks of it. Christian lifts her up, teaches her things she'd never know if it weren't
for him. 'You led a sheltered life before I came along, didn't you,
Em?' he'd joked the other day. But it's true. More than he
realises.

They're alone in her flat this morning: Kirsty didn't come
home last night, and Erin must be at Andre's. It's only six a.m.,
but slivers of late-February sunshine filter through the blinds,
and dust motes dance through the room.

'You're staring at me,' Emily says, pulling the duvet up
further, covering up every inch of her body. She's had a
boyfriend before, and is no stranger to intimacy, and by now
Christian knows every inch of her, yet in the harsh light of
morning, she's self-conscious being naked around him.

'I'm sorry,' Christian says, stroking her cheek. 'I love the way your hair fans out across the pillow when you're sleeping. It's cute.'

'It's messy,' she counters, pulling at a straggle of wavy hair.

'No,' he says, gripping her hand. 'Don't do that. Don't put yourself down. You just... it sounds corny, but you stop my breath. I can't believe how lucky I am to have you.'

Emily almost can't comprehend his words; no one has ever told her things like this, not even Isaac at school. That was kid's stuff, she realises now. Fumbling around in empty parks and fields. Isaac trying to feel her flesh while she constantly pushed his hands away, placing them over her clothes instead of under them. A clandestine relationship she was constantly in fear of her mother discovering. In the end Isaac had told her he didn't want to be a dirty secret, and he moved on to the next girl. Rather than being upset, Emily had been relieved. No more living in fear of her lie being exposed. Yet here she was, doing it all again.

'Yes, you *are* lucky,' she tells Christian.

The smile disappears from his face and he looks away.

'What's wrong?' she asks.

'Nothing. It's just... when you said that... I just can't stand arrogance. You know, girls thinking they're better than me. That's exactly what my ex was like.'

'I'm so sorry – I was only joking. I didn't mean anything by it. Of course I don't think you're the lucky one. *I* am.'

'No,' he says. 'We both are.' He smiles again. But this time his mouth is barely a thin line.

'You never talk about your ex,' Emily says, turning over to face him. 'What was she like?'

The minute she asks the question Emily realises her mistake. Silence fills the room, heavy and loaded with tension. But all she wants to know is whether the girl has curly black hair and likes wearing fur coats. Emily's seen her a few times, sashaying through the corridors at university. Self-assured. Just like Christian.

'Let me make breakfast for you,' Christian says after a moment, ignoring her question. 'A fry-up. How does that sound?'

'Um, like heaven,' she says. 'But I don't have much in the fridge. I usually just have cereal for breakfast.'

'That's not a problem,' Christian says, sliding out of bed. 'I'll pop to the shop across the road.'

'Okay, great.' Emily tries to focus on the impending smell of sizzling bacon that will soon fill the flat. It helps her forget Christian's strange reaction just now.

Breakfast is already on the table once she's showered and dressed. It smells as good as she's imagined, and her stomach rumbles in protest at being kept empty for too long. 'I can't believe you did all this,' she says.

'Yep, that's me – unbelievable! Come, sit. It will get cold.'

They sit at the round wooden table in the corner of the kitchen. She likes having him here in the morning. And she's doing her best to ignore what happened earlier. Perhaps it's no big deal: he just didn't want to talk about his ex. It doesn't matter; the only important thing is that he's here now with her.

'Do you have plans today?' Christian asks, slicing into his toast.

'I have to see my mum. I've been putting it off for as long as I can but... she likes me to go at least every other weekend. If she had it her way it would be every week. It used to be, but lately I've been busy, haven't I?' She smiles, hoping that she's making things right with him.

'I'll come with you,' Christian says. 'It's about time I met your mum, isn't it?'

'What? No... you can't.'

Christian places his fork down and frowns. 'Why? Are you ashamed of me?'

'No, course not.'

'Then I'm coming. She'll love me, Em, you'll see. I can charm anyone.'

How can she tell him that this won't be the case? That she could bring home any man in the world and he wouldn't be acceptable to her mother. 'I know, but... you don't understand.'

He rests his elbows on the table. 'Then help me to. What's going on? This can't just be about your mum being overprotective. You're an adult. You can have a boyfriend.'

'It's not about you. It's just... she won't exactly be happy that I'm seeing someone.' Her first and only boyfriend until now was a major secret she'd managed to keep from her mum.

'That doesn't make sense,' Christian protests. 'You're nineteen! You don't even live with her.'

'I know, she just... she's really strict. It's always just been the two of us. I'm sorry. Maybe soon. I just need to find a way—'

'I'm going to the shop.' Christian pushes his plate aside and jumps up, ignoring her plea for him to stay. He stalks out of the kitchen and grabs his coat from the hook in the hallway, not even turning back to look at her.

'Christian, wait!' Emily follows him, but he's already slamming the front door. She stares at it, as if somehow it will open again, and Christian will be standing there laughing, telling her it's all been one of his jokes.

Ten minutes later she's still staring at the door.

Coming back to her mum's house is always difficult. They aren't a normal family, whatever normal is. When they're together, the atmosphere is fraught with tension, usually with Emily waiting for her mum to have an episode.

And now Emily stands outside the three-bedroom house her mother inherited from her grandparents – a home that's always been too large for the two of them. When her dad was around they'd lived in a flat in Woking, but moving here had been the best thing for her mum.

She waits to be let in; she's forgotten her key and her mother won't like that. It had taken Emily long enough to convince her to let her have her own key in the first place. 'I'm too nervous to let you have one,' she'd always insisted. 'You might lose it, then someone could get in our house and attack me. There are horrible people in this world.'

She refused to believe this. There were more decent people than not in this world, weren't there? Yet her mother had repeated this theory so often that eventually Emily gave up asking until she went off to university. She'd somehow managed to convince her mum it was essential she have her own key, in case her mum got ill or had an accident and Emily needed to get in.

'Where's your key?' her mother asks, peering past Emily as she ushers her inside, and shuts the door, bolting it from inside. 'Please don't tell me you've lost it? I'll have to get the locks changed right now.'

'It's not lost. Sorry – I just forgot to bring it. It's safely locked in my desk drawer.' A harmless lie to keep her mother from panicking – the key is on top of her desk where it usually sits.

'You're very late again. I was starting to think the train must have crashed. You could have texted me. Didn't you get mine? I sent you about four. Lunch is ready. They had a special offer on some ready meals, so I grabbed a few.'

Emily doesn't point out that the fridge is always stocked with ready meals, whether there's a supermarket promotion on or not. Instead, she sighs and offers an apology, blaming the trains and buses as she usually does. And a dead mobile battery.

But in reality she's late because she was fretting about Christian walking out that morning, and what it means. Is their relationship over? It's her fault – she made him feel that she doesn't care, when that couldn't be further from the truth. All he'd wanted to do was meet her mum.

But I need to keep this part of my life separate.

Her mother gestures to Emily's clothes. 'For goodness' sake, that coat's hardly warm enough, is it? It's not summer, Emily. It's February!'

'I've got a scarf and gloves, Mum, I'm fine.'

Her mother shakes her head. 'And aren't those jeans a bit tight? Do you want men leering at you? Men are predators, don't give them any reason to get ideas.'

'Mum! These are normal jeans like everyone wears.' Emily rolls her eyes. 'Are we going to eat, then? I'm starving.'

Most of the meal is eaten in silence. Formal. Uncomfortable. Emily wants to scream, just to get a reaction, but she'd never dare do it. She needs her mum to think she's doing everything she expects from her.

She's clearing away the plates when the doorbell rings.

'Who could that be?' Her mother tuts. 'It's Sunday. I'm not expecting anyone. And I definitely haven't ordered anything.'

'Shall I get it?' Emily offers.

'No!' Her mother stands. 'You stay here. I'll go.'

While she heads off to answer the door, walking so slowly that Emily's sure whoever it is will be long gone before her mother reaches it, Emily begins washing up. There's a perfectly good dishwasher next to the fridge, but her mother doesn't trust them. She doesn't believe it washes the dishes properly.

She hears a male voice – familiar yet incongruous – and she turns from the sink so abruptly she almost drops the plate she's been scrubbing. She hurries to the front door, dripping bubbles across the hall.

Christian is standing on the doorstep, while her mother peers out from behind the door.

'This man insists he knows you,' her mother says, frowning.

'Do you know him, Emily, or do I have to call the police? He seems to know everything about you.'

She forces down the bile in her throat while she racks her brain for a way to explain Christian's presence. 'Yeah, we... um—'

'I've just come to pick Emily up,' Christian says, smiling broadly. 'I don't want to intrude on your family time, but we've got an exam tomorrow and everything's riding on it.' He leans forward to shake her mother's hand. She looks like a stone statue, not reaching for his hand, but staring at him with wide, disapproving eyes.

'And you must be Emily's mother,' Christian continues, seemingly unperturbed by her reluctance to respond to his greeting. 'I'm Christian. Emily and I are on the same course. She's actually helping me a lot. With studying. Such a bright daughter you have. I'd be lost without her.'

'Oh,' her mother says, hesitantly taking his hand. 'Emily never mentioned you. But then she never mentions anything to me. And you didn't tell me you have an exam tomorrow, Emily.'

'I'm sorry,' Christian says, before Emily can respond. 'I'm always saying how important it is to talk to our parents, and let them know what's going on in our lives. I'm sorry if she isn't doing that.' He turns to Emily. 'Maybe you could make more effort with your mum, Em?'

At a loss for words, all she can do is nod.

'I'm Laura,' her mother says, after a moment of silence. She's not exactly smiling, but neither is it a dismissive scowl. Emily's not sure how Christian's done it, but he's managed to break down a barrier, and her mother isn't rushing to get him out.

'I think I'd better get back now, Mum,' Emily says. 'Get some studying in before tomorrow.'

Her mother frowns and turns to Christian. 'How did you

get here? Did you drive?' She peers past him and scans the road outside. 'You won't go too fast, will you?'

Christian takes her mother's hand. 'Mrs Thomas, you have my word that I will drive Emily home carefully. I've never even had a single point off my licence.'

Silence once again floats around them all for a moment before her mother gives a small nod. But Emily knows she's watching them closely as they make their way to Christian's car across the road. This won't be the end of it; her mother is just too shocked to register what's happening.

And her mother is still standing at the door when they drive off.

Emily doesn't speak until they're out of her road and heading towards the A3, back to London. 'What's going on?' she asks finally.

'What do you mean?'

'You walked out of my flat this morning and now you've just turned up at my mother's house. How did you even get the address?'

'Kirsty let me in, and I found it in your room.'

She turns to him. 'You've been through my things?'

'No! Of course not. What do you take me for? There was a letter right on top of your desk. The address was right there. I'm not some kind of stalker. I wasn't going through your stuff.'

She should be angry with him, but as mad as she is that he's done this, she's also flattered that he's gone to all this effort just to see her. She's being too hard on him again. 'I know you're not a stalker,' she replies.

This doesn't seem to appease him, though, and for the rest of the drive, Christian barely says a word,

It's not until they pull up outside her flat that Emily dares to ask him if he's okay.

'It just made me feel like shit,' he says, staring out of the side window. 'That you wouldn't let me come with you. Your mum will grow to like me. She just needs to be able to trust me. And how can that happen when you keep me a secret?' He turns to face her. 'Which makes me wonder even more why you didn't want me to meet her. She didn't seem as bad as you've made out.'

'You were there for two minutes,' Emily explains. 'And she was having a good day. You haven't seen her at her worst, Christian. Everything I said is true. I'm still shocked that she let you in the house. I'm sure I'll get hell when I speak to her next.'

'But she's hardly the person you made her out to be,' he insists.

'That's because she didn't realise we're together. She thought we were just friends.'

Christian stares at her. 'Whatever you say.'

She reaches for his hand but he pulls away. 'Aren't you coming in?'

'Not today. I just need to be alone right now. This has... I won't lie – I feel hurt.' Without waiting for a reply, Christian gets out and walks round to open the passenger door. 'I'll walk you to the door then I'm going.'

She tries to change his mind when they get to the main door of her block, but Christian is adamant about leaving. 'I just hope this doesn't happen again,' he says, shaking his head. He kisses her cheek before he heads back to his car, a gesture which does nothing to assuage Emily's guilt.

Inside, she pulls off her coat and heads straight to the kitchen to get some water. Kirsty sits at the table, her head buried in her laptop.

Her flatmate waves without looking up. 'This damn assignment. It's driving me insane! I could be at the bar but instead I'm stuck here. Know anything about coastal erosion?'

'Um, no. Sorry.'

'Well, what kind of flatmate are you?' Kirsty laughs. 'Just kidding. You're pretty great, actually. You don't make a mess or too much noise. We barely even know you're here most of the time.'

Invisible. That's how she's always felt. Emily forces a laugh. 'Sorry about Christian turning up earlier. He didn't realise I was going to my mum's.'

Kirsty looks up. 'What?'

'Christian. He came to get something from my room. He said you let him in.'

She shakes her head. 'Er, no. I've been by myself all day. Actually wishing someone would disturb me so I can have a break from this.' She turns back to her laptop. 'He definitely didn't come here.'

Emily frowns. This is weird. Christian had definitively told her he'd come here and that's how he'd known where to find her. 'I must have heard wrong,' she says. 'Do you want coffee?' She busies herself with boiling the kettle.

But Emily knows she hasn't got this wrong. Christian has lied to her.

SEVEN

NOW

The day looms ahead of me, stark and unnerving. If I knew exactly what Christian has planned for me then I could face it head-on – but he's deliberately keeping me in the dark, making me stew. All I know for sure is that he won't stop until he's had his revenge.

All morning the image of Ella plays in my head. Is Christian planning to tell her? That would have devastating consequences for me, but also for him. I never knew about Ella. If I had, I would have done something to make amends.

I spend the morning drafting a letter to her. I can leave it on her car. I don't even have to sign my name, but I can explain everything. Several times I change my mind, and shred what I've written, but then I have the letter ready. There will be a chance to do it. I will do this for her. I place it in the shoebox I keep my passport and other important documents in and put it back on the top shelf of my wardrobe.

When my stomach begins to groan, I force myself to make a ham sandwich, but I can't bring myself to eat it. Instead, I drink two glasses of water to fill my stomach, and stare at my phone, wondering when the call will come. Because I know it will. Christian is unstable, and there's no reasoning with him.

At four o'clock, my mobile rings. I should be relieved that it's Jeremy, but somehow I'm not. Until Christian calls and I know what he wants next, I can't work on a way to stop him.

'Are you okay? Missing me?' Jeremy asks.

'Of course,' I tell him. 'How's Canada?'

'I do love it here. But I'd rather be home with you and Lexi. I feel awful leaving so soon after the wedding.'

'We knew that would be the case, though, didn't we?' I'm used to Jeremy's gruelling schedule – I was fully aware that being the wife of a pilot would mean long absences. 'We were lucky you could take those three days off. And we had a lovely pre-wedding honeymoon.' Yet my memories of Kefalonia have now been tainted.

'I still feel bad, though. How did it go dropping Lexi at Tia's? I just spoke to her and she seems fine.'

'Tia was okay to me,' I tell him, choosing to keep quiet about her warning to be careful. I'm sure it didn't mean anything – it's not the first time she's made a snide comment to me.

Jeremy pauses. It's still hard for him to talk about his ex-wife. He tries not to show it, but I feel it in his heavy pauses and silences. 'Good. What are your plans tonight?'

Waiting to find out what my puppet master will force me to do. 'Not much. Early night for me, I think. A book. Netflix.'

'Two more days then I'll be home.'

For a short while. Then he'll be off again and I'll be stuck here with Christian. And who knows what will happen?

We say goodnight, and when I tell him I love him, a flood of doubt washes over me, threatening to drown me. How can I love him as he deserves when our whole relationship is based on a lie?

Another hour passes and there's still no word from Christian. I sit on the sofa with the book I took to Kefalonia, daring to believe he might leave me alone. Maybe he's realised he doesn't want to do this after all. There must be a heart buried somewhere in his body. I wouldn't have fallen for him otherwise, would I? But I know it's not as simple as that. And when I picture how he was in the early days of our relationship, the image is hazy, unreal, as if it never existed. There was no way I could foresee what would happen.

The doorbell rings, cutting through the silence, and I freeze. Praying I'm wrong about who will be standing at my door, I slowly head towards it and peer through the peephole. It's him. Looking directly at me and smiling; he knows I'm watching him.

He rings the bell again. 'I know you're in there, Emily. What will the neighbours think if you leave me standing out here?'

I open the door and stare at him. 'What are you doing here? Lexi could have been home!'

He steps inside, pushing past me. 'But she's not, is she? She's with her mother. You told me that.'

Even if I had mentioned it, Christian has already proven that he can find out anything he wants about me. 'I don't want you in here.'

He pushes the door shut. 'I don't like your attitude, Emily. You need to show me some decency.'

'You could have called!'

Christian ignores me, pulling off his coat and wandering through the hall. 'Nice place you have. Bet you never dreamed you'd end up with all this.'

'It's just a house,' I try to convince him. 'Possessions don't mean anything.'

He smiles. 'You're right. When it comes down to it, it's only people who mean anything.'

'Just tell me what you want. You've proven you're in

control. Can't that be enough? Taking me to Ella was enough. Please, Christian.'

He smiles and picks up a photo of Jeremy and me with Lexi. 'Aren't you even going to offer me a drink? Oh, don't worry – I'd have to say no. I drove here, after all. You and I have somewhere else to go, and I don't want to be over the limit.' He places the photo down.

As I stare at him, I fight back the urge to pummel my fists into his chest. 'Please don't do this, Christian. You've done enough already. Turning up like that ruined my wedding day. I'll never be able to think of it without remembering, will I? Every time I look at our wedding photos I'll think about it.'

He appears to mull this over, glancing at the paintings on the walls, taking in my home. 'Yep, that's unfortunate. But what you did to me is far, far worse. And it's payback time. I've told you that already, Emily. We don't need to go around in circles.' He walks past me into the living room. 'Anyway, we're wasting time. I'm always punctual. Do you remember? We need to leave in a minute and you're not ready.'

'Ready for what?'

'We're having dinner with my father and brother. I haven't seen them since my mum's funeral. They'll never forgive me for not coming back to see her before it was too late. And I can't explain to them now that she was in touch with me the whole time. That would change the way they think of her, and I can't have that when she's not here to defend herself. And that's all because of you.'

I shake my head. 'I don't make your decisions for you. And Audrey decided to keep it from your dad. You can't blame me for that.'

'You stole so much time from her,' Christian says. 'From me. And now she's dead there's no way I can make it up to her. My dad can barely look at me because of what *I* did. And how can I blame him for hating me?'

Christian is right about this. His family didn't deserve any of what happened. 'I'm sure your dad doesn't—'

'Shut up!' Christian yells. 'He doesn't know what to say to me. What to think of me. And now you're going to help me put that right.'

'Why don't you tell them the truth right now? You could put an end to it all. To me.'

'Believe me, I've thought about that. But this is a much better way. Making you pay, and getting everything I want from you.'

'You're sick in the head,' I say.

Christian steps towards me and grabs my wrists, twisting my skin so tightly it burns. It's all I can do not to scream.

I've made a mistake calling him out. I need to keep Christian onside. He knows what happened that night, and I can't risk him exposing me. I will go along with him for now, until I can work out how to stop him. How to silence him. 'I'll help you,' I say. 'You're right, I owe it to you.'

He lets go of my wrists and pushes me against the wall. 'You can't go like that,' he says, pointing to my jeans and T-shirt. 'Wear a dress. It's still warm out there.'

I shudder, and fight away flashbacks of the old Emily. 'I'm fine as I am,' I insist. I need him to know that, despite everything, I will stand up to him.

He shrugs, and I believe I've won this battle until he saunters over to me and leans into my ear. 'Put something nicer on or I'll be making some phone calls. Starting with one to your husband.' He begins reeling off Jeremy's mobile number.

'Stop! I'll change. Just wait here.'

Christian smiles. 'There was a time when you liked me to watch you getting undressed. Remember?'

Bile rises to my throat, and in my head I visualise running from the house, from him, escaping this nightmare. Instead, I nod. 'That was a long time ago. Everything's changed.'

'Because of your actions.'

I turn away from him and head to the bedroom, feeling the weight of his eyes upon me.

Christian doesn't say anything as I walk away, and somehow his silence is far worse than any words he could throw at me.

EIGHT

NOW

We arrive in Reading too soon. Being in the car has felt like we're in no man's land; neither safe nor dangerous. And as much as I've loathed every minute of being alone in a car with Christian, at least he didn't speak for most of the journey. Instead, he turned up a talk radio station and left me alone with my scrambled thoughts. I'm trapped, with no idea yet how I'll escape.

Everything changes when we pull up outside an unfamiliar house, on a street I've never set foot on. Christian is no longer at ease, and this spells trouble for me. He stares at the house, and I realise it must be just as unfamiliar to him as it is to me. Christian's parents moved here a few months after he disappeared, so he never lived in it. It's a three-storey townhouse, offering more space than his father needs now. But knowing Anthony as I used to, I'm quite certain he will never entertain the idea of downsizing, especially when memories of Audrey still live there.

I turn to Christian and notice how pale his skin has become. And just for a second, I almost feel sorry for him. But I won't allow myself to get sucked back in. 'Bringing me here won't help you,' I say. 'You're just lying to your family. Again.'

He nods. 'I suppose I am. You'd know all about that, wouldn't you?' He takes a strand of my hair and holds it for a second before letting it drop. 'We're so alike, aren't we? As much as you don't want to believe—'

'I'm nothing like you!' I spit my words at him.

The door opens, leaving him no time to respond, and his father stands there, squinting at us. He seems smaller than I remember him, as if Audrey's death has diminished him. I remember him as a powerful man, intimidating. With his light brown hair and green eyes, he is a glimpse of the future Christian at sixty-four. 'I didn't think you'd come,' he says to Christian. 'Finally ready to answer some questions, I hope?' He doesn't wait for a reply, and instead looks me up and down. 'Well, there's a face I never thought I'd see again. Come in, Emily. It's good to see you.'

Silently, Christian walks inside and I follow, holding out my hand to shake Anthony's.

Instead of taking my hand, Anthony hugs me, and beside me I sense Christian's discomfort. I'm pleased, and remind myself that despite being forced to come here, I won't let Christian win. I can't.

'I've decided to order food in for dinner,' Anthony tells us. 'It's Thai. My favourite. Of course, I have no idea what food you like these days, Christian.'

'It's perfect,' I say.

'Emily's not fussy,' Christian says, turning round and taking hold of my arm. 'And I'll still eat anything.'

'Well, how would I know that?' Anthony says. 'Go through to living room – Tyler's in the kitchen on a work call. I'll check if he's finished.'

Anthony disappears, leaving us alone in the hallway. I study Christian's face; I've never seen him look this anxious, this far out of his comfort zone. 'You're not being natural,' he hisses in my ear. 'Do better.'

'I'm trying my best, Christian. Your dad's just upset—'

'Just stick to the story.' He squeezes my arm, and it takes all my willpower to suppress a scream. 'And next time don't flinch when I touch you. You're my girlfriend, remember? You need to be more... loving.'

Anthony pokes his head into the hall and beckons us into the kitchen. 'Don't just stand there, come and say hello to your brother.'

Christian reaches for my hand, and I fight the urge to pull away. I can't make a scene here. Christian's dad might appear to like me, but he wouldn't if he knew the truth.

In the kitchen, Tyler gets down from his kitchen stool and walks over to us. I can't help but stare at him – he's no longer the young kid I remember. He must be around thirty now, and his dark hair and brown eyes make him the stark contrast of his brother. 'Well, well, well,' he says to Christian. 'You're actually here. You wouldn't say a word to us at Mum's funeral so I didn't think you'd turn up today.' He slaps Christian on the back. 'I think you've got some explaining to do.'

'All that can wait,' Anthony says. 'The food will be here in a minute. I've ordered several different dishes and we can all share.'

'It's fine,' Christian says. It's funny how the formidable figure of his father can diminish him.

Tyler walks over to me and holds out his hand. But just as I reach for it, he pulls me into a hug instead. 'This is a huge surprise,' he says, staring at me as if I can't be real. 'I didn't think we'd see *you* again,' he says. His tone is softer with me, and I remember he was always kind to me. With an eight-year age gap between them, Christian never had time for his younger brother – but I always made sure I did.

'Love conquers all, doesn't it?' Christian says, squeezing my hand.

My phone rings, and I freeze. Christian's grip tightens: a silent warning. 'Sorry,' I say, pulling out my phone. 'It's a work colleague. I'll call them back.' I cut off Jeremy's call and switch off my phone.

'They're always calling Emily for advice,' Christian explains. 'Shows what a fantastic teacher she is.' He twists my fingers so tightly it feels as though they'll snap. Neither of the others notice I am at his mercy.

'Isn't it the summer holidays?' Tyler asks. 'Surely you should be having a break?'

'We all share lesson ideas for next term, so it's never-ending.' I'm able to look him directly in the eye as I answer – at least this is not a lie.

Tyler smiles. 'Well, they say teaching is a vocation, not just a job, don't they?'

'What do you do now?' I ask. 'I remember you wanted to be a vet.'

'That's exactly what I am,' Tyler says, smiling. 'I'm surprised you remember.'

'Emily never forgets a thing, do you?' Christian says, squeezing my hand again.

It's a relief when the food arrives and the aroma of Thai spices fills the kitchen. Anthony directs me to sit opposite Christian. Even though he can't physically do anything to me while we're eating, my body remains rigid. Ready for flight.

'So how have you been all these years, Emily?' Tyler asks, digging his fork into his rice. 'How did the two of you find each other again? You couldn't have been in touch all this time – I know you would have told my parents if you knew where Christian was.'

'Of course I would have. I had no idea where he was until a

few months ago,' I say. 'The same time as you.' I glance at Christian. 'He found me on Facebook.' Christian has briefed me on the details, I just need to get it all right. I worry what he's capable of if I don't. But we're both on a knife edge: if Tyler pushes further about Facebook, then all our lies will be exposed. I've never been on it, or any other social media site. How can you hide from someone if your life is plastered all over the internet?

Anthony frowns. 'Well, I hope it lasts this time. I hope you can stop him running again. Not telling his own family where he is for fifteen years. Are you sure you didn't know where he was?'

'No, I really didn't.'

'Don't talk about me as if I'm not here,' Christian says quietly.

'Well, you weren't here for fifteen years. So it's a bit hard to get used to. Your mum—'

'Dad, don't,' Tyler urges.

'We told the police, you know. Fat lot of good that did. They barely even tried to look for you.'

'Because he wasn't a kid, Dad. He wasn't vulnerable.' Tyler spoons some chicken onto his plate. 'So, you never got married, Emily?'

I've been instructed to say no. That I was in a relationship but I left him because I realised I still loved Christian after all this time. It's delusional to think they will believe this, but I will play his twisted game for now. I spew out the words I've been forced to learn, studying their faces for disbelief. It surprises me when Anthony nods and says he's glad our paths crossed again. 'You were good for him,' he declared. 'I always thought that. I'm surprised you've forgiven him for leaving.'

'It's all in the past,' I say. 'We're only looking forward now.'

'Sounds super healthy,' Tyler says. 'And what would we do without social media?' He looks at me for too long and I feel my face flush; my lies are scrawled all over it, and it's only a matter of time before I'm exposed.

'So, how have you been, brother?' Christian asks.

'Top of the world. You know me. Never let anything get me down.'

It's clear that Tyler is taking a dig at his brother. 'So is Christian,' I say. 'Did he tell you he has his own business in America?

'What's all this, then?' Anthony asks, turning to Christian. 'What's Emily talking about?'

'Well, I had to earn a living,' Christian says. 'Can't live on thin air.'

'Oh? I'm intrigued,' Anthony says. 'What's the business exactly?'

For the first time since we've been here, Christian seems at ease as he gives them details of his cyber security business. Although I understand little of what he's saying, it's clear how much this means to him. Which means it is a weapon I can use against him.

'Well, you make it sound impressive,' Anthony says. 'You managed to pull it off even though you left university before you finished.'

'I learnt everything I needed to,' Christian says.

'If you don't abandon it. We had high hopes for you when you were studying business at university, and then you just... gave it all up. Disappeared. Like a ghost. If you hadn't packed up all your things, we'd have thought you were dead.'

'Just goes to show you can be wrong sometimes,' Christian says. 'Even you, Dad.' He raises his glass. 'Cheers to me, then. For making a success of myself against all your expectations.'

Neither Anthony nor Tyler lift their own glasses, instead turning their attention back to me. 'So, the two of you are back together then?' Tyler asks.

I freeze. Even though I already know that's what Christian wants them to believe, hearing his brother say it chills my bones.

'Fate brought us back together.' Christian smiles. 'You can't fight what's meant to be.' When he leans across and kisses my cheek, I only just manage to suppress a scream.

'As long as you don't go disappearing again,' Tyler says, under his breath.

We all hear him, but nobody responds.

I feel Tyler's heavy stare resting on me, and I look down at my hands. They're trembling. I'm trapped here, powerless to go against anything Christian says. And surely it's just a matter of time before someone catches me out?

Tyler stands up. 'I hope it works out for you both this time. Stroke of luck, Emily being single.'

Christian bangs his fists on the table. 'What the fuck did you say?'

'Calm down, I was just joking. Where's your sense of humour?'

'I don't have one,' Christian says, glaring at his brother. Then, as if a switch has flicked in his brain, he smiles. 'But you're right. I'm a very lucky man. This time I won't be making the same mistakes.' He glances at me.

'Well, that's more like it,' Anthony says. 'This get-together is supposed to be about building bridges, not burning them. Now, come on – eat up.'

Christian excuses himself to go to the bathroom, and I once again burn under Tyler's stare.

A few seconds pass before anyone breaks the silence. 'So, you're giving him another chance,' Anthony says. 'After him disappearing the way he did. Dropping out of university. Leaving us all to wonder whether or not we'd ever see him again.'

'Ghosting,' Tyler explains. 'He ghosted his own family.'

Only Christian and I know they're wrong about this, but

the truth will never escape my mouth. 'Like I said, that's all in the past. I forgive him,' I say. 'He's not the person he was.'

'And what person was that?' Anthony asks. 'Someone unreliable who lets his family down. Someone who can just disappear without any thought to what he was putting his mother through. It destroyed her. And all that money we spent on his education. He could have done anything he wanted to. Instead of drifting through life relying on his charm.'

'I don't think that's fair,' I say. 'He's made a success of himself. He has his own business.'

'That's what he says.' Anthony turns away.

'We all make mistakes.' My words are cold and detached, and with Christian out of the room, I don't even attempt to make them sound believable.

'Isn't that exactly what *you're* doing?' Tyler asks.

'What?'

Before he can answer, Christian comes back in, pulling on his jacket.

His dad frowns. 'You're not going already? You've just got here. This is ridiculous!'

'No, I'm not leaving,' Christian says. 'In fact, I thought Emily and I could stay the night. It's a long drive back and I want to spend time here with my family.' He smiles. 'We would like a walk though, wouldn't we, Emily?'

I open my mouth to protest – I feel safer with Anthony and Tyler around – but Christian walks over to me, placing his hands on my shoulders. 'Won't it be lovely to stay? A night away from the London chaos.'

'Of course you'll stay,' Anthony says. 'Tyler's staying too, but there's plenty of space. And as Emily doesn't have work in the morning, there'll be no arguments.'

'Actually, I do have to go into school. Setting up the class-room and getting all my resources ready.' I glance at Christian.

I'm taking too big a risk here. 'But it's nothing that can't wait until the afternoon.'

'Emily loves her job,' Christian says. 'So much so that she often forgets to make time for herself. She's totally dedicated to those children she teaches. She can't imagine doing anything else.' He turns to me. 'That would be the worst thing for you, wouldn't it?'

Anger swirls around my body. 'No, and I'll never have to.'

'It's great that you've found your vocation,' Anthony says.

'She certainly has,' Christian says, and I'm the only one who sees how sinister his smile is. 'Come on, Emily, let's go for that walk.'

Without hesitation I stand and pick up my plate. 'I'll clear this away. Thank you so much for dinner, Anthony.'

'My pleasure,' he says. He looks at me for a fraction too long, as if he's about to say something else, but then he begins clearing the rest of the food.

As soon as we're outside, I turn to Christian. 'Why have you forced me to go for a walk with you. I was doing what you asked in there. Fighting your corner. What the hell is this about? Now they're wondering what we're doing!'

Christian grabs my arm. 'It's time to regroup, Emily. Go over our strategy. Come on. It's still warm, isn't it. A perfect night for a stroll.' He lets go of my arm but takes my hand instead. The gesture is such anathema to me that I flinch and almost pull away.

'Play your part,' Christian warns. 'We're being watched.'

I turn back to the house and see Tyler standing by the living room window with his arms folded. He lifts his hand and gives a small wave, but we both ignore him.

Christian's hand feels so different to Jeremy's – his skin is dry, and I'm sure it never used to be. But then, I've blocked out so much of my past that it's no wonder I can't recall small details.

We head along Nelson Road, Christian gripping my hand so tightly it feels as though my skin is burning. 'Tyler knows something,' he says, when we reach the end of the road and turn left.

I freeze. 'That's impossible.'

'No, it's not Emily. You must have always known this could happen.'

'But why do you think that? Did he say something? He was fine with me at dinner. Kind.'

'I know my brother. He knows something. The way he kept asking you questions. He doesn't trust either of us. Don't you see? This causes a huge problem. Because it's in my interests that nobody finds out. Not while you're doing everything I want you to. If anyone's ever going to expose what happened, it will be me.' He pulls his hand away and walks faster.

Looking around at this endless residential road, where it seems nothing exists beyond the rows of houses, I picture myself running. I'm wearing flat shoes and I'm fast. Christian used to be faster, but I can cling to the hope that the years – however he's spent them – have gnawed away at his fitness.

Instead, I turn away from him and focus on my shoes scuffing the pavement as I walk. 'You don't know for sure that he knows. You're being paranoid, just like—'

He grabs my wrist. 'We need to find out. We need to watch him. I don't trust him.'

'He's your brother! He wouldn't do anything to—'

He shakes my arm, so hard it feels as though my bones are rattling. 'Stop questioning me, Emily!'

I'm convinced this is nothing but Christian's paranoia, but I keep my mouth shut. For now, it's easier to go along with him. 'I'll be more careful.'

'Then start listening to me.' He lets go of my arm. 'I'll try and find out what he knows, but in the meantime be extra careful around him.' He takes my hand again and this time I don't flinch. If this is what I need to do in order to stop him, it's a small price to pay.

'You owe me,' he reminds me, as we continue walking.

I nod, unable to speak at this mention of the past.

'We'd better get back,' he says. 'I'd love to be a fly on the wall right now. I know they're talking about us.'

'We've just disappeared for a walk by ourselves when we're supposed to be spending time with them,' I say. 'What are they supposed to think?'

He stops walking and leans into my ear. 'That we're so into each other we needed to be alone.' His mouth brushes against my lips as he speaks.

There are three floors in this house, and Anthony has told us that Christian and I will be sleeping in the spare bedroom at the top. 'You'll have some privacy up there,' he said. 'And your own bathroom.' But privacy is the last thing I want.

A double bed takes up most of the space in the spare bedroom. There's no room on the floor for anyone to sleep, and with the low sloping ceiling, no space for a wardrobe. I would gladly let Christian have the bed to himself. I've tried to bargain with him, but he won't give in. He's enjoying having this control, and the more I beg, the more pleasure he gets.

'I'll just sleep sitting up on that,' I insist, pointing to the chair in the corner.

'No, you won't. How would that look if someone came in and saw? There'd be no explaining that away.'

The worrying thing is that Christian seems to believe his words, almost as if saying them makes it all real. He has forced me into a box, a repeat of those years we were together. But of course, it's far worse now. I watch as he pours himself a beer on the bedside table and climbs into bed fully clothed.

I need to get out of here.

'Are you sure you don't want one?' he asks, holding up his glass. 'I've brought plenty up here.' He gestures to the floor by the bed, where he's put a box of beer bottles.

I shake my head and settle back into the chair, folding my arms. If he keeps drinking, perhaps he'll fall asleep and not realise until it's too late that I haven't come to bed. The plan has been forming in my head since we went for a walk earlier. I'll leave a note explaining that I've had a family emergency and need to get back. I'll say that I'll be back to pick up Christian in the morning. That should buy me some time. And I'll deal with his rage later. Surely he won't expose me over this – not when he's so sure he can get everything he wants out of me.

He wants to destroy my life. Nothing less. I can't lose sight of that.

Pulling out my phone, I begin tapping a message to Jeremy. It's hard to let myself think of my husband – a kind, selfless man – while I'm forced to be here with Christian, but I need to let him know I'm okay.

'What are you doing?' Christian asks.

'Messaging Lexi. I need to check on her.'

'Why? She's with her mother.' A smile creeps onto his face. 'Oh, that's right. Tia Long. I know all about her. Jeremy doesn't have much luck with women, does he? Still, as bad as that marriage was, what he's walked into with you is far more destructive, isn't it? I mean, what's a little issue with alcohol compared to what you bring to the table?'

I ignore his jibe. It shouldn't surprise me that Christian knows about Tia, not when he seems to know everything about my life and everyone in it. 'People get divorced. It happens.'

'Yep, and now he's met you. Lucky, lucky man.' He takes a sip of beer. 'But as I said, you don't need to check on Lexi when she's with her mum, who as far as I know doesn't touch alcohol any more.'

Again, I resist the urge to smash my fists into his face. Not just for this but for everything he did to me. Everything that followed was because of him. I turn back to my phone, try to focus on Jeremy. *I love you*, I type. There's so much more I want to write to him, but every word will be tainted because of where I am, and who I'm with.

When I glance up, Christian is still watching me as he sips his beer. His silence disturbs me more than his words, because I fear what his mind is capable of conjuring.

Yet when he finally speaks, I immediately wish he hadn't. 'Thinking about Ella? How you messed up her life? From what I can see, all she does is go to work then go home. Lives by herself. Two cats. Everyone needs someone to love, don't they?'

Ignoring him, I stand and walk to the small bookcase in the corner of the room. Ella has been permanently on my mind since Christian took me to the university, and the only way I can deal with it is to remind myself I will make it up to her.

The bookcase is filled with paperbacks, and I scan the spines, pulling out a John le Carré novel I assume must be Anthony's. I take it back to my chair and open the cover. None of the words will sink in, but at least it's an excuse to stay on this chair.

Christian leaves me alone for some time, perhaps close to an hour, but I'm aware of his eyes on me every so often when he glances up from his phone, and I lose count of the times he refills his glass. *He's nervous of his dad. Something I can use against him?*

'Do you ever think about it?' he slurs. 'I'm sure you do. How could you not?'

'I look forward, never back.'

He takes another drink. 'It was just you and me against the world, wasn't it? At one time.' His words blend into each other without a pause.

Christian wants me to apologise. To say I'm sorry. But that

is not the regret I hold on to, the one that is my constant companion.

'Never mind,' he says, when I don't respond. 'You're going to make up for all of it now.' He places down his glass so heavily I'm surprised it doesn't smash. 'What's that about?'

'What?'

'The book you've been reading for the last hour. I'm asking you what it's about. Tell me.'

I have to think fast. 'A spy. He has to find a way to track down a Russian spy.' I only know this from the blurb on the back of the book; I've barely read a word of the first chapter.

'Sounds riveting,' Christian says. 'My dad loves those books. Wouldn't have thought it was up your street, though. Anyone would think you were avoiding coming to bed.' He rests his head on the pillow and closes his eyes. It's only a matter of time before he slips into sleep. From what I remember, Christian slept deeply, especially after drinking, and was never easy to rouse.

It's another ten minutes before long deep breaths float from his mouth, convincing me he's finally asleep. I get up and hover over him, thinking how innocent he looks. How peaceful. Nobody would believe that behind that façade lurks a monster. I need to get out of here, forget leaving a note and just run.

I scoop up my bag and denim jacket and leave the room, closing the door softly behind me.

The house is bathed in darkness, and I make my way down the stairs, which creak with each step. Anthony and Tyler must be asleep; no light spills from any of the doors. Navigating my way through an unfamiliar house with nothing to light my way slows me down, especially with two staircases to negotiate, but I make it to the front door and reach for the handle.

A heavy hand lands on my shoulder. 'And where d'you think you're going?'

NINE

NOW

Slowly I turn to face Tyler. He's wearing a black towelling dressing gown, tied at the waist. 'I needed to get something from the car,' I say.

He studies my face for a moment. 'Oh, what?' He pauses. 'No, forget it. Sorry, it's not my business. I just heard something and... I thought Christian might have been leaving in the middle of the night.'

My blood runs cold at the mention of his name. 'No, just me. But I understand you might be worried he'll disappear again. I worry about that too.'

Tyler nods. 'Thing is... when I realised it was you, I thought you might have been trying to leave.'

'Why would I do that?'

'It's late, isn't it. Not safe.' His words are reminiscent of my mother's, but the memory is too painful so I wrap the thought tightly, trapping it so it can't touch me.

'Well, I wasn't. Just getting something.' I dangle Christian's car keys in front of him.

He nods. 'I thought everyone was asleep. It's kind of late.'

And now it's my turn to hesitate, as I recall Christian's

warning: *I know my brother. He knows something.* I'd dismissed it as paranoia, but what if it's true?

'*You* weren't,' I say.

He smiles, melting some of my apprehension. Unlike his brother's, Tyler's expression seems sincere. Warm. 'Guilty as charged. I have dreadful insomnia. It's like my mind can't switch off. I'm always running through the things I need to get done at work the next day. Wish I could switch off.' He glances upstairs. 'I was about to make coffee if you want one?'

I almost smile. 'That's not going to help you sleep, is it?'

'Nope, but it tastes good.' He laughs, and beckons me to follow him.

In the kitchen, I sit at the table while Tyler sets about making coffee. Now that I'm out of Christian's presence, I can think more rationally. Tyler has done me a favour – it was too big a risk to leave in the night, especially when I know how unpredictable Christian is. Besides, I would never have got out of here tonight, given that Tyler won't be sleeping any time soon.

He joins me at the table and watches me for a moment. 'I know it was years ago, and forgive me for saying this, but I never thought of you and Christian as a good match.' He holds up his hand. 'That's no reflection on you, I promise. He's just... I can't explain it.' Tyler shakes his head. 'I know he's my brother but you seemed too... good for him.' He averts his eyes.

I compose my thoughts, choosing my words carefully, as I've been doing since we got here. Did Tyler know about us all along? We just thought he was a kid, lurking in the background and never paying attention, but now I'm thinking otherwise. 'Things change. People change,' I say. Despite my best effort, these words are half-hearted, and I wonder if Tyler will see through me.

'Do you know what my mum always used to say to us?' Tyler asks.

I shake my head, picturing Audrey and how she always seemed so wise. So together. The contrast of my own mum.

'People never change. Not permanently, at least. We are who we are. The core of us doesn't change. We can try, of course, but we always revert to what comes naturally. She was right.'

I agree, but I can't let Tyler know this. My unwritten script has to be performed to Christian's approval, every word I say carefully calculated and analysed for consequences before it's left my mouth. 'He's a good man,' I say, the words slicing into my throat like carving knives.

'If you say so.' He drinks some more coffee, his eyes upon me the whole time.

I look away. 'So, you never got married, either?'

Tyler shakes his head. 'Nope. I'm seeing someone, but can't say I'm in a rush to get a meaningless piece of paper. Katerina and I are both happy this way. We don't need a ceremony to validate us.' He rolls his eyes. 'Much to her parents' annoyance. They're very traditional.'

I ask him about Katerina; it's a distraction from Christian and the dangerous area our conversation is heading towards.

'She's one of those women who are just, you know, fundamentally kind and compassionate. She's an animal rights activist. Selfless. Always puts others before herself.' His mouth stretches into a thin smile. 'Sometimes I'm not sure I deserve her.'

'She sounds... perfect.' *Too good to be true?*

His eyes narrow. 'But there's no such thing, is there? We grow up believing there is, but it's all bull. That quest for perfection leads us down a worrying path.'

This sounds like a conversation I don't want to have with Tyler. And if there are cracks in his relationship, I don't want to know about them.

'Want to hear something funny?' he asks. 'I used to have a

huge crush on you when you were a student.' He laughs and rolls his eyes. 'I know. I was just Christian's annoying little brother, and you were this amazing... grown woman.'

'Hardly,' I snort. 'I was a kid myself.'

'But you weren't sixteen. I was so envious of Christian. He was always so... confident with women. And then he brought you home and I couldn't believe you'd go for him. You were so shy and a bit awkward, but underneath that you had a mind he didn't deserve. Not when you look at the girls he'd been with before.'

I try to recall my interactions with Tyler those years ago, but there's nothing left in my mind other than a hazy blur. Christian didn't have much to do with him – the eight-year age gap meant they were always in different phases of their lives.

Tyler's words have surprised me, and now I wonder if Christian knows what he's just admitted to me. Perhaps this is contributing to his paranoia. 'Tyler, I don't think we should be having this—'

'It's okay. I'm not saying I feel that way now.' He laughs. 'Please don't think it means anything – it was a long time ago.'

And I am not the person you think I was.

Tyler takes his mug to the dishwasher and haphazardly places it inside. 'Did you really miss Christian all this time? And want him back? Did something happen with you two?' He comes back to the table.

'No. Christian leaving had nothing to do with us.' I force myself to look him in the eyes.

He frowns. 'One minute you were there, love's young dream – and the next he'd disappeared. It didn't make sense then and it still doesn't now. What did you do after he left? Did you try to look for him?'

Keep lies simple. Stick to the truth as much as possible. 'I told your parents at the time, Christian leaving had nothing to do with our relationship. A few weeks before, we'd already agreed that it wasn't the right time for either of us. I was too focused on my studies and we just... drifted. I hadn't even seen him in that time before he disappeared.' The lie sticks in my throat. 'And it's not that I missed him all this time. I'd carried on with things because I had no choice. I had a degree to finish, and then teacher training. But when we found each other again, it brought back all the feelings I had for him. That happens. It's not unusual.' I sound too defensive. I need Tyler to believe me.

'I know, but are you—'

'Well, this is cosy.'

We both turn to see Christian leaning against the door frame. Neither of us heard him approach, and I have no idea how long he's been standing there, how much he's heard. I try to recall if I've said anything he won't like, but I can't remember now.

'I couldn't sleep,' I explain. 'And I found Tyler up too.'

Christian walks into the kitchen and stands behind me, placing his hands on my shoulders. 'Is that right?' He glances at my shoes. The denim jacket I'm still wearing. He leans down and tenderly kisses my cheek, and then turns to Tyler. 'Have you always had trouble sleeping?' he asks Tyler. 'Or is it just tonight?'

'It's since you vanished, actually. That kind of thing has an effect on people. You know, the unanswered questions. The wondering if you're alive or dead.'

'Let's not do this now,' I say.

'No, let's not,' Christian agrees. 'I'm afraid, brother, Emily and I have to go tonight. Something urgent's come up and I need to be back for the morning.'

I'm about to protest, but Christian is already taking my arm, coaxing me up from my chair.

'That's crazy,' Tyler says. 'It's nearly one a.m.'

'London's not that far,' Christian insists. 'And I don't want to get stuck in rush-hour traffic in the morning. Better this way.'

Tyler stands. 'You can't just leave. Dad will be disappointed. He was making us all breakfast. You're supposed to be repairing the damage you've done, not making it worse.'

'He'll understand,' Christian says, gently tugging my arm.

'Sorry,' I add. 'Work's a priority for Christian at the moment while he builds his business. It must be important, otherwise we wouldn't have to leave so suddenly.' Hopefully this will ease Christian's anger at me for talking to Tyler.

'Bye,' I say. It's all I can fit in before Christian rushes me from the room.

I turn to him when we reach the car. 'You shouldn't have done that. Tyler was already asking a lot of questions. Now you've made him even more suspicious. Why did you lie? There's no emergency, is there?'

'You and Tyler were getting too cosy. You didn't even notice what he was doing. Trying to get information from you. What exactly did you tell him before I found the pair of you?'

'Nothing,' I insist.

'But he was trying to squeeze information out of you, wasn't he?'

'No. We just talked about his partner. Katerina.'

Christian flings open the car door. 'Get in. You'll have to drive. I've had too much to drink.'

Without a word, I do as he asks, grateful that he won't be behind the wheel. It means – for a little while at least – that I will be in control.

On the motorway, it occurs to me that I could put an end to this right now. There aren't many other cars on the road and I'd only have to put more pressure on the accelerator, turn the wheel so that we veer off into the barrier. I press my foot down firmer, feel the car jolt forward. But there's no way to guarantee the outcome, and I could never put my own life at risk – not when it would destroy Jeremy and Lexi. I ease my foot off the accelerator.

'What are you doing?' Christian demands. 'Trying to kill us both?' He thumps my arm, enough to make me jump so that the car lurches sideways. 'I said be careful!' His shout pierces my eardrums.

It will do no good pointing out that he is the one who caused me to momentarily lose control of the steering wheel. He wants a fight and I won't give it to him. This is the same old story. A chameleon shedding its camouflage, suddenly showing its true colours.

'You'll have to stay at my place tonight,' Christian says, once we're back in London, cruising through darkened streets.

'No. I have to go into school tomorrow. Early. I don't even know where you live.'

'Barnet,' he says. 'Miles from Putney. And if you drop me there, how do you think you'll get home?' He points to the dashboard. 'It's nearly two a.m.'

'I'll get the night bus.'

'Well, that's hardly safe, is it? How could I ever forgive myself if something happened to you?'

Once again, I fight the urge to smash my fist into his face, to erase the grin plastered across it. How is this a man I once loved? The one I would have done anything for.

'I'll be fine,' I insist. 'I take care of myself.'

'And that's always been your problem. Drive to yours – I'll stay at your place instead. Will be good to get a real feel for how you've been living.'

'No!' I squeeze the accelerator.

'I don't think you have a choice. It's yours or mine. So hurry up and make a decision.'

I won't have him spending the night in my house. In Jeremy's house. That would be a further betrayal of my husband and stepdaughter. 'Your place,' I say quietly, my voice cracking, a seed of nausea rapidly growing in my stomach.

He clasps his hands together. 'Good. I knew you'd see sense.

There's plenty of time for me to visit your lovely home again, isn't there? Now slow the hell down. And you need to take this next left if we're going to mine.'

Silently, I obey, anger raging inside me that once again Christian is calling the shots. I need to stop him, no matter what it takes.

We reach Barnet and Christian directs me to turn into a quiet, tree-lined street. 'This is it,' he says, ordering me to park up. Street lights glow in the darkness, a picture of serenity. 'Nice, isn't it?' he says, pointing to what appears to be a new building. The lawn surrounding it is neatly mown, with pale pink dahlias and blue hydrangeas lining the walls. 'You live there?'

'Don't act so surprised. Where did you imagine I'd be living? In some hovel?'

'No. I didn't imagine anything. I haven't thought about you at all. Not once. I blanked you out of my mind as if you never existed.' I fire my bold words at him like bullets, preparing myself for the ricochet.

'Well, I find that hard to believe,' he says, smiling. I used to think Christian's smile was sexy; now it's sinister, unnerving.

'Can we just go inside?' I beg. 'I'm tired. And I'm sleeping on the sofa.'

'Suit yourself,' he says, getting out of the car.

Inside, his ground-floor maisonette is immaculate and barely looks lived in. It's a show home, devoid of life, with only a few of Christian's belongings. The walls are stark and white, and there isn't a single decorative item to lend warmth.

'I'm not here much,' he says, as if reading my thoughts. He was always able to do that, somehow, burrowing into the darkest recesses of my mind before I even knew myself what I was thinking. I shudder to remember how I could never hide anything.

I sit on the sofa and pull my legs up to my chin. I don't have a toothbrush or any nightwear so I'll sleep in my clothes, and escape the moment dawn breaks.

'I've got to find out what Tyler knows,' Christian mumbles, more to himself than to me. He paces up and down. 'Tonight didn't go well. I thought you being there would help them see that they don't have to worry about me. I thought it would put a stop to their questions. It didn't work. And now my brother is even more suspicious.'

'He doesn't know anything,' I say. 'If you haven't told him, then there's no way. We're the only ones who—'

'We can't just assume that, Emily.' He stops pacing and sits on the edge of the sofa, clasping his hands together.

I hear Tyler's words again. *I used to have a huge crush on you.* 'He was just a kid. And if he knew, why wouldn't he say anything?'

'To torment me. I don't know.'

'And he'd keep it a secret for fifteen years? You're deranged if you believe that.'

He moves closer and grabs my arm. 'You just keep pushing your luck and see what happens.' He flings my arm away, but I won't show him that he's hurt me.

Christian is paranoid. I'm not safe here in his home.

He inches even closer, and I shuffle away, wedging myself against the arm of the sofa.

'You're scared of me,' he says. 'But if you just stop fighting me, we can work together. We need to stop my brother talking. Or anyone else.'

He means Ella. Is there any way she could know?

'It's in your interests as well as mine,' Christian continues.

I nod, because he's right. I don't believe Tyler knows anything, but if I can get proof of that for Christian, it might help end this sooner.

'Call him tomorrow,' Christian says. 'Say you want to apologise for us leaving in the middle of the night. Find a way to meet up with him and find out what he knows.'

'No. Keep him out of this. He's your brother. Doesn't that mean anything to you?'

'That's very touching, but once again, what choice do you have? Just do what I say, Emily.'

I lean forward and rest my head in my hands, taking a deep breath to staunch my anger. 'I need to use the bathroom,' I say, standing up.

'Down the hall at the end. Don't go snooping through my things now, will you?' He laughs. 'Not that you'll find anything.'

When I come back, Christian is asleep on the sofa. Dark thoughts rush through my head. There's only one way to stop what he's doing.

And that's to make him disappear.

Tears stream from my eyes; he's destroyed my life once before and I won't let him do it again. I pick up my bag from the floor and throw it over my shoulder, glancing back at him before I tiptoe to the front door.

It's locked. Frantically I search the house for the key, but I can't find it anywhere. I stare at Christian. It must be in his pocket, but I can't risk searching. I try the back door, but again, it's locked, and none of the windows open, either.

He knew what I would do; he predicted my actions before I thought of them myself.

I leave Christian on the sofa and find his bedroom, shutting the door and curling up on his bed. The sheets smell of floral fabric softener, something I can't imagine him buying for himself. Is this even his place?

Eventually my eyelids begin to droop, and sleep plays a tug of war with my desire to stay alert.

I lose the battle, and when my eyes pop open again, daylight streams through the window. I check my phone and it's six a.m.

I turn on my side and reach for my phone, but it's not on the bedside table where I left it last night.

Scrambling up, I step into the hallway, listening for any sounds. But all is silent. There is no sign of Christian in the living room. The sofa is empty of anything but the cushions, and even these look as if they haven't been disturbed.

He's not in the bathroom, and the second smaller bedroom is empty other than a bed and desk.

And I know he's not in the kitchen even before I open the door and check inside.

None of this makes sense; unless he was telling the truth about having an emergency he needed to deal with.

At the front door, I take a deep breath and turn the handle.

Locked. Just as it was last night.

I can't get out. I'm imprisoned. Here until Christian decides I can leave.

TEN
BEFORE

Emily has avoided Christian for days, ignoring the constant flood of texts asking her if she's okay, and why she's not replying. She feels cruel, and has almost given in a few times, but ignoring him is for the best.

As much as she likes him, this relationship feels too intense, and it makes her claustrophobic. And why did he lie to her about how he got her mum's address? She doesn't understand any of it; all she knows is that there should be no distraction from her studies. She's got it all wrong – it's not Christian who will get her away from her mother, it's finishing university and then applying for a teaching job far from Surrey. Far from London. She quite likes the idea of Devon or Cornwall, although she imagines teaching posts are in short supply in rural areas.

She's in the university café, grabbing an egg and cress sandwich for lunch before her next lecture, when Christian appears in front of her. Emily's taken aback – she's already carefully scanned the room and there'd been no sign of him.

'How have you been?' he asks, shoving his hands in his pockets. He seems nervous, which is out of character for him.

'Okay.' The queue moves forward, so Emily steps away from him.

'That's good,' he says, catching up with her. 'Look, I'm sorry I got funny about you not wanting me to meet your mum. I've missed you so much. I've been an idiot. I don't blame you if you can't forgive me. But I wasn't ending our relationship, I swear.'

She shrugs. She'd been so adamant, but now his words are powerful, drawing her in.

'Are you free now?' Christian asks. 'We could go and get something nicer than that.' He points to her sandwich. 'My treat. Please let me make it up to you, Em. I've been such an idiot. I don't want to mess this up.'

Emily's so surprised to see this side of Christian – humble and remorseful – that she's not sure how to respond. 'Um, I have a lecture in fifteen minutes. I was just grabbing this quickly. Didn't have time for breakfast.' It's not exactly a rejection, but this explanation should speak for itself.

'You need to look after yourself,' Christian says, as if she's a child. Does he see her as someone he needs to parent? 'Breakfast is important.'

'Yeah. Anyway, I'd better hurry.' The longer she stays here talking to him, the harder it will be to pull herself away, and up until now she's done so well. She doesn't want his words to seep into her mind and disrupt her thoughts.

'Will you give me a chance to explain?' he begs.

'It doesn't matter. There's nothing to say. I don't know how you got my address, but you lied to me. I won't be lied to by anyone,' she says, and the student in front of her turns to stare.

A frown spreads across Christian's forehead. 'No, you've got it wrong. I didn't lie.'

She shakes her head. 'Kirsty said you never went round there. So how did you really get my mum's address?'

Christian stares at her, opening his mouth then closing it

again. 'Oh. I see. I get it. Now it all makes sense.' He shoves his hands in his pockets.

'What are you talking about?'

Christian pulls her out of the queue, ignoring the tuts of everyone behind. 'I can't believe she'd do this. Well, actually I *can* believe it.' He ushers her further from the queue. 'Kirsty's lying to you, Em. I *did* go round there. How else would I get your mum's address? Kirsty was there and she let me in. We chatted for a bit and then she... she came on to me. I wasn't going to say anything. She's your flatmate and you have to live there, but it's true. She's always staring at me whenever I'm at your place. I should have known and stayed well away from her. I'm not interested in her. Never.'

Emily's face crinkles. 'No. Kirsty wouldn't—'

'I swear to you it's the truth. You don't really know her that well, do you? You've lived together for a few months but she's hardly ever there. You're not really friends, are you? You're just flatmates.'

Christian has a point. How can she be so sure Kirsty didn't come on to Christian? How well does she really know her? Once again, she hears her mother's words as if she's standing beside her. *Don't trust anyone, Emily.*

'She got upset when I rejected her,' Christian continues, 'and told me to get out. I'm guessing this is her payback. She probably felt humiliated.'

'I... I can't...'

Christian takes her hand. 'I wouldn't lie to you, Em. I know I'm not perfect but I'm not a liar. I really like you. *Really* like you. I've never had these feelings before. Maybe that makes me act a bit crazy sometimes, but it's only because I don't want to mess this up.'

She stares at him, scanning his face, trying to make sense of his words. Christian seems so genuine, yet she can't imagine that Kirsty would do that to her. But then again, Kirsty is a bit unpredictable. Emily's learnt that much in the few months she's known her. Her priority is having a good time, so it's not beyond reason that she might have taken a liking to Christian. And Kirsty does seem to believe she can have anyone she wants – she's as much as said it before.

'I'll have to talk to her,' Emily says, moving back towards the line for the till.

'You could,' Christian says, grabbing her arm. 'But think about it from her perspective – it's a bit humiliating, isn't it? And you've still got to live together, at least until summer. Maybe just ignore it, but keep in mind what she's like. We both need to be careful around her.'

'But she knows we're together. She shouldn't have—'

'I know.' Christian takes her arm. 'But it's going to take a lot more than that to destroy us. You'll find this out, Em, but lots of people will be jealous of what we have. People who don't have it for themselves will try anything to tear us down. Come on, you go and find a seat and I'll pay for your sandwich.' He pulls it from her hand. 'Five minutes with you is better than nothing.'

Emily watches him join the queue and wonders what just happened.

Despite vowing not to get distracted from her studies, over the next few weeks Emily sees Christian every day. She's not sure how it's happened, but they've subconsciously fallen into a routine, and neither of them mention spending time apart.

They avoid her flat as much as possible, though Kirsty is rarely there. 'I don't trust Erin either,' Christian had said the other morning. 'They've known each other for ages, haven't they? Stands to reason she'll side with Kirsty. It's obvious she doesn't like me.'

Emily didn't argue, even though she's not sure she agrees. Erin seems like a fair person, and she's too busy with her studies, and Andre, to get involved in whatever happened. Erin's never said anything against Christian, at least not in her presence.

It's easier to stay silent – she doesn't want to argue – even though she knows she shouldn't let him control her, just like her mum does. *I'm my own person, perfectly capable of speaking my mind.* But she doesn't, not this time, and spends most evenings at Christian's, avoiding any mention of her flatmates.

'You should move in with me,' he says one night when they're lying in bed, the duvet tangled around their naked bodies. At moments like this she is at peace, when the outside world is shut out, and it's only the two of them. The only light comes from the television on Christian's chest of drawers, and it casts dancing shadows across their skin. It's peaceful. Serene. Until Christian made this statement.

She lifts her head from the crook of his arm. 'What?'

'It makes sense, since Matty's moved out. I'm sure we can sort it with the accommodation department. They won't care.'

Despite her shock, and her unease, Emily is flattered that Christian wants to take this huge step with her.

'You don't even have to pay half the rent,' he continues. 'I'll cover most of it and you can just chip in, say, a quarter? Or less if that's too much. What do you think? It means you can work less. You'll have more time for studying.' He kisses her. 'Go on – say yes. You've got nothing to lose!'

She considers what he's saying for a moment, sighing when she realises it's a pipe dream. 'My mum would never go for it.'

Christian pulls away. 'Jesus, Em – you're nineteen. You can make your own decisions.'

'I know. But it's not as easy as just saying *screw her* is it?'

Christian sits up in bed. 'Do you know what this feels like,

Emily? It feels like you're always looking for reasons to stop us moving forward. Sabotaging our relationship. I've kept quiet for weeks now, but I really feel like that's what you're doing. And how do you think that makes me feel? Especially after what my ex was like.'

Emily sits up too, pulling the duvet up to her chin. She wishes she knew more about what his ex was like, but all she ever hears are vague references to her. 'Is that what you really think I'm doing?'

He nods. 'I feel like I'm the only one invested in us.' He untangles the duvet from his legs and gets out of bed, pulling on his clothes.

'Don't you understand?' she says. 'I know your mum is great, but you have huge issues with your dad.'

'The difference is I don't try to please him when he's being a jerk. His unrealistic expectations of us don't mean anything to me.'

Yet Emily knows this can't be true. Hadn't Christian been the one to say that parents mess you up? Now he's pretending that he doesn't care what his dad thinks of him.

She reaches for him but he shrugs her off, and she's sure his eyes are glistening.

'Let me think about it,' she says. 'I could try and talk to her. Maybe she'll understand.'

No she won't – Mum will spiral out of control. I can't let that happen, but I don't want to hurt Christian either.

He turns to her and she notices a tear in the corner of his eye. *What am I doing to him?* 'Thanks,' he says softly. 'I know you can make her understand.'

Christian is distant for the rest of the evening. And when Emily says she might go back to her flat, he doesn't try to stop her.

Later, when she's alone in her room, guilt washes over her. She had no idea she was being so cruel to Christian, always putting obstacles in their way. She will have that chat with her mum, it's the least she can do. She sends Christian a text to say she'll call her mum tomorrow.

When she wakes the following morning, there's still no response from him.

ELEVEN

NOW

I've never known time to move so slowly. I'm trapped in Christian's home – if this place does belong to him – and I have no idea where he is or when he'll be back. My phone is missing too – I've searched the flat and there's no sign of it, nor is there a house phone.

There's nothing in this place of Christian's – no photos or personal papers. No passport. Nothing. No mail addressed to him.

Surprisingly, the kitchen cupboards are stocked with food, so I make myself a cup of tea and some toast, just to ease the hollow ache in my stomach. I sit on the sofa to eat, scattering crumbs as I bite into the toast. I watch them fall through the gap between the seat cushions.

My agitation grows when there's still no sign of Christian at two p.m. He's doing this on purpose. I try to stay calm, but when I can bear it no longer, I scream into the silence. His manipulation and control weighs down on me, crushing my lungs so that I struggle to breathe. I wonder if this is what a panic attack feels like. After that night, I only ever felt an ice-cold numbness, gripping me, compressing everything.

I must have dozed off on the sofa because I wake to find Christian towering over me, smiling. Instinctively, I reel backwards.

'Oh good, you're still here,' he says. 'Had a good day?'

I straighten up, rub my eyes. 'Why did you lock me in? I need to go. I have to message Jeremy or he'll worry about me. And Lexi might have tried to call me. There could be an emergency with Tia and she might need me to get Lexi.'

'You're not her mother,' Christian says. 'I'm sure her actual mum can look after her.'

'I needed to be at school today. I've got work to do!' I stand up. 'Where's my phone?'

'Sorry, I must have locked the door without thinking. Habit, you know. There's plenty of food, though – you weren't going to starve.'

'My phone!' I repeat. 'Why did you take it?'

He pulls something from his pocket. 'Oh, this? Yeah, sorry. I accidentally picked up yours, thinking it was mine. We have the same iPhones – see?' From his other pocket he pulls out his own. 'Didn't realise mine was already in my pocket until it was too late.'

I snatch my phone from his hand. The battery is dead. 'Where did you go?' Not that it matters; most likely he just left to drive around and make me squirm in here. Make me anxious. Fearful.

'I had an emergency, remember? That's why we had to leave Reading last night. Are you losing your memory, Emily? It would be a shame if that was happening. Didn't that happen to your mum? Along with everything else?'

'Don't talk about my mum. Don't you dare.' I won't let him do this to me.

'Sorry, touchy subject?'

'You were lying last night to Tyler. There was no emergency, you just wanted me away from him. Worried we were talking about you? I have to go. Now.'

He puts out his hand to stop me moving.

'I need to go, Christian. Then I can work on doing what you asked me to. If you want me to find out if Tyler knows anything, then I need to get things in motion. And I can't do that from here.' I wave my phone. 'My battery's dead.'

Christian doesn't respond, and I imagine he's about to protest. 'You're not a prisoner here,' he says. 'I'm not going to keep you here like a caged animal.' He laughs, triggering flashbacks that force their way into my head. Pounding fists against his bedroom door, pleading to be let out. Screaming, wailing, crying. All of it futile.

'Get on with handling Tyler,' Christian continues. 'Before this situation is beyond our control.'

Without another word I gather my bag and jacket and leave as quickly as I can, relieved to find the door unlocked this time.

Only when I'm on the Tube home does it occur to me that getting away just now was far too easy.

My house is eerily silent, and it won't be long before darkness sets in. I'm floundering, fearful. I thought I'd left all that behind me, and feeling like the old Emily only intensifies my anxiety.

I call Lexi – I need to know she's okay, and hearing her voice will lift my spirits.

'Hi Em,' she says, once Tia's passed her the phone. 'Is it time for me to go home yet?'

'Tomorrow,' I say. 'I'll be there straight after breakfast, okay?'

'Okay. And Dad will be back?'

'He lands first thing in the morning, so yeah, hopefully he'll be home by the time I've picked you up. Are you having a nice time?'

'Yeah. But Mum's been out a lot. Urgent stuff. Mrs Jenkins next door has been looking after me. But I don't mind cos she has the cutest dog. Her name's Lolly. That's a funny name for a dog, isn't it? Mrs Jenkins says it's because when she was a puppy she was always trying to steal her grandchildren's lollies.'

I lose myself in Lexi's chatter, letting her words envelop me like a warm blanket.

'Mum's calling me for dinner,' she says after a while. 'She promised she'd make my favourite.'

There is something so innocent and normal about Lexi's words, and I long for her to be here with me. 'Let me guess – pizza with sweetcorn and peperoni? You'd better run. I'll see you in the morning. Love you.'

'Love you too, Emily.'

We hang up and I cradle my phone for a moment, devastated that I have to lie to the two people I love most in the world. The phone vibrates in my hand. Christian.

Here's Tyler's number. You know what to do.

I stare at the digits for a moment, weighing up my options. I find it hard to believe that Tyler knows anything. He's always been different from his brother. More laid-back and at ease with himself. Probably because he has a different relationship with his dad. His revelation that he used to like me when he was younger might mean that he could be on my side. I need to find out if I can trust him, though. And Christian's demand that I talk to him will provide the perfect smokescreen.

I send Tyler a message, apologising for leaving so abruptly last night. It's a first step and I need to tread carefully; like Mum always said, there is nobody I can trust.

When there's no reply after a few minutes, I make myself cheese on toast and sit on the sofa with my plate on my lap. Jeremy wouldn't be happy to know this is all I'm having for dinner; I can picture the frown on his face, as if he's sitting across from me. Thinking of him grounds me, makes me even more determined to fight for my family.

After I've eaten, I wash up my plate before going through the house, checking every door and window. If I know anything about Christian, it's that he's unpredictable. It's feasible that he's suddenly decided threatening me isn't enough punishment, and that he needs to do something worse.

When I'm satisfied that every entrance is secure, I brush my teeth and climb into bed, pulling the duvet up to my chin. I'm exhausted, but my brain fights to stay active. I close my eyes and wait.

Before my eyes snap open, I already sense someone's presence in the house. My vision is blurred, and it takes a moment to focus on the figure standing over me.

Christian's here. He's found a way in.

'Em? Are you okay? It's nearly nine o'clock.'

Jeremy's comforting voice infuses my body with a surge of relief. For now, at least, I am safe.

'I must have overslept.' I pull myself up and check my phone. Eight fifty-seven. The latest I've woken up in years. 'Lexi. I promised her I'd get her straight after breakfast.'

'I can pick her up, don't worry.'

'No, I promised. She'll be expecting me.' It's a small detail, but I won't let her down when I made a promise.

'Okay,' Jeremy says. 'If you're going, then I'll jump in the shower.'

I climb out of bed and he gently pulls me towards him. 'I missed you,' he says, breathing in the scent of my hair. 'It's hard being away from you and Lexi.'

'But you also love your job. How many people can actually say that?'

He nods. 'True. We're both very lucky in that sense.' He kisses my forehead. 'Any problems with Tia when I was away?'

'No, not this time. She actually seemed quite... I don't know... reasonable? And apparently yesterday she was cooking Lexi's favourite meal.'

Jeremy raises his eyebrows. 'Hmm. Reasonable is not a word I've ever used to describe her. Maybe she's actually changing.'

Tyler's words drift into my head. *People never change.* 'Maybe,' I say.

'I forgot to say – the wedding photographer emailed me the photos. Let's go through them and decide which ones we want.'

Before Christian turned up, I would have been desperate to look at the photos, painstakingly choosing which ones I want to display throughout the house. Now, though, I don't think I can bring myself to look at them. 'Can we do it when Lexi's back?' I suggest. 'It would be nice to look through them with her.'

'Okay,' Jeremy says. 'But I'm surprised you can wait that long.'

While he's in the shower, I get dressed.

'I'll cook dinner tonight,' he calls from the bathroom. 'That fish pie Lexi likes. Tia's not the only one who can cook her favourite meals.' He laughs. I know he's joking, but I wonder if a small part of him does feel as though he's in competition with Tia.

'Fish pie sounds good,' I say, dabbing concealer on the grey shadows under my eyes.

'I love you,' he calls as I'm leaving the bedroom. And as much as I want to say it back, as much as I feel it, the words won't leave my mouth.

I lose myself in Lexi's infectious giggles and chatter. It's impossible to sink into despair when she's in the room, lighting it up. My phone is on silent, but vibrates constantly with messages screaming to be noticed.

We're on the sofa, Jeremy on one side of me and Lexi on the other; the weight of her head resting on my shoulder is reassuring. This is a peaceful family moment. Only I know what lies beneath it.

'Your phone keeps buzzing,' Lexi says, pointing to the coffee table. 'Don't you want to see who it is?'

'I'm too comfortable to move,' I reply. 'And it won't be anything more important than the two people here with me in this room. Now, I want to hear all about your weekend with your mum. Did you do anything fun?'

Lexi sits up. 'She took me shopping. And got me a new pair of leggings. They're a bit big, but she said I'll grow into them.'

'You will. Better too big than too small. I'm glad you went shopping,' I offer.

'I suppose.'

'It sounds as though she's trying really hard to do fun things with you, Lex,' I say. Tia might not like me, but she's a mother, and I know it's not easy being a parent. It's not her fault that she's had issues in the past. What matters is that she is trying to change now.

'But it was weird – she kept asking me loads of questions about you and dad.'

I sit up straighter. 'Oh? Like what?'

'About the wedding, that kind of thing.'

'And what did you say?'

'I just told her it was nice. And I told her about your friend who turned up.'

My body freezes, and a wave of nausea hits me. 'I see. Well, it was nice of Christian to come all that way, wasn't it?'

'That's what I told Mum. She thought it was weird, though.'

'What else did she say?'

'She just asked about him. And then she started saying how things were going to be different from now on.'

'What does that mean?' Jeremy says, deep lines creasing his forehead. Up until now he's been silent while we've spoken about Tia.

Lexi shrugs. 'I don't know. I think she meant better for me when I'm there. She said she's going to slow down with work or something like that.'

Jeremy stands. 'I'll go and check on dinner. Should be nearly ready.'

'This is great, Lexi,' I say, when he's gone to the kitchen. 'Everyone deserves a chance to do better, don't they?'

Lexi hugs me. 'You're right. You're such a kind person, Emily. We're so lucky to have you.'

I fight back tears, turning away so Lexi can't see them.

It's a relief when Jeremy calls from the kitchen that dinner is ready, and Lexi jumps up. 'Fish pie!' she cries.

Slowly, I follow her, wiping at my eyes in case either of them notices the shine of tears.

I make sure we don't talk about Tia while we eat, instead focusing on where I can take Lexi as a treat before school starts back.

'Disney World?' she suggests, and I'm pleased when Jeremy laughs, back to himself again.

We're halfway through our dinner when the doorbell rings. 'Have you ordered anything?' I ask Jeremy.

He shakes his head, and my stomach somersaults. I jump up, but I'm too late – Lexi is already rushing to the door.

'Wait!' I call, but she doesn't listen.

My worst fear is realised when I reach the open front door, and Christian is standing there, smiling at Lexi as if we've all been expecting him. 'You remember me, don't you, Lexi?' he says.

Lexi nods, turning to me. 'Emily, your friend is here.'

'Why don't you go and finish your dinner?' I say. 'I'll be right there. And please don't answer the door again without us – it's not safe.'

'Yeah,' Christian says. 'You never know who'll be standing there.'

For a second, nobody moves, time temporarily paused. 'Okay,' Lexi says, bounding off.

'What are you doing here?' I hiss at Christian, as soon as Lexi's out of earshot.

'That's no way to greet your old friend, is it?' He looks past me. 'Hey, Jeremy. How's it going?'

Jeremy is beside me, placing his hand on my shoulder. It's a tender gesture I know will incite Christian's rage.

'Yeah, good, thanks. Sorry, were we expecting you?' He frowns at me. 'Em must have forgotten to mention it.'

Christian smiles. 'No, not her fault. I was seeing a friend in the area and thought I'd stop by and see how the newlyweds are.' From a bag I hadn't noticed him holding, he pulls out a bottle of champagne. 'Felt bad for turning up at the wedding without a gift, so this is for you both to enjoy.' He hands it to Jeremy.

'You didn't need to do that, but thanks.' He pauses and looks at me. 'Um... come in, I guess. We were just eating.'

I know Christian won't decline this offer.

'If you're sure I'm not intruding,' he says, stepping inside.

I'm desperate to object; I want to catch Jeremy's eye – to pass on a silent hint that this isn't a good idea, but once again Christian has got his own way.

'There's loads more food,' Lexi says when we reach the kitchen. 'Christian can have some!'

'I'd love to,' Christian says, catching my eye and winking.

I turn away and start dishing up another plate.

'So, Lexi,' Christian says, when we're all seated at the table.

'You must love having Emily as your teacher. I bet you learn loads from her.'

'Yeah. But she's not my teacher any more. That was in Year 3 – I'll be in Year 5 when school starts back. I'm ten. And she doesn't even teach Year 3 any more; now she teaches Year 4.'

Christian lifts his fork to his mouth. 'Well, change is good, they say. And you certainly are all grown up.'

Lexi giggles, while my insides churn.

'So, you've been in America, then?' Jeremy asks. That's about all I've told him about Christian; I haven't dared to mention much more, in case I get caught out in my dreadful lies.

'Yep. Left straight after uni. I haven't been back here until now.'

'It must feel strange after all this time?' Jeremy says.

Christian shrugs. 'I guess. But I have things I need to be here for. And I feel like I've been away for too long.' He fixes his eyes on me.

'Oh?' Jeremy says. 'Sounds intriguing.'

Christian smiles. 'Yeah. Good to have goals, isn't it? What's life without dreams to work towards?'

'So, no partner back in the US?' Jeremy asks.

Again, a smile spreads across Christian's face. He's enjoying using Jeremy to get to me. 'There was someone special. It didn't work out. But she's still in my life. Always will be, I reckon. We seem to have a bond that can't be broken, even though we're not together.'

'I get that,' Jeremy says. He turns to me and takes my hand. 'Reckon we're the same, aren't we, Em?'

I nod, and force a smile.

The dinner drags on, and each mouthful of food sticks in my throat. It's not enough that he's blackmailing me; Christian is escalating the threat by being here in my house, getting close to Jeremy and Lexi. My world. He is charming Jeremy, an actor deserving of an Oscar, winning my husband over. Just like he did to me from the moment I talked to him in that bookshop. Unable to bear it any longer, I tell everyone that Lexi needs to get ready for bed.

'Oh,' she protests. 'Can't I stay here with you for a bit? It's the holidays.'

'Maybe not tonight,' I say, unable to offer an explanation why, as I normally would.

'You go up with her,' Jeremy suggests. 'I can entertain Christian while he finishes his drink.'

I don't want to leave them alone, but I'm fairly certain Christian won't say anything to Jeremy – not yet at least.

An hour later, Christian is still in the kitchen with Jeremy when I go back down.

'Sorry,' he says. 'I've been talking your husband's ear off. All my fault.'

Jeremy laughs. 'No wonder you two were such good friends – this guy's hilarious, Em. Good fun. I can see why you two got along so well.'

I suppress a shudder and nod instead, filling a glass with water so that I don't have to speak. Christian might be comfortable with all these lies, but I'm not.

'Well, let me get out of your hair,' he says, patting Jeremy on the back. 'Thanks for your hospitality. There's not enough kindness in this world, is there? It's great to have found it in you two.' He holds out his hand for Jeremy to shake, then heads over to me and kisses my cheek. The scent of his Fahrenheit hurls me back in time. He's worn it on purpose.

It takes all my restraint not to smack his arm away, but he must sense my body turning rigid. And with his back to Jeremy, Christian takes the opportunity to turn to me and smirk, before his eyes narrow to slits.

'I'm taking you both out for dinner,' he says, turning to Jeremy. 'To celebrate your wedding, and my new business venture.'

'No, you don't have to do that,' Jeremy says.

'Course I do. Emily's one of my oldest friends. It would be my pleasure.' He turns to me. 'I'll message Emily with some dates.'

'I'll see you out,' I say.

At the door, I step outside into the fresh, cool air, and pull it almost closed behind me.

'What the hell are you doing?' I hiss.

'Now, now. I've told you before about speaking to me like that.'

'It's one thing for you to force me to do stuff, but stay away from my family.'

'Or what? You'll go to the police? Hmm, I don't think so, do you?' He turns away. 'Night night, Emily. Sleep tight.'

I watch him walk down our path. He's not a man, he's a monster. And time is running out for me.

TWELVE

BEFORE

Christian has been acting strangely lately. Distant. He still wants to be with her all the time, but when they're together it's clear that his thoughts are elsewhere. Maybe it's because they've had a few arguments lately. Disagreements, Emily prefers to label them. But surely Christian sees, like she does, that they're not important, that they don't define their relationship.

The worst thing is, they're all about silly misunderstandings, like Emily getting the time wrong for when they were supposed to meet. Or her not replying to his texts, when she tries to tell him that she did. And then there was the time she booked a session at the new swimming pool. She thought he'd be happy to do something different, but the second she told him, he'd hit the roof. 'You know I can't swim!' he'd insisted. 'I told you about the accident. How could you forget something like that?' But Emily had no idea what he was talking about. 'I fell into that pool in Greece when we were on holiday, and I stay well away from the water now. It traumatised me.' But Emily doesn't remember him ever mentioning it. And surely she wouldn't have forgotten something like that?

But she won't give up on her relationship. When something's broken, you should try to fix it before you throw it away. This is what she believes, at her core. It's what she values. Her parents couldn't manage it, but Emily won't make the same mistakes.

'Daydreaming again?' Justine says.

Emily turns to her colleague, who's busy tidying the rails of clothes, even though they've barely been disturbed. It's always quiet on menswear, especially during the week. Here, unlike the other side of the store on ladieswear, her customers generally come in, grab something, pay for it and then leave as quickly as possible, which makes Emily's life easier. Sometimes Emily even reads when the manager isn't around, keeping her book hidden under the till.

It's her turn to stay by the till today, and she snaps to attention when Justine addresses her. 'Sorry, I—'

'Oh, no need to apologise to me. I remember what it's like being your age. Wishing you could be anywhere else but at work.' Justine laughs. 'And for me, I come here to escape the kids!'

Emily studies her. She's not sure how old Justine is, but she has two school-aged children, so she guesses at mid-thirties.

'Plus, I've noticed you've been here a lot these last couple of weeks. Please don't tell me you've dropped out of uni?'

Emily increased her hours for the next few weeks; it's Christian's birthday in a couple of months and she wants to buy him something decent. Not just some aftershave or a DVD. It has to be something that shows him he's special to her. So that he knows.

'No. Nothing like that. Just need some extra money.'

'I get that,' Justine says. 'Good on you for earning your own money while you study, and not just relying on the bank of mum and dad.'

Emily forces a smile and begins sorting through the drawer

under the till. It's a mess in there. Stationery. Clothing tags. Size cubes.

'You looked worried. Are you okay?' Justine asks, walking over to the till.

'Yeah, I'm fine. Just tired.'

'You should sneak off early,' Justine suggests. 'Go on, it's fine. It's so quiet and we're closing in a couple of hours. I can manage here by myself. No one will notice, or care.'

Emily is horrified. 'It's okay. I'd feel bad to leave early. And I don't want to get into trouble.'

'Oh, don't worry about that,' Justine assures her. 'You always go the extra mile, so you deserve an hour off.'

Emily hesitates. It's a tempting offer; she still has five hundred words to add to her assignment on *Othello*, and it's due in tomorrow. She's never normally this behind, but all the time she's been spending with Christian has made it hard to keep up. 'I can't really,' she says.

'Oh, let me guess – that fella of yours is meeting you at six, isn't he? You've got a kind one there, always meeting you after work to walk you home. Every time without fail.'

'Yeah.' Emily looks away, scared that Justine will see her face flood with shame. Every day for months, Christian has dropped whatever he's doing to come and meet her at the shop. They don't even discuss it any longer, he just knows when her shifts are and he makes sure he's always there. It's sweet. He just wants to make sure she gets home okay.

'Just message him and let him know you're leaving early,' Justine suggests. 'Have a nice walk home on your own. Sometimes we need space to clear our heads, don't we?' She looks intently at Emily, and it feels as if she's transmitting a silent message. A warning.

'Actually, I think I will go,' Emily says. 'If you're sure.' She can text Christian on the way to her flat and get that essay finished before six o'clock. He might even be relieved that he doesn't have to come out to meet her. He won't admit it, but Emily thinks his course workload might be affecting him.

Stepping outside onto the street, with the warm May sunshine brushing against her skin, she's surprised to find herself relieved that Christian isn't there in his usual spot, leaning against the rail. It's as if she can exhale after holding her breath for too long.

Everyone needs time by themselves. It's normal. Healthy.

As soon as this thought flickers through her mind, she shuts it down. She loves Christian. What kind of girlfriend is she to have these kinds of thoughts? Still, she's content as she heads home, walking slowly to make the most of it.

Approaching her road, Emily calls Christian, but there's no answer. He should be home by now, and it's too early for him to have left to meet her. He's probably knee-deep in his assignment, so he'll be pleased that he doesn't have to come and meet her. She wants to do something nice for him; she needs him to know how important he is to her, and that this isn't all one-way.

She turns around and heads towards Christian's place. She'll surprise him, and get some pizza for them to have for dinner. There's a takeaway place just around the corner from him, and Emily makes her way there, convinced this is the right thing to do.

There's only one other customer in the pizza place, and when he turns around, Emily recognises his face, though she can't place him. He smiles at her. 'You're at my uni,' he says. 'English lit. You probably don't recognise me.'

'I do, actually,' Emily says, holding out her hand. 'I'm Emily.'

'Niko,' he says. 'I wouldn't blame you if you didn't recognise me,' he adds. 'There are literally hundreds of us in those lectures.'

'I know what you mean,' Emily laughs.

'Although I am quite unique,' he says. 'Look at this hair!' He pulls at a lock of dark curly hair. 'How many guys do you know with curly hair this long?'

Again, she laughs. 'It suits you.'

'Your pizza,' the man behind the counter says, handing Niko a box. 'Enjoy.'

'See you around,' Niko says. 'And now you know who I am, maybe you can say hi sometime?'

'I will,' she says. 'See you.'

She watches him leave, wondering why her stomach is fluttering.

Emily feels content when she reaches Christian's flat, clutching the pizza box. It might unsettle him that the plans have changed, but he'll soon come around when he sees she's got them dinner.

She rings his doorbell and waits. Seconds tick by but there's no answer. Emily stands back and stares up at his window, hoping he'll appear. When there's no sign of any movement, she places the pizza box on the doorstep and pulls out her mobile.

It rings for a few seconds and she's just about to hang up and text him when he answers.

'Hello?' he says, as if he hasn't seen her name appear on his screen.

'I'm at your house,' she says. 'I finished work early and wanted to surprise you.'

There's a pause, and the phone becomes muffled. 'I'm not well,' he said. 'I'm sick in bed.'

She only saw him this morning and he seemed fine. Maybe he was a bit quiet, but he definitely wasn't ill. 'Just let me in. I'll come and look after you. I've got pizza. You must be hungry?'

'No, can't eat,' he says, coughing into the phone.

His words don't ring true, but she doesn't want to push him when things are already tense between them. 'Okay,' she says, deflated. 'I'll go home, then.'

'I'll see you when I'm better,' Christian says. 'Going to try and sleep now.'

Emily's barely had a chance to say goodbye when he hangs up.

She walks away, turning back to glance up at his window, and she swears she sees movement at the blinds.

Kirsty's in the kitchen, and the overpowering smell of garlic fills the flat. 'Wow, you're back!' she says. 'I was beginning to think you'd abandoned us. I would have called the police if I hadn't seen you at uni today.'

'Sorry, I've been—'

'With Christian? We guessed as much. How is he?'

Emily has never confronted her flatmate about Christian's claim that she tried it on with him. She's wanted to, but could never form the words, so it was easier just to hole away at Christian's. Now, though, looking at Kirsty, Emily's filled with doubts. She wants to believe her boyfriend, yet Kirsty has never done anything to suggest she's interested in him. And he was lying to her just now, she's sure of it.

'Actually, I've been at work. I'm doing extra shifts.'

Kirsty smiles. 'How is he anyway?'

Why is she asking about Christian? She never does. 'He's... busy with assignments. We all are, aren't we?' Emily replies, unable to look directly at her. Instead, she focuses on the saucepan Kirsty is vigorously stirring with a wooden spoon. 'What are you making?'

'Oh, don't get too excited. It's just pasta sauce. It's the only thing I can rustle up. Tastes amazing, though. Do you want some? I've got loads of pasta. Always do too much.'

'Thanks, but I've got this.' She places the pizza box on the kitchen counter. 'It's probably cold now.'

Kirsty laughs. 'Cold pizza is the best! Even better for breakfast. Save me a bit for the morning.'

Emily nods. 'Can I ask you something?'

'Course, ask away.'

But Emily's mouth won't open, the question she wants to ask trapped inside it like a prisoner. Once she speaks the words, she will never be able to take them back, and if Christian has been lying, Kirsty will never forgive either of them. And Emily still has to live here. As much as she loves Christian, she can't let things change by moving in with him. She can't do that to her mother. 'Can I borrow a teabag? I've run out and forgot to get some.'

Kirsty smiles. 'My mum always says you can't borrow something if you're not giving it back.' She laughs. 'Take one, I've got loads.'

Emily thanks her and boils the kettle for a drink she doesn't want.

'Can I say something?' Kirsty asks, placing down her wooden spoon and leaving a pool of tomato sauce on the worktop. 'I know you and Christian are all loved up, and it's great and all that, but he does need to give you some space sometimes too.'

'I've been at work,' she says. 'I haven't seen him this evening.' Feeling defensive, Emily's about to add that it's no different to Erin and Andre, but once again she stops herself saying something she'll regret.

Besides, Kirsty is far more intuitive than Emily has given her credit for.

'I need to finish my assignment,' Emily says, walking out of the kitchen.

'Don't forget your pizza!' Kirsty calls after her – but Emily has lost her appetite.

. . .

For the next few hours she sits in her room, tapping away on her laptop and throwing herself into knocking her assignment into shape. She's consistently been getting high marks, and she won't let herself down now. This degree means everything to her, and she won't let Christian's behaviour interfere with her goals.

But as soon as she types the last sentence and rereads what she's written, her thoughts become consumed with him. He's lying to her, and shutting her out, and she at least deserves to know why.

It's nearly midnight, but she calls him anyway.

'Just checking you're okay,' she says to his voicemail. 'Hope you're getting some rest.'

As she hangs up, Kirsty's loud laugh drifts into her room.

Emily shuts it out and flicks through her messages. So many from Christian. Not a day goes by when he doesn't inundate her with texts.

Yet now there is radio silence.

THIRTEEN

NOW

When I wake, for a fleeting moment I believe the man lying next to me is Christian. I pull myself up and am about to jump out of bed when Jeremy stirs. 'Hey, you okay?' he asks. My panic eases at the sound of my husband's familiar, comforting voice.

'Just need the bathroom.'

In the en suite, under the glare of the bright light, I tie my hair up in a bun and splash cold water on my face. It stings my skin but I relish the pain. At least it means I'm still living.

'You okay in there?' Jeremy calls after a few minutes, gently tapping on the door.

I open it and pull him towards me, throwing my arms around him.

'Hey, what's going on? Are you all right?' He pulls back and studies my face.

'I am now,' I tell him. I wish I could believe my own words. 'It was just hard you going away so soon after the wedding. We missed you.'

Jeremy sighs. 'I knew I should have asked for more time off.'

'No, no, it's fine. I don't think I slept well last night.' I turn back to the mirror and wonder if Jeremy can see how different I look. Pale. Haggard. A shell of myself.

'I could tell. You were mumbling in your sleep. It's funny, I've never heard you do that before.'

I freeze. What truths have I revealed subconsciously? 'What... was I saying?'

Jeremy shrugs. 'I'm not sure. It didn't really make much sense. Your words were a bit garbled.'

My shoulders drop. 'Must have been having a nightmare,' I say. I glance past him to the alarm clock; it's only six fifteen. 'You should still be sleeping,' I say.

'No, I need to get back into UK time. For the next two weeks at least. What are your plans today?'

I tell Jeremy that I need to head into school for a few hours, not mentioning that it's to catch up on the things I should have been doing over the last couple of days. Instead of being locked up at Christian's flat, or being forced to visit his father and brother.

Tyler still hadn't replied by the time I went to bed last night. I scoop up my phone from the bedside table and check my messages. There it is, sent just after midnight.

Sorry for the late reply. Insomnia again. Maybe I'd better start giving my midnight coffee a miss! No need to apologise to me about anything.

He ends it with a smiley face, and somehow this puts my mind at rest. I don't believe Tyler knows anything – it's nothing but Christian's delusions.

'I think I'll take Lexi to visit my mum,' Jeremy is saying, 'if you're going to be out.'

'Good idea,' I agree, only half listening. I type a reply to Tyler.

How about you let me buy you a coffee? As an apology.

When he doesn't reply, I wonder if I've pushed too far, too quickly. How will he interpret my message? I quickly send a follow up:

As I'm in Christian's life again, it's important I get to know his brother.

It's only when I've finished my shower and dried my hair that his reply comes.

Coffee sounds good. About 13:00? Hammersmith okay? Antipode Coffee is right by my practice.

I put my phone down and breathe deeply. I'm doing what Christian wants. I need to prove to him that Tyler knows nothing, so that he can stop involving his brother. The fewer players in this twisted game, the better. And he's still little Tyler to me, the young boy who once adored his older brother.

I sit in the coffee shop, waiting for Tyler to bring our drinks. It's too loud in here, and the constant hissing and clatter mingles with a myriad of conversations, clashing around my skull. My nerves are shot, and I wonder what Tyler thinks of my invitation to have coffee together.

I can't discount the possibility that Christian is right, and Tyler knows something, even though I struggle to believe it. I watch Tyler walk back to our table, smiling as he waves to someone on the other side of the room. All I can hope for is that he thinks I want to build bridges, and get to know my future brother-in-law better.

'They'll bring the coffees over,' Tyler says, sitting at the table. 'I have to say, I'm surprised to hear from you. The way you and Christian disappeared like that – I didn't think I'd see either of you again. Call me paranoid, but... well, to be honest, I never know what to expect from him.'

'I'm sorry. This business venture has been stressful for him. He just wants to make sure it all runs smoothly. I'm sure you get that. Aren't you a bit of a workaholic too?'

'Guilty,' he says, holding up his hand. 'But I also wouldn't disappear on my family for fifteen years, and let them believe all kind of things could have happened to me. It's astounding when you think about it. And no explanation either. He just sent a text message to Mum saying he needed space from everyone.' He shakes his head. 'And all those fees my parents paid for him to go to university. Right down the drain.'

I should defend Christian again – that's what any girlfriend would do – but I can't conjure up any words.

'You know, his disappearance put such a strain on my parents' marriage. They were never the same afterwards. Dad even threw accusations around... questioning what kind of parent mum was if their son would leave like that and want nothing to do with them.'

I stare at Tyler. I can't imagine Anthony accusing Audrey of this. As formidable as he is, it was clear to everyone how much he loved her.

'I honestly thought they'd end up divorced,' Tyler continues. 'Before that, I don't think I'd ever heard an angry word between them.'

I recall how I'd only ever scratched the surface of Christian's troubled relationship with his dad. Tyler might be the only chance I get to know the truth about what was going on.

'Can I ask you something? Christian used to tell me how he... couldn't connect with your dad.'

Tyler nods. 'They were just... two different people, I

suppose. Rubbed each other the wrong way. I can see both sides of it.'

'What do you mean?'

'Dad likes things done his way. He's always right. You know how he is. He was like that with both of us, but I think he was harder on Christian. Maybe because he's the oldest. Dad's all about appearances and how things look from the outside.' He pauses. 'His sons have to be successful, otherwise it reflects badly on him.' He sighs. 'There's no room to be human. To struggle with anything. It's just work, work, work. Be successful, no matter the costs.'

'You seem to have dealt with it okay.'

He considers this for a moment. 'I had more space to find my way. He wasn't breathing down my neck as much. Plus, I was too scared to do anything other than succeed.' He laughs, but I'm sure there is pain behind his joviality. 'Dad's not a bad person, though. He's a product of his upbringing. As are we all.'

'Do you forgive Christian?' I ask, steering the topic away from parents.

'I don't forgive him for what he did to Mum and Dad. Not giving them any explanation about why exactly he was disappearing from our lives. That just made them believe it was their fault somehow.'

'It was never your parents' fault,' I assure him. 'Christian's just—'

'What?'

'Nothing. Forget it.'

'He needs help,' Tyler says. 'Anyone who disappears like that needs to talk about what made them do it. What's he hiding?'

Our coffees arrive, enabling me to avoid responding. But while we both stir sugar into our cups, I realise that Tyler has just opened up an opportunity for me. I might not be able to speak aloud all the things Christian is doing to me, all the night-

mares from the past, but I can help his family to see for themselves that he's unstable. That he needs to be stopped.

'Christian's... fine,' I say. 'He's fine now.'

'What do you mean *now*?'

'Nothing. Please don't read into that. I'm just... this is difficult. Talking about him like this when he's not here to defend
himself. It feels wrong.' I stir my coffee, just for something to do
to hide my anxiety. So much is riding on this conversation going
the way I need it to.

'The trouble is, Emily, talking to him when he's right in
front of us does no good. It's like he's... I don't know. I can't
explain it.'

He's out to destroy my life and that's all he can focus on.
That's what Tyler senses but will never know.

Tyler takes a sip of coffee. 'You know, I used to think that he
was weird with you sometimes. Like a switch would go off and
he'd just be blank. Act as if you weren't there. Or as if... he
didn't want you to be there. But then the next time I saw you
together he'd be fine, cuddling up to you as if you were the only
person in the world who mattered to him.'

It chills me to remember Christian's coldness. How he
would push me away. Make me believe the way he felt was all
my fault.

'All relationships have rocky patches.' I lift my own cup to
my lips, take a sip of strong espresso.

'True,' Tyler admits. 'So, do you really believe he's okay,
then? That your marriage will work?'

I hesitate, just long enough for Tyler to doubt me. 'One
hundred per cent.' I stare into my cup, avoiding his questioning
gaze.

'Does he talk to you about those missing years?'

'No,' I say. 'Other than what he did with his business.'
Despite my outward confidence, my insides churn. I hate everything I'm doing. Tyler doesn't deserve this, and neither does

their dad. But if it's the only way I can stop Christian, then I have to see this through. 'It will all work out. Christian's fine. There's nothing to worry about.'

'I hope so,' Tyler says.

'Anyway, I came here to get to know my future brother-in-law better. Tell me all about your work. And about Katerina. We'd love to meet her soon.'

Tyler smiles, and becomes animated when he speaks of his job. And his girlfriend. I listen attentively, taking in all the information I can. And by the time he's finished speaking, and our coffee cups lie empty in front of us, I'm more convinced than ever that he knows nothing about what happened that night.

Lexi greets me at the door the second I step inside and pulls me into the living room. 'Guess what?' she says. 'Grandma's here and she gave me my first proper piano lesson today. I loved it. Look!'

She sits down at the piano and begins tentatively playing scales, starting again when she misses a note. Pam sits on the sofa and claps.

'That's amazing, Lex! I'm so glad you're starting to learn.'

I walk over to Pam and give her a hug. 'It's lovely to see you,' I say. 'You'll stay for dinner?'

'Not today, I'm afraid. I was just dropping Lexi off and thought I'd stop in and see how you are. We didn't get much chance to talk after the wedding, did we? You had to go out with your friend, didn't you?'

Perhaps it's the trauma of Christian turning up that's making me paranoid, but I sense Pam's words are laced with mistrust. 'He's been living in America for fifteen years. Haven't seen him in all that time.'

Pam stands and places her arm on mine. 'Just remember where your priorities lie,' she whispers, before turning back to

Lexi and clapping again. 'How about one more time? Practice makes perfect!'

'Where's your dad?' I ask Lexi. I need to get out of this room.

'He's in the bath,' Lexi says, tapping the piano keys again. 'He was listening to me play and then he said he needed to relax in some nice hot water.'

I head upstairs and find Jeremy in the en suite.

'Hey,' he says. 'Come in and join me. We haven't done that for a while.'

I hover by the door. 'Not with Lexi and Pam downstairs. But I'll sit in here with you for a bit.' I cross to the bath and sit on the floor, trying to be present with Jeremy.

'How has your day been?' he asks. 'I hope you don't need to go in again tomorrow. You deserve a break,' he continues. 'Some time to relax. We didn't have long in Kefalonia, did we? And school starts back soon. I feel awful that we haven't had a proper honeymoon. I've been talking to Mum about that – and she's happy to have Lexi in the week so we can get away somewhere. Just the two of us.'

Christian will never let this happen. 'I'm fine,' I assure him. 'We can sort something out soon. I really don't need a break. This *is* a break. I have all I need right here.'

Jeremy leans out of the bath to kiss me, dripping bubbles onto my hair. I try to lose myself in him, but all I can see is Christian looming over me. Always there. I slowly pull away. 'Is your mum okay?' I ask.

'Yeah. Why?'

'I don't know. She seemed a bit... oh, it's nothing. I'm just tired. I'd better get some dinner sorted,' I say. 'Lexi will be starving.'

Jeremy offers to do it instead, and I jump at the chance. As soon as he's gone downstairs, I find my laptop and sit on the bed, waiting for it to wake up and silently urging it to hurry, in case Jeremy comes back up and wonders what I'm doing.

When I'm finally logged in, I go straight to Google and search for the Mental Health Act – I need to know if there's a way I can stop Christian. For almost an hour I scan webpages, soaking up information that I need to store in my mind and never commit to paper.

From what I can determine, a close relative needs to make the move to get Christian sectioned. There are many ways I can prove that he is not of sound mind, I just need to make sure he isn't aware of what I'm doing.

It will have to be Tyler or Anthony who question his sanity. Despite what they believe, I'm not Christian's girlfriend, and if anyone digs too deep, the whole house of cards will fall.

And I will lose Jeremy and Lexi, and my career.

Satisfied that I have what I need, I close my laptop and head downstairs. My phone vibrates before I reach the bottom. It's Christian.

What's happening with Tyler?

Short, cold words I wish I could ignore.

Saw him today. Don't think he knows anything. Will keep working on it.

His reply stops my breath.

Time is running out for you.

FOURTEEN
BEFORE

Days stretch endlessly before her now that summer is here. She's been dreading the end of this semester, and the thought of having to go back home. It's affecting Christian too – he barely wants to be away from her, and when they're watching TV together, he grips her hand tightly, as if she'll disappear if he lets go even for a second.

Christian has been sweet to her lately. As if he's making up for something. But Emily pushes those thoughts away. 'You don't have to go back,' he'd said to her the other night. 'Just take on more shifts at Next, and then your mum will understand why you have to stay. She can't object to you working.'

The seed was planted and Emily gave life to it, compromising with her mum that she would come back for the first week of the holidays. Christian had become silent and withdrawn when she'd told him her plan, refusing to admit what was wrong when she questioned him.

Now, sitting across from her mum – who is a shrunken figure on the sofa, with a blanket pulled around her – Emily regrets coming back home. Her mother looks like a child wrapped in that blanket, with only her head peeking out. And it's hot in here, so Emily has no idea why her mum is layering up.

'You don't look well,' Emily says. 'Are you feeling ill?'

Her mother glares at her. 'I haven't been sleeping. For weeks now. It's because of that... that neighbour across the road. In the house that faces ours. I don't know his name. He keeps watching me.'

Emily frowns and glances at the window. 'What? Who?'

'Everywhere I go, I see him. Just standing there, watching me. Right across the road. And when I look out the window, he's there too. Staring. He doesn't even try to hide.' She shakes her head. 'I don't know what to do. It's hard to avoid him when our windows face each other.'

Emily stands and crosses to the window, peering through the slats in the blinds. 'There's no one there now.'

Her mum sighs, and pulls the blanket down slightly. 'Probably because he knows you're here. I'm not alone. That's why you haven't seen him. He's clever, Emily. He doesn't want any evidence left behind.'

She wants to tell her mum that she's not making any sense, but of course she won't. 'Doesn't he work? He must do something.'

Her mother shrugs. 'No idea. All I know is that I keep seeing him, and he just stares at me.'

'How old is he?'

'How would I know? I've never spoken to him. We're not friends, Emily.' She tuts, and pulls the blanket up to her chin again.

Emily's never heard her mum speak like this before, even with all the warnings and scaremongering she loves to preach – this is something different.

'Okay, well I can go over there and find out what's going on,' Emily suggests.

'No, don't do that. It's not safe.'

'Mum, it's just across the road. Nothing's going to happen to me.' But even as she says this a flicker of apprehension passes over her. She doesn't know this neighbour. What if her mum is right?

'Does he live on his own?'

Her mother nods. 'Must do. I've never seen anyone else leaving or going in that house. Maybe he's divorced? That could be why he's fixated on me. It's very frightening, Emily.'

'Oh, Mum. Please don't worry.' Emily sits next to her on the sofa. 'While I'm here for the week, I can keep an eye out for you? Just from the window, I mean.'

Her mother stares at her, and her eyes are large and wild, something Emily's never seen before. Panic, yes, but never this vacant expression. 'That would be nice. Thank you. As long as you don't go over there.'

'I think maybe you're coming down with something, Mum. You don't seem yourself. Why don't you rest and I'll make us some dinner?'

Her mum lies back and rests her head on the sofa arm. 'I'm not ill, I just need to sleep. My head's pounding.'

Emily prays it is just lack of sleep, and not a virus; she doesn't want to catch anything and be stuck here for longer than a week. Especially when her mum is acting even more strangely than usual.

Christian calls while she's cooking spaghetti and meatballs. 'I can't really talk now,' Emily says, keeping her voice low. 'Mum's not feeling well and I'm making dinner.' She peers into the living room to make sure her mum's still asleep.

'Oh? What's wrong? I hope she's okay.'

'Not sure. She's not been sleeping.' With her free hand she stirs the meatballs. 'I don't know really.'

'I'm sure she'll be okay. It's probably her anxiety taking its toll. I miss you, Em.'

'I do too. But it's only a week, remember. What are your plans?'

There's a pause before he speaks. 'I'm out tonight and tomorrow. With Matty. We're heading to the West End, then we'll see where we end up.'

Emily's surprised to hear this. She'd expected Christian to be begging her to come back, to be laying it on about how much he misses her. Not making other plans. It's for the best, though. She can't leave her mum in this state, and at least she doesn't have to feel so guilty now.

'It's good you're keeping busy,' she says.

'I'd rather be with you, of course,' he says. 'But Matty's a good laugh. Seeing him will help pass the time until you come back.'

The phone becomes muffled, as if he's covering up the speaker. 'What's going on?' Emily asks.

'What?'

'It sounded like you covered up the phone.'

'I didn't. Why would I? It's just a bad connection. You know what my phone's like.'

She's sure he did, but she doesn't question him further. The last thing she needs is to fall out with him when they're miles away from each other.

They finish the call and Emily turns her attention back to stirring the meatballs. She dishes up dinner and takes their plates through to the living room, and finds her mother still sleeping soundly on the sofa.

Emily watches her for a moment, surprised by how peaceful she looks when she's asleep. She can't remember ever seeing her mum at peace like this. Normally her pain and anxiety are etched across her face, like tattoos.

Not wanting to wake her, Emily eats in the kitchen, and covers her mum's plate to reheat later.

Feeling guilty that she's relieved she doesn't have to talk for now, Emily slips on her shoes and heads outside. She doesn't know what's going on with this neighbour, but she needs to find out what's bothering her mum.

The previous neighbours, the McAllisters, moved just after Emily started university, so she hasn't been around to see who bought the house.

She walks up to the front door and rings the bell. It's not long before someone answers, but it's not the male neighbour she's expecting to see. It's a woman around a similar age to her mother, with dark blonde shoulder-length hair.

She smiles at Emily. 'Hi, can I help you?'

'Hi, I... um, I live across the road with my mum.' She turns and points to their house. 'And I was just wondering... um, my mum seems to think there might be a man who's been watching her. A lot. She's a bit worried about it.'

The woman frowns and peers out, looking up and down the street. 'Oh. Oh dear. I haven't seen anyone hanging around. Have you called the police?'

The enormity of what she's doing hits Emily. How can she turn up here and accuse this woman's husband of stalking her mum? 'Um, no. I just wanted to check first whether it's just someone who lives on our road, and Mum's just got a bit confused.' She smiles apologetically. 'Can I ask – do you live here with anyone?'

'Nope. It's just me. I have two daughters but they moved out a while ago. They share a flat in Woking. I do miss them, but I'm glad they've got their own space now that they're adults. That's important, isn't it?'

None of this fits in with what her mum has told her. 'Yes it is. Mum seems to think a man lives here on his own? Divorced, she thinks.'

'Oh, no. No one like that. Just me. Never married. I've always been a single mum, and had IVF to have the girls.' The woman smiles proudly, and it strikes Emily that she couldn't be more different to her mother, though they are both single mothers. This woman is clearly an over-sharer, while her mum barely likes to talk about what she's having for dinner with anyone. *Our private business is all we have to cling to in this world*, she always tells Emily. *And is of no concern to anyone else. Never give too much of yourself away. It's a recipe for disaster.*

'What about next door?' Emily asks the woman. It's possible her mother got confused about which house it is.

She shakes her head. 'Well, there's only Margot and Alfie on that side, and they're in their eighties at least.' She gestures to her left. 'And on that side is a young family, but there's no man living there. Just Sadie and Jasmine and their two kids. Lovely children. So polite and respectful, and they're only four and six.'

Her mother had been clear that the man lived in the house opposite, hadn't she? So there's no point enquiring about any other neighbours on this side.

'Well, sorry for bothering you,' she says. 'I'll see you around, I'm sure.'

'Oh, it's no bother, dear. I'm happy to meet the neighbours. I don't think I've even seen your mum.'

'She doesn't leave the house much. That's probably why you haven't seen a lot of her.'

'Oh, work from home, does she? Yes, that's so common nowadays.'

Emily hesitates before answering. 'Yeah.' There is no way she will reveal to this stranger that her mother hasn't been able to work for years. That she is more than likely agoraphobic, but won't set foot outside to see the doctor.

'Well, tell her that whenever she needs a break, she's welcome to pop over for coffee.' She holds out her hand. 'I'm Valerie.'

'Emily. And my mum's Laura. I'd better get back.'

'Bye then, Emily. Don't forget to tell your mum to pop round. I'd love to meet her.'

Emily lets herself back in the house, saddened to think that if things were different, if her *mum* was different, the two women might have ended up friends. Valerie seemed nice.

Now, though, there are bigger things to worry about – who is this man her mum has been talking about? Does he even exist? Emily opens the living room door, prepared to let her mum know what she's found out, even though it could bring on a row.

But she's still sleeping on the sofa, one arm dangling to the carpet. Emily tucks the blanket around her mum, careful not to wake her. She still looks peaceful, and it haunts Emily that this is the only time her mother gets any respite.

The house is so stuffy; Emily is desperate to open at least one window. But if her mum wakes up and finds it open she would have a huge panic attack.

'I wish I could talk to you,' Emily whispers. 'I know you went through hell with Dad, and I think that must be what's done this to you.' It feels good to let these words out.

She makes herself a cup of tea and takes it up to bed, pulling out *A Doll's House* to read. She needs to get ahead of her reading for next term. But she only gets through a few pages of the play before her mind wanders. She pulls out her phone and texts Christian to see how he is.

But Christian doesn't reply.

She's woken in the middle of the night by a thump. When she opens her eyes, her mother is standing in the doorway.

'Emily, are you awake? He's there! He's there by the window, staring at me again. I'm scared. Why does he keep doing this?' Her mother clutches her head, twisting hair around her fingers. 'I can't do this again. Not tonight. I just want to sleep!'

Emily throws the duvet off and springs up. 'Mum, it's okay – I'm coming. Let's go and see what's going on.'

But she already knows as she follows her mother downstairs that there is no man. None that exists outside her mind.

They reach the window. 'He's gone,' her mother says, sighing. 'He was there, though, Emily. He's always there. And now he's gone. He'll have been watching the house and he'll know you're here.'

Emily takes her arm and leads her from the window. 'We'll look out for him tomorrow, Mum. But you're safe now. I'm here with you.'

'Oh, Emily, haven't you realised by now? Neither of us is safe. Not until we're... not until we're dead.'

FIFTEEN

NOW

It won't be long before Jeremy notices something is wrong. With each passing minute, I'm finding it harder to maintain the pretence of normality. It's crippling me to act as though there's nothing out of the ordinary. And I'm running out of time.

Last night, Jeremy had reached for me, longing for intimacy that I was unable to give him. There is only so much pretending I can do; I wanted to, but my body wouldn't respond. The disappointment on his face crushed me. He doesn't deserve this.

'Emily, can we go to the playground?' Lexi asks this morning.

It's Saturday, and the three of us are eating breakfast together before Jeremy goes to his regular football game. I've made French toast in an attempt to distract myself. It hasn't worked, though. Losing myself in distractions is no longer working. Christian is ever present.

'Course we can,' I say. 'We can take your bike too, if you like.'

Lexi smiles. 'Yes! I've hardly been on my new one.' She finishes her last mouthful of toast and rushes upstairs to brush her teeth.

'Are you okay?' Jeremy asks. 'You don't mind me playing football, do you? I know we haven't spent much time together since the wedding.'

'No, not at all. You miss it when you're working, so don't cancel.'

He takes my hand. 'Thanks. Are you sure you're okay, though? You seem... quiet.'

I've got to get better at this; this isn't the first time that Jeremy has asked about my wellbeing. 'Just thinking about school starting in a couple of weeks. Wondering if I'm ready for the new term.'

Jeremy smiles. 'Course you are. When have you ever not been ready for anything?'

With Christian.

Despite planning for it, knowing it would happen one day, I wasn't ready for him to turn up when he did. How naive of me to believe it would simply be a case of grabbing my packed suit-case and disappearing.

'I'm sorry about last night,' I explain. 'I think I might be coming down with something. I'll be fine, though. I'm looking forward to getting out this morning with Lexi.' I begin clearing the table.

'Promise me no work today?' Jeremy says. 'It's not healthy to work twenty-four seven. It'll do you good to have a break.'

He leans in to kiss me and I let myself get lost in him for a moment, pulling away when I picture Christian's face instead of my husband's.

'What is it?' Jeremy asks.

'I've just remembered – Sue messaged me yesterday and I forgot to reply. My phone's upstairs.' I rush off, leaving Jeremy staring after me.

I head to our en suite and lock the door. I check my phone for messages, relieved to find there are none.

I need to move things along with Tyler, to firmly plant those seeds of doubt about his brother. It shouldn't be too difficult – he already has doubts of his own. Christian didn't do himself any favours by disappearing on his family like that. I begin typing a message:

Thanks for the coffee the other day. Not sure Christian was too pleased about it. Shh – please don't tell him I've said that.

It sickens me that I'm lying to him – yet another person – but I need him to trust me.

While I wait for his reply, I wash my face and brush my teeth, staring at my reflection in the mirror. Other than looking older, not much about my appearance has changed. Inside, though, it's a different story. I'm damaged. My dark hair is still shoulder length, falling in soft waves around my face. Before meeting Christian, I never wore it loose, always tying it in a ponytail instead. He was the one who encouraged me to wear it down. And of course I listened. Now, I grab a hair tie from the bathroom shelf and scrape my hair back in a ponytail, so tightly it hurts.

My phone pings, and I sit on the side of the bath to read Tyler's message.

Trouble in paradise? Be careful, though, Emily. I'm serious.

Without replying, I slip my phone in the pocket of my jeans. For now, planting those seeds is enough.

The playground is walking distance from our home, set next to an expansive park, where dog walkers and joggers flock to make the most of the sunshine. Even in winter it's a beautiful space, one that the three of us often frequent. There are no triggers for me here, nothing that will hurl me back fifteen years.

Marta, one of Lexi's schoolfriends is in the playground when we arrive, and I watch as the two of them rush off to play. I barely know Marta's mother – she's a good friend of Tia's, so I'm more than happy to keep my distance. She gives me a tentative wave, and I wave back before turning away, hoping she'll assume I'm being professional rather than rude.

I sit on the bench and consider how to reply to Tyler. I don't want to rush it, to make him suspicious, because then it will all fall apart. While I'm still figuring out what to write, a text message from Christian appears.

Don't you just love lazy Saturday mornings? The sun shining, birds humming in the trees. Peace.

And underneath his words there is an emoji of a bomb exploding.

I delete the message immediately without replying. But as soon as it's vanished, I realise I should have kept it. It could help me prove Christian is not of sound mind. I need to be less rash from now on, and start building up a picture of him.

Lexi runs over and asks if she can have some ice cream. I look towards the car park and see the ice cream van parked in its usual spot, silently beckoning children to grab a quick sugar fix. 'Okay,' I say, fumbling for my purse. Lexi usually eats fairly healthily so I won't begrudge her the odd treat. I hand her a five-pound note. 'Get one for Marta too.'

'Thanks, Em – you're the best!' She runs off, grabbing her friend's arm on the way to the ice cream van.

My phone pings again.

I'm enjoying watching you squirm. But it's nothing compared to what you did. Enjoy every moment you can.

Fighting back nausea, I look around, making sure no one

can see how sick I must look. I wonder if I could convince Jeremy that we could live abroad somewhere. There are plenty of English schools in Europe, or I could teach English as a foreign language. And being such an experienced pilot, Jeremy would get snapped up by any airline. But the thought quickly evaporates. I can't uproot Lexi – she has friends here, routine and familiarity. Her mum. Everything that's important to a child.

Despite my earlier vow to build a trail of evidence, I delete Christian's message, though the words stay with me.

Switching my phone to silent, I turn to the ice cream truck, squinting at the queue. But there is no sign of Lexi. Nor is she anywhere I can see in the playground. Her bike is still chained to the railing.

I bolt towards the truck, shouting her name. She doesn't answer, and there's still no sign of her. Across the playground, Marta is walking towards her mum.

I've never known such deep penetrating fear.

'Lexi!' I shout, scanning every inch of the playground equipment as I sprint towards Marta and her mother.

'Where's Lexi?' I cry. 'I can't see her anywhere!'

'Oh, my!' Marta's mum exclaims. I wish I could remember her name. She turns to her daughter, addressing her in Hungarian.

'She was over by the ice cream van,' Marta says. 'I just came here to show Mum what I got. I thought she was right behind me! Maybe she needed the toilet?'

I race off, almost knocking into another mum as I navigate my way through the playground.

The toilet block is on the other side of the car park, and I push through the doors, shouting Lexi's name.

'There's no one in here, love,' a woman washing her hands at the sink says. She doesn't turn around but watches me in the mirror.

I check the toilets are all empty just to be sure. 'Did a ten-year-old girl come in here? Light brown hair, blue eyes? Wearing an orange hoodie?'

'Not since I've been in,' the woman says, shaking water from her hands. 'That damn hand dryer's broken again.' She rolls her eyes. 'They really need to sort this place out. These toilets are a disgrace.'

I don't respond, but rush outside, shouting out for Lexi again, questioning every person I pass. But nobody's noticed her. And why would they when this playground is full of children?

I rush towards the park, checking every face I pass. Marta's mum is striding through the playground, speaking on her phone, and I wonder if she's calling the police. Is it too early to panic? But there's no sign of Lexi anywhere.

With each step I take, I'm crushed by the fear that I'll never see her again. That I will have to explain to Jeremy and Tia that it's my fault Lexi is missing, that I couldn't keep her safe.

'Lexi!' I shout again, repeating her name so much that it stops sounding like a word.

A woman holding her toddler rushes over to me. 'Don't panic. She'll be here somewhere. I'll help you look.'

'She's never done this before,' I say. 'She always stays close by or lets us know what she's doing.'

Saying this out loud spurs me on even more, and I rush around the playground, begging people to help me look.

Within minutes everyone has rallied together to help me search. Minutes tick by, and I have no idea how long we've been looking; all I know is that it feels like hours. Someone tells me they've called the police, because it's never too early when it comes to children.

I'm making a circuit of the park when a hand lands heavily on my shoulder.

I spin around and Tia is standing in front of me, her face distraught.

'Tia, I'm sorry,' I begin. 'One minute she was over by the ice cream van – the next she... she wasn't there.'

'I know. Anna's told me everything. She called me. You should have called me.'

'It's only just happened. I... I've been looking.'

Tia ignores me and rushes off, calling Lexi's name, just like I've been doing.

I run in the other direction, past the tennis courts and out onto the other side. I'm sure Lexi wouldn't have ventured this far, but I have to try.

As I run, struggling for breath, I see a girl in an orange hooded top by a tree in the distance. It's Lexi. I know it. And she's talking to a man. Summoning all my stamina, I run faster, and only when I get closer do I realise who she's with.

Christian.

'Lexi!' I scream.

They both look round as I finally reach them, struggling to catch my breath.

'Emily, look who's here!' Lexi says, smiling. 'It's Christian!'

Doubled over, my hands resting on my thighs, it takes me a moment to speak. 'I've been looking for you everywhere. Why did you go off without telling me? You mustn't ever do that, Lexi. What are you doing all the way out here?'

'She's fine, aren't you?' Christian smiles. 'I saw her when I was jogging in the park and thought I'd say hello.'

I stare at him: black T-shirt and charcoal joggers, Nike running trainers. AirPods in his ears. He didn't come all the way here from his house in north London for a run, but he won't care whether I believe him.

Lexi tugs at my arm. 'Christian said he'd seen a red squirrel by this tree. I had to come and look! They're so rare, aren't they?

I've never seen one before! You only ever see grey in this country.'

I stare at Christian, desperate to expose his lie, but knowing I can't.

'Your mum's here, Lexi! We've all been looking for you.'

'Sorry,' she says, scanning the park for Tia.

'Did you see it, then?' I ask Lexi, as my breathing slowly begins to regulate.

She sighs. 'No. It was gone by the time we got here. We probably scared it off. But we've been looking for it. Sorry, Emily. I got so excited I dropped my ice cream, and I forgot to tell you I was coming over here.'

What worries me even more is that Christian knew exactly how to lure Lexi away. He's supposed to be my close friend, so why wouldn't she trust him? Her love of animals and nature is something only those who've spent time with her would know – so how does *he* know this?

I put my arm around her. 'Come on, Lex. Let's go and find your mum.'

But there's no need – Tia is already rushing towards us, screeching Lexi's name. She's wearing a mint-green summer dress and white slip-on trainers.

Lexi rolls her eyes. 'I'm *fine*, Mum! I was just with Christian.'

Tia grabs Lexi and wraps her arms around her. 'I was worried sick when Anna called. I rushed here as quickly as I could.' She turns to Christian. 'And who are you?'

I stand helplessly by as Christian reaches out his hand to take Tia's. 'Hi, I'm a good friend of Emily's. Christian.'

'Ah, yes.' Tia smiles. 'Lexi's told me all about you. What exactly happened here?'

'I'm so sorry for the misunderstanding,' Christian says. 'I did message Em to say I'd bumped into Lexi. I said I was showing her where I'd just seen a squirrel across the other side of the park.' He turns to me. 'I would have told you in person but I couldn't see you. We didn't want to miss the squirrel.'

'I didn't get any message from you,' I say, as calmly as I can manage. He's messed up now – there was no message.

'Really? That's strange. Check your phone.'

I pull my phone from my pocket. And there it is – an unread message from Christian. Sent at 10.33.

Just bumped into Lexi – taking her over other side of park to see a squirrel! Meet us over there x

I open my mouth to speak but can't find any words. The message is there – I have no idea how I didn't see it. Then I remember: I switched my phone to silent so that I could ignore Christian's messages. Most likely he sent it way after I started looking for Lexi, but I have no way to prove that. I lost all sense of time when I realised she'd gone.

'I don't know how it was on silent,' I say. 'Sorry, Tia. I made you worry for nothing.'

Tia sighs. She's surprisingly relaxed, given that moments ago her daughter was missing. 'No harm done. Lexi's fine – that's all that matters.' She turns to Lexi. 'I need to get back now – I've got builders coming to give me a quote this afternoon. I'll see you next weekend, though, as normal.'

'Okay,' Lexi says.

Tia grabs her hand. 'Tell you what. We'll go out for lunch on Saturday – how does that sound? You can choose where. And we can invite Marta and Anna too. We haven't done that for ages, have we?'

'Thanks, Mum,' Lexi says, giving her a hug. I'm glad Tia wants to spend time with Lexi, but I feel a twinge of sadness too.

'I apologise again,' Christian says. 'Please let me make it up to you.'

Tia waves him off. 'Really no need. As I said, no harm done.'

'Can Christian come and eat with us?' Lexi asks me.

'Not today.'

'Don't worry, Lexi,' Christian says. 'There'll be lots more chances. And I can tell you all about the wildlife in America that you don't find here.' He turns to Tia. 'Are you walking to the car park? I'll walk with you.'

I watch helplessly as Christian heads off with Tia, both of them engrossed in conversation. He couldn't have planned all of this, but now he's met Tia, he has entwined himself even more tightly into my life.

And it's only a matter of time before he makes his final move.

SIXTEEN

NOW

For the rest of the day, I'm numb, undertaking household chores on autopilot. Christian crossed a line by approaching Lexi this morning, making me believe she'd gone missing. I've never felt terror like that before, and he knows it. I can deal with whatever he wants to do to me, but I won't let him drag Lexi into this. This escalation is forcing my hand.

I'm vacuuming the upstairs hallway, so I don't hear Jeremy until he's right in front of me. 'Jesus!' I scream, jumping back and dropping the vacuum cleaner nozzle so it clatters to the floor.

'Sorry! I thought you saw me coming up.'

'No... I... I didn't even hear you. Is Lexi okay?'

'She's fine.' Jeremy smiles. 'I think you're the one who's traumatised by what happened.'

'It's not funny. I thought someone had taken her. It happens all the time.' I sound like my mum, and it makes me shudder. But this was a real threat. 'I didn't know Christian was in the park!'

Jeremy moves closer and wraps his arms around me, and I try to let the feel of him comfort me. But all I see is Christian. It must have taken some planning to make that happen today; there's no way he would have known we were there unless he'd followed us from the house. Which means he'd been waiting, with no idea when, or if, we'd venture out today.

'It must have been a terrible shock.' Jeremy pulls back and smooths my hair from my face. I almost flinch, until I remember that it's my husband doing this. 'Lexi's fierce, though,' he continues, oblivious to my torment. 'She would have screamed blue murder if anyone had tried to drag her away. She's got some lungs on her.'

I nod, pleased that this is true, and somehow I'm able to smile. Lexi *is* the type of girl who will let her voice be heard, no matter what. So different to the young girl I was, constantly shrinking into the background.

'You've been cleaning since you got back,' Jeremy says. 'Come and have a break. I promised Lexi we'd have a movie afternoon. Think she wants to watch *Harry Potter* for the hundredth time. Or is it the millionth? I've lost track.'

Nothing would make me happier than spending time with the two of them, and shutting out everything else, but I can't sit around while Christian painstakingly destroys my life. 'Actually, I really need to go food shopping. The cupboards are bare.'

I hold my breath, hating that I'm lying to Jeremy. *I'm doing this for you, Jeremy. For you and Lexi.*

He frowns, and I wish I could erase it like a mistake in a drawing. 'Didn't you go the other day? Surely it's not that urgent.' He's doubting me – something I never wanted to happen.

'To be honest, I could do with getting out. I need a long walk to clear my head. This morning really got to me.' Going for long walks by myself is something I've always done, and the supermarket is right by the nature reserve, so Jeremy won't question why I'm driving. 'I'll get the shopping on the way back,' I explain.

His face softens. 'I know it was a tough morning. Remember you can talk to me. And if it's Tia who's bothering you, then don't let her. She can hardly complain about your parenting, can she?'

In the car, I head towards the north circular, filled with doubt about whether I'm doing the right thing. But then I think of Lexi, and how terrified I was when I thought I'd lost her. Taking Lexi is the worst thing he could do to me, far worse than exposing the truth.

A car horn blares, and I realise I've swerved into the other lane, narrowly missing hitting a silver Golf. Shaken up, I warn myself to be careful.

Outside Christian's flat, I waver. He won't take kindly to me turning up like this, taking away some of the control he's so desperate for.

But I force my legs to move forward, up to his door, for the sake of Jeremy and Lexi.

I press the doorbell and wait. He answers after only a few moments, dressed in black joggers and a red T-shirt. For a fraction of a second, I catch a glimpse of the man I once loved – I always told him red suited him.

Then he narrows his eyes and it all comes flooding back to me. He steps outside, pulling the door behind him so it's almost closed. 'What are you doing here?' he hisses.

'Let me in. We need to talk.' My voice is firm – I need to show him that no matter how he terrorises me, I'm not afraid.

'*I'll* decide when we need to talk,' he says. 'Just get out of here. Now.'

'No!' I try to brush past him but he shoves me away.

'Just go, Emily,' he insists. 'I didn't invite you here. Don't ever come to my home without being asked.'

'You went too far today, Christian. Keep Lexi out of this. Your problem is with me, not her!'

'Keep your voice down,' Christian hisses. He tries to cover my mouth, but I inch back out of his reach.

Then I realise what's going on. 'Why won't you let me in? The other day it was the opposite and you wouldn't let me out.' I try to see inside. 'Who's in there with you?'

'That's none of your business.' He pushes me away.

I stare at him. 'Girlfriend, is it?' I try to see through the small gap in the door. 'Why don't you introduce us? Come on, Christian. I'm sure she'd love to meet your old friend.'

Again, he pushes me away. 'Get in your car and drive back home,' he says, his words slow and measured. 'And don't ever turn up here without an invitation again. Do you understand?' He turns around and steps back inside, slamming the door in my face.

But not before I hear a woman's voice calling his name.

Back in the car, I send the text without fully considering what I'm doing.

Can we talk?

I'm running out of time, and I need him onside. There's a chance Christian is right and his brother does know something, but my instinct tells me I can trust him.

Tyler's reply comes after a few minutes, letting me know he's at home and I can meet him there.

The address Tyler has texted me is in Clapham – far from Christian – and the further away I get, the more relief I feel. For now, at least, I know where Christian is, and he's nowhere near Lexi or Jeremy. Tonight he's likely to be busy with whatever woman he's entertaining in his flat. Whoever

she is, I pity her – and I hope she doesn't end up how
I did.

People don't change.

I knock on the door of a Victorian terrace house and realise
I'm holding my breath. But I don't need to – it's Tyler who will
answer the door, not his brother.

I'm stunned when a woman answers. She's around thirty,
with wavy blonde hair tied in a loose ponytail, and a red head-
scarf wrapped around it. 'Hi, you must be Emily.' She smiles
and holds out her hand. 'I'm Katerina. Tyler's just on a call – he
won't be long. Come in.'

Her friendliness puts me at ease, but I'm still surprised that
she's here, given Tyler never mentioned that they live together.

The hallway is filled with family photos – but not Tyler's.
'This must be your place,' I say. 'I thought it was Tyler's.'

Katerina laughs. 'It may as well be – he's always here.
Reading is just so far from his work. Can I get you a drink while
we wait? Tea or coffee? Something stronger?' She laughs again,
and it strikes me as a nervous gesture.

'Just water, thanks.'

I follow her into the kitchen, impressed with how
welcoming and homely the house feels. How lived in. A stark
contrast with Christian's cold and sterile place.

'I'm guessing you haven't met Christian properly yet?' I ask.

'No. I only saw him at their mum's funeral.' She lowers her
voice. 'I have to admit, it's all been a bit of a shock. All the years
I've known Tyler, he never spoke about his brother. I knew he'd
disappeared and never contacted them, and I didn't want to
open up old wounds, so I've never mentioned it. When their
mum died, no one expected Christian would just turn up. I
mean, it's good that he came for the funeral.' She smiles, and
hands me a glass of water. 'I know Tyler just wants them all to
try and repair their relationship. For their dad's sake.'

'I see how it must feel strange,' I say. 'But Christian had his reasons for leaving. And now he's back, he just wants the same as Tyler.'

Katerina nods. 'I'm so happy to meet you,' she says. 'It's felt a bit like... like Tyler's been keeping me away from Christian on purpose. I was beginning to think it's because Tyler's, well... oh, it sounds so silly now.' She bites her lip. 'Worried about me meeting him? Ashamed, maybe?'

'Of course not! Why would he be? He told me all about you at dinner the other day and he was so proud of everything you do. He couldn't be more smitten.'

She exhales loudly. 'That's a relief.'

'I'm sure he just wants to make sure Christian's... okay before he introduces him to you.'

'What do you mean?'

We're interrupted by Tyler bounding into the room, sliding his phone into his pocket. 'Hi Emily, sorry about that. Problem at work. At least it's given you a chance to meet Katerina.'

'I feel like I already know her,' I say. And this is the truth. I've learnt to make quick assessments of people, because misjudging Christian was the biggest mistake of my life.

'Well, sorry to rush off,' Katerina says, 'but I'm meeting a friend in fifteen minutes, and it's a twenty-five-minute drive in good traffic.' She takes my hand. 'I really wanted to meet you, though, Emily. And I hope I'll get to meet Christian soon too. Maybe we can all go for a meal?'

'That sounds lovely,' I force myself to say. 'I know he's looking forward to meeting you.'

Katerina crosses to Tyler and kisses him. 'See you later.'

'Are you sure you just want water?' Tyler asks, taking a seat at the kitchen table.

I tell him I'm fine and sit down opposite him.

'Okay. Then how about telling me the truth about what's going on with Christian?'

SEVENTEEN

BEFORE

Emily feels uncomfortable at Christian's parents' house today. It's not as though this is the first time she's visited, yet somehow she feels as though she doesn't belong here.

And there's no way of knowing how Christian will behave here. He's already on edge. Several times she's caught him staring at her, studying her when he thinks she's too engrossed in something to notice. And it worries her, because she has no idea what he's thinking. It makes her self-conscious. She glares at him, willing him to stop. He simply smiles.

They're sitting at the table, tucking into an extravagant Sunday roast that Christian's mum has spent hours preparing.

'Thanks for this, Audrey,' Emily says. 'You really didn't have to go to all this trouble.'

'Nothing's too much trouble for my boys,' Audrey replies. 'Especially when I barely see one of them.' She smiles at Christian, and pats his hand. 'I get it. Too busy living life.'

Anthony grunts. 'No one should be too busy to visit their own parents.'

Christian glares at him. 'And no parent should be too busy working to see their children.'

We all stare at Christian. He's never said this aloud to his dad before; it's always been something that simmers in the background. Embers rather than flames.

'Are you looking forward to your second year at uni, Emily?' Christian's mother quickly asks, changing the subject. She's a petite, stylish woman, with a blonde pixie haircut that very few people can pull off. Emily can't recall a single time she's seen her dressed casually.

'Yes,' Emily replies. 'It took a while for me to settle in last year, but now I think I'm doing okay.'

'Tyler can't wait to start,' Audrey says. 'He wants to be like his big brother.' She laughs.

Anthony rolls his eyes. 'I wish my sons would realise that it's hard work.' He ignores the warning glare Audrey shoots him. 'It's serious. Time to knuckle down and plan your future, not just mess around partying every night.'

The room falls silent, and Emily forces herself to speak. 'Lovely roast, Audrey. Thank you again.'

Later, Emily helps Audrey clear up while Anthony and Christian engage in a heated debate in the living room. It's politics this time, something Emily has little interest in. And up until now, she thought Christian felt the same. Yet he and his father will argue about anything, even if it's of no interest to either. They can never see eye to eye, neither of them able to see the other's viewpoint. But both of them determined to wind the other up.

Audrey leans in to her. 'I wish Christian was more like you in that way. He seems so disengaged with his studies. I don't know what's going on. He was so excited to change to a business degree. He's always talking about setting up his own business. Something to do with computers. He's always been good with all that technical stuff. He's got big dreams, so I have no idea why he's so half-hearted about his studies.' She stops loading the dishwasher. 'Have you noticed anything wrong?'

Emily shakes her head. 'No. I think he's just desperate to be finished and start working. Like you said, he's ambitious, Audrey. I think he feels tied down at university.' She looks away and focuses on the dishes she's drying.

Audrey frowns. 'Hmm. He's always been that way, since he was a young boy. But he's not a young boy any more, and he needs to get settled. We've told him so many times that this degree is the foundation for everything he wants to do in the future. How can he run a business when he hasn't learnt how they work?' She shakes her head, but quickly smiles. 'At least he's settled down with you. You make him happy, I can tell. You're a breath of fresh air, Emily Thomas.' Audrey pats her arm. 'I hope you're happy together. Sometimes I—'

'What's all this?' Christian appears in the kitchen, making Emily jump.

'Nothing for you to worry about,' Audrey says, turning back to the dishwasher. 'Where's your dad? Was that the front door I heard?'

'Yep. Tyler just called. He's stuck somewhere and needs a lift. Again. I can't believe Dad's actually going to pick him up. He's got legs, hasn't he?'

'We could have gone to get him,' Emily says. 'Save your dad having to go out.' It bothers her that Christian doesn't spend any time with his brother, or even pay him much attention. She would have loved a sibling, but her mum had always insisted that childbirth can kill you so there was no way she would risk doing it again. And by the time Emily was thirteen, it was too late.

Christian sighs. 'We're supposed to be relaxing here before uni starts next week. I'm not his chauffeur.'

'Be kind to your brother,' Audrey says.

'Come on, Em, let's go upstairs.' He doesn't give her a choice, but reaches for her hand and guides her out of the kitchen. But not before she's glimpsed the frown on Audrey's rosy-cheeked face.

Upstairs, Christian sits on the bed and pulls out his phone. Emily's on the verge of enquiring who he's messaging, but she won't do it. Even though he wouldn't hesitate if it were the other way around. Instead, she sits on the floor and pulls out her own phone.

Nothing. Of course there isn't. Not even from her mum, who has become more withdrawn lately. While it's a relief to not have the chore of constantly replying to her mum's panicked messages, Emily is more worried that she hardly hears from her. She knows she needs to help her mum; she's just not sure how.

And she's lost touch with all her school friends since she moved to London. Time eroding any connections she's ever made. As for Erin and Kirsty – they probably wouldn't notice if Emily never went back to the flat.

'Any messages from anyone?' Christian asks. He's mocking her.

'Never mind,' he says, when she doesn't reply. 'It takes so much effort to maintain old friendships.' He continues tapping on his phone. 'You're a different person now – living your life in London, while they're still stuck in the same place.'

'Not all of them,' Emily insists. 'Rosanna's gone to uni in Southampton.'

'Even more reason not to force that friendship. When would you have time? We're so busy, aren't we? With studying, and *us*. It's about priorities, isn't it?' He smiles, proud of his words, clearly liking how small he's making her feel. 'Besides, you're pretty much looking after your mum now, aren't you? I'm hoping I'm wrong, but she doesn't seem to be getting any better.'

She's surprised to hear him mention her mum. They seem to have established an unspoken rule to avoid talking about their parents.

Now that Emily's met his dad, she can't see what makes him

such a bad father. Maybe he's a bit set in his ways, and puts his work first, but that's not the worst thing he could do. And Audrey is kind and warm, and clearly dotes on her sons. Still, Emily won't pry. It's just the two of them in their own little world. That's what Christian loves to say.

He doesn't look up at her as he speaks, still busy texting on his phone. She's itching to ask him, and for some reason, the image of fur-coat girl at Freddie's Bar forces its way into her head. Emily never did find out who she was.

'I need the bathroom,' she says, rushing out.

Locking the door, she sits on the side of the bath and stares at the mirror on the opposite wall. The reflection looking back at her is a stranger.

I don't know who I am any more.

It's not good for her to be here in this house, not while there's so much friction in their relationship. She's been ignoring it, shoving it aside as if it'll disappear if she doesn't think about it.

As if she is a character in her own life, playing a part she's been given by someone else. *Is that all we ever are?*

Christian's been lying to her. She often senses something isn't right. Like there's a piece missing from them that she can't work out. But then he is all over her, and amnesia sweeps through her body, making her bury her doubts.

There's a knock on the door.

'Won't be a sec,' she calls, dabbing her face with the hand towel.

'Er, sorry but I need to come in.' It's Tyler, not Christian coming to check on her.

She opens the door and he rushes in. 'Sorry, I fell off my bike and got filthy.'

'I see that,' she says, taking in his mud-soaked jeans and T-shirt. 'Are you okay?'

'Yeah, thanks. We were racing and I stupidly didn't see a huge twig in my path.'

Emily suppresses a giggle. His cheeks are flushed red and she doesn't want to embarrass the poor kid further.

'Well, at least you're okay,' she says, brushing past him. 'We're thinking of watching a film tonight – want to join us?'

His face brightens, but then quickly dulls again. 'Um, I don't think Christian will like that. But thanks for asking.'

'Okay,' she says. 'But the offer's there if you change your mind.'

Christian's not in his room when Emily opens the door. He must have gone to get a drink, or some popcorn for the film. Voices drift from outside so she crosses to the window and peers out. Anthony is out there talking to the next-door neighbour.

Then she notices Christian's phone lying on his bed. It silently beckons her to pick it up. To scroll through his messages.

I can't. It's an invasion of his privacy.

But Emily finds herself kneeling down by the bed, glancing at the door before reaching for the phone. Christian has no idea, but she already knows his passcode. She's seen him tapping it in, and was surprised to realise it was a mixture of their birthdays. She types it in now, and the phone comes to life, glaring at her, daring her to click on his messages.

It takes a few seconds of wrestling with her conscience, but eventually she gives in.

And reading the first message, Emily quickly wishes that she hadn't.

EIGHTEEN
NOW

I stare at Tyler, the walls of the kitchen closing in on me. It takes a gargantuan effort to stifle my panic and remain composed, which is what it will take to convince Tyler that he's wrong about everything.

But Christian has evidence. After all these years he still has it. Because he's always known that he would come back for me.

'What? What do you mean?' I ask, forcing myself to lift my glass of water and take a sip.

'I know something's going on,' he says. 'None of it makes sense. And Christian's behaviour is just plain bizarre. Turning up like this after fifteen years without a word about where he's been or what he's been doing. The two of you getting back together.' He sighs. 'I think you're in some kind of trouble, Emily, and I wish you'd talk to me. I know you probably still think of me as Christian's pain in the arse little brother, but I'm not that kid any more. Neither of us are the same, are we?'

I barely hear his words – I'm too focused on the fact that Tyler hasn't actually revealed he knows anything. It's just his instinct alerting him that something's going on.

I take a deep breath. 'I'm not in trouble,' I begin, looking away. If I play this right, Tyler confronting me could work to my advantage.

'Okay,' he says. 'But if there is anything – anything at all – I want you to know that you can always talk to me. Or Katerina. She's a good listener too. And I don't want her thinking she's not part of this family.'

'I appreciate that,' I say, studying his face briefly before I look away. 'Everything's fine, though.'

Tyler studies me too closely and I shift in my seat. 'It's just... the way he rushed you out of Dad's house the other day when he saw us talking together. It just felt... weird. And he hasn't explained why he disappeared for all those years, or what he's been doing. We know he set up a business in America – but that's about all we've got from him. I googled him and his cyber security business does appear legitimate, but why won't he tell us anything else? What's he hiding?'

The ball is in my court now, and it's time for me to make my play. I glance at the door. 'I don't know,' I say. 'But... '

Tyler leans forward. 'What? What is it? I get the feeling you've been trying to tell us something.'

'Nothing. Forget I said anything. I'd better go.' I stand up and scoop up my bag.

'Please, Emily, wait,' Tyler pleads. 'Christian's my brother. If there's anything you need to tell me, then please just say it. Whatever it is, we'll find a way to work it out. As a family.'

I sit down again and pause for a moment. 'I *have* been a bit worried. About Christian's... you know... mental health.'

Tyler's brow creases. 'Go on.'

I look away and silently count to five. Tyler's got to believe this is difficult for me to talk about. 'It's little things, but when you put them together... maybe there's a pattern.' I shake my head. 'I shouldn't be saying this. I love him. Talking about him like this isn't right. It's not fair when he can't defend himself.' I look at Tyler. 'Besides, I'm sure it's nothing. Probably just me overthinking things. I do tend to do that.'

'Please, just tell me what's going on.'

I take another deep breath. 'Sometimes it's like... one minute he's on top of the world – you know – laughing and happy, and the next he's got this... rage.'

'Please don't tell me he hits you? If so, you need—'

'No, he never hurts me,' I lie. 'I mean, sometimes he might throw things, but never *at* me. I wouldn't stand for that. I'd be straight out the door.'

Tyler sighs. 'I should have expected this. It all fits.'

'Please,' I beg. 'Can we talk about something else?'

'Emily, this is important. We're trying to piece together who he even is now. You're the only one who can help us.'

I shake my head. 'This doesn't feel right. Please don't tell Anthony any of this. I don't think he'd understand.'

'Don't worry about my dad.'

I nod. 'After Christian gets into these rages, he can go right back to smiling again, in an instant. I'm sure it's just the pressure of setting up a business. But his behaviour has been...'

'Worrying?'

'I just never know which Christian I'll be coming home to.'

For a moment we fall silent as Tyler tries to make sense of what I'm telling him. And I watch him closely, praying that he's buying every word of it.

'How long has this been going on?' he asks.

'Pretty much since we found each other again. It was immediate. But I've just been hoping it's the stress of trying to get his new business off the ground.'

'He's got an investor now though, hasn't he? And nothing's changed?'

My hands are shaking. 'Not really.'

Tyler nods. 'He needs to see a doctor, Emily. He's not right.'

'I've tried. He says they'll just try to lock him up. He's terrified of that happening.' I think of my mum, how adamant she was that she didn't want help, and hope my experience of caring for her lends weight to my words.

Tyler's eyes widen, and I wonder if I'm going too far. I'm not meant to be giving away too much too soon; I'm just planting a seed for now, and then slowly things can escalate. 'I'll keep trying, though,' I say. 'He'll be fine. I'll make sure he is. I'm sorry I've burdened you with all this. I can help him, Tyler.'

Tyler stands and walks to the kitchen doors, folding his arms as he stares at the garden. 'I think I'll need to let Dad know what's been going on.'

'Is that a good idea? Can't we try to sort this out ourselves, without worrying him?'

'I don't know. Dad's worried about him. But at the same time, I don't think he has any understanding of mental health issues. I'm ashamed to say this but he thinks we should all just soldier on, brush things off. He can't seem to understand anyone who doesn't do that'

'We're only human,' I say, thinking of Mum. I know what he'll say.

'Dad isn't,' Tyler replies, turning back to me. 'He's a machine.' He laughs, but behind it I sense his pain. 'He *is* worried about Christian, though. Keeps saying we don't know what could have happened to him all these years. Or what made him disappear in the first place. I told him it's got to have been something traumatic. Is that what you think?'

Heat engulfs me and I struggle to maintain my composure. 'Christian's never told me why he left, other than that he just needed to get away from everyone. Please don't talk to your dad about any of this. I shouldn't have even spoken to you – I've broken Christian's trust, and I'm the one person he *does* trust.'

'He's got us too,' Tyler says.

'I know, but he doesn't feel he can trust anyone.'

Tyler's body sags, as if he's been deflated. 'Fine, I won't say anything for now. But will you promise to tell me next time anything happens?'

I assure him that I will, and tell him I'd better get back before Christian wonders where I am.

The house is shrouded in darkness when I park up. It's eight o'clock, too early for Lexi to be in bed, but even if she is, there's no way Jeremy would be. And his Audi sits in the driveway, so unless they've walked somewhere, they must be here.

Confused, I check my phone. Somehow I've managed to miss a message from Jeremy, and three calls. I'd turned my phone on silent at Tyler's so that my cover isn't blown, and once again I've neglected to switch it back on. Cursing myself for another oversight, I read Jeremy's message.

Where are you? Christian offered to take Lexi to the aquarium. An apology for what happened earlier. We're all grabbing some food now. Been calling to see if you can meet us there but too late now. Home soon.

It sickens me how Christian has so easily insinuated himself into our lives. But as long as Jeremy is with them, Lexi will be safe. He would never have let Christian take her by himself, no matter what he believes about how strong our friendship supposedly is.

Clambering out of the car, I grab the shopping bags and head inside.

'Emily.'

I spin around, dropping one of the bags.

Pam walks towards me, her mouth set in a straight line. 'I was hoping you'd be home soon. I've been waiting a while.'

'Is everything okay?' I lean down to pick up the bag. I know something's wrong, though – Pam never turns up unannounced.

It's an unspoken rule that seems to exist between her and Jeremy.

'When Jeremy mentioned he'd be out with Lexi, I thought this would be a good time for us to talk.' She nods towards the door. 'Shall we go in?'

'Course, come in.' I fumble with the key, trying to force it into the lock.

Once we're inside, Pam hands me a small pink cardigan. 'Lexi left it the other day. I know she loves it so I wanted to bring it as soon as I could.'

'Thanks. You didn't have to do that. It could have waited. Lexi has plenty of—'

'Actually, I wanted to speak to you. Alone.' She peers into the kitchen. 'I assume we have the house to ourselves.'

'Is something wrong?' I ask.

She brushes past me and heads into the living room. Having no choice, I follow and perch on the arm of the sofa. 'You're not ill are you?' I ask. 'Please tell me it's nothing like that.'

She shakes her head. 'No. This isn't about me. It's about you.' She looks straight at me; there's no awkwardness about her. Pam's always been a straight-talking woman.

And now I'm drowning underneath a wave of guilt and shame. 'Oh. What is it?' I venture.

'You know, Emily, I've never been an overprotective mother. I've always let Jeremy make his own decisions, always tried not to influence him. I've done the best I can to teach him to make good choices in life. That's all a parent can hope to do, isn't it?'

I nod, unsure where she's going with this.

'I've been very trusting,' Pam continues. 'And I trusted Tia. We all did. What she did – no one saw coming. But I've learnt a lesson. I will not sit by and let Jeremy make the same mistake again.'

'Pam, I can assure you I would never—'

'I bumped into your friend the other day. The one who unexpectedly turned up at your wedding.'

My heart hammers in my chest, and heat floods to my cheeks. 'I don't—'

'We had a very interesting chat. And I don't believe for one second that you were just friends.'

'That's ridiculous! What did he—'

'It's not what he said. It's what I was able to intuitively work out. From the way he talked about you. Things he said without realising. So many hints about the two of you. Very chatty, isn't he? And now seeing how your face has turned bright red, I know for sure I'm right.' She stands up. 'I think it's best you stay away from him, don't you?'

'There's nothing going on,' I insist. 'I would never hurt Jeremy.'

'I don't know what you're playing at by seeing so much of him and letting him become part of your lives, but it needs to stop. Otherwise I'll have no choice but to tell Jeremy. I should anyway, but I don't want to cause him any pain. Just stop whatever it is you're doing.'

'I... there's nothing—'

'No need to see me out.' She stands up and strides out.

I'm rooted to the spot. Christian must have engineered this chance meeting with Pam, just to prove he's the puppet master. To show how my life hangs by a thread.

A message comes through, breaking the agonising silence.

Having a great time with Jeremy and Lexi. How does it feel to know you're about to lose everything?

NINETEEN

BEFORE

Her mother is rapidly deteriorating, a flower withering away, while Emily stands helplessly by, not sure how to help. She is her mother's sole carer, and with her studies and Christian to factor in, she's barely managing to surface for air.

The other day Dr McCready came for a home visit, but somehow Emily's mother managed to convince her that she doesn't need help. She dismissed Emily's concern and insisted she wasn't unwell, and was just having difficulty sleeping. 'It makes you a mess, doesn't it?' she'd said to the doctor. 'Not sleeping plays havoc with everything else in your life. I'll be fine if I can just get some rest.' She'd sounded so rational that for a moment Emily *did* question herself.

No, Mum is sick. She's just good at acting when she has to be.

Dr McCready prescribed her mother sleeping pills and that was it, much to Emily's despair.

Spending every weekend with her mother is taking its toll on her relationship with Christian. Even though he doesn't say it outright, almost every sentence he speaks is laced with irritation, as if her mum is a fly who needs to be swatted. Emily ignores this; her mother has looked after her for years so she wants to do the same. It's not her fault that she's ill. Illness isn't just physical, she pointed out to Christian. That didn't go down well. He believes her mother likes depending on Emily for everything, and that she doesn't want to get better.

This weekend Emily has cleaned the house from top to bottom, washed all the dishes by hand – twice because according to her mother, once is not enough to kill all the germs – and put on three lots of washing. She's given up trying to convince her mum that she doesn't need to change her clothes four times a day, and wash them after only a few hours' wear.

And while Emily's worked tirelessly to make things more comfortable in the house, her mother has sat curled up on the sofa, staring at the wall.

'Mum?' Emily joins her on the sofa, exhausted. Her mother doesn't move up to make space, but once Emily's sat down, she rests her head on Emily's arm, like a child. 'Are you okay?'

'I don't like you going outside,' her mum mumbles. 'It's fine when you're here. I can relax. But when you leave... And that car you've got – is it safe? It's really old, isn't it?'

Emily was proud that she'd saved up for over a year to afford a second-hand car, but her mother has only ever made her feel guilty for buying it, even though it means Emily can visit her more regularly. It's not straightforward to get to Shere from west London.

'It's perfectly safe, Mum,' she replies. 'It's just had an MOT, so there's nothing to worry about.'

Her mum's eyes widen. 'Except other drivers. You might think you're safe, but you can't control what others do. People drink and drive, you know. Or smoke stuff then get behind the wheel. You might think I don't know what young people do, but I do, Emily. And do you know how many road traffic accidents there are each year?'

Emily tunes out while her mum throws statistics at her. She

has no idea how accurate they are, but clearly her mum's given this a lot of time and thought.

'I know, Mum,' she says, when the lecture finishes. 'But I have to be able to get around. I wouldn't be able to visit half as much as I do without it.'

'If you lived here, you wouldn't need a car.'

'Mum! I have to finish my degree. I've only got a year and a half to go.'

'And then what? Where will you go? What will you do?'

Emily sighs. She hates being exasperated with her mum, but it's becoming increasingly difficult to humour her. 'I don't know. I'll get a job hopefully. Teaching. I'll have to do a PGCE first, though.'

Her mother's eyes widen. 'In London? You could teach anywhere, you know. You could come back here. There are plenty of good schools right on our doorstep.'

'I haven't thought that far ahead. I'm just trying to get my degree first.'

Her mother shrinks back into herself. Emily is astounded at how thin she's become. How frail-looking. And she's only in her early fifties. It shouldn't be like this. She should be out having fun with friends, maybe even dating. But her mum hasn't so much as looked at another man since her dad.

Without warning, her mother grabs Emily's arm and pulls her towards her. 'You're seeing that student, aren't you? Christian. You pretend you're just friends, but I know you're *with* him. You haven't listened to anything I've ever said, have you? I warned you. He's no good, Emily. Why won't you listen to me?'

Emily ignores her. 'Shall I make us some food? We could have a roast, but I'll have to go and get what we need.' There is barely a crumb in the kitchen cupboards. Her mother's been existing on air, and the odd ready meal.

'No, thanks. I can't eat. There's too much to do.'

At least she's stopped mentioning the supposed man across

the road, although Emily suspects this is because she just doesn't leave the house any more.

'There's nothing to do, Mum. I've cleaned the house and done all the washing. You can just... rest.' Emily glances at the bookshelf on the wall, where she'd moments ago found a thick layer of dust. 'You could read? You used to read loads, remember? When I was little. You always had a book in your hand.' Emily smiles, but it fails to lift her spirits, contrary to the advice in all those self-help books. She can't feel it in any inch of her body.

Her mother vigorously shakes her head. 'If I've got my head stuck in a book then I'm not being alert, am I? And then what will happen?'

Emily wants to scream that nothing will happen, but of course she smothers this urge. She's learnt not to even attempt justifying anything to her mum. Laura Thomas, a woman who must have been reasonable and logical at one time, has gone, replaced by this frail shell of a woman. Still, at least she no longer mentions the supposed man across the street.

As Emily holds back tears, she glances at the photo of her mother on the mantelpiece. She's young and vibrant, smiling brightly at whoever was holding the camera, her long silky hair floating around her shoulders. It was taken before she married Emily's dad, and Emily doesn't remember her mother ever looking this carefree or happy. She'd been an office manager in a school then, and had loved her job until Emily's dad had left.

She takes her mum's hand. 'It's okay, Mum. I'll stay here with you tonight. I don't have lectures until eleven, so I can just leave in the morning.'

For a second her mother's face brightens, but then shadows cross it once more. 'We'll have to be careful. We're vulnerable here on our own, aren't we? Anyone could break in. And who knows what they'd do to us. Have you checked the door's double-locked?'

There are a thousand responses Emily could give to this, but instead she leans in and hugs her mum, shocked to feel so much bone through her clothes. 'I'll keep watch through the window,' she whispers. 'But there's one condition of me staying. I'm making us some food and we're both going to eat it all.'

Her mother smiles briefly, and it strikes Emily that she can't remember the last time she witnessed even a hint of happiness on her face. She wishes she could reach her mum, and find a way to pull her out of herself.

After dinner, Emily tucks her mum into bed then attempts to clear up the kitchen. It's been a few hours since she's heard from Christian, which is unlike him. Unless he's angry with her about something. *Again.* She checks her phone, just to be sure, but there's no reply to her last message.

To distract herself from worrying about what this might mean, she grabs the recycling bin and makes her way outside, slipping on her trainers at the door.

Even though she knows her mother was imagining the man in the house across the road, Emily looks up anyway, relieved to see all the lights off, and that nobody is standing by any of the windows.

An arm grabs her, pulling her away from the bins. Emily screams, and a cold hand smacks across her mouth. She struggles and instinctively kicks backwards.

'Woah, it's me! Stop!'

She spins around and glares at Christian. 'What are you doing? You scared the hell out of me! Jesus! Why didn't you tell me you were coming?'

He stares at her, and seconds tick by before he speaks. 'I texted you three times. Didn't you get my messages?'

'No! I've had no messages from you since this morning. When you asked me what I'd had for breakfast.'

He pulls out his phone and begins scrolling, shaking his head when he can't find what he's looking for. 'I must have deleted them.' He shrugs and places his phone back in his pocket. 'Anyway, I think it's time you got a new phone, don't you?'

Her pulse quickens and she feels nothing but anger towards him for turning up and terrifying her like that. 'You shouldn't be here. I don't want Mum to see you. She's not in a good way, Christian.'

He looks offended. 'I thought it would be a nice surprise. I thought you'd be happy.'

Emily softens. 'I am... it's just... Mum.'

He wraps his arm around her. 'Then let me come in. I'm assuming you're planning on staying another night? So, if that's the case, then at least let's spend an hour together. She must be asleep by now?'

Loathing herself just a fraction, Emily agrees.

They make it upstairs without disturbing her mum, and Emily closes her bedroom door, relieved that her mother's room is right across the hall and not next to Emily's.

'This doesn't feel right,' she says, as Christian wastes no time pulling her onto the bed. 'Not with—'

'Shh!' He places his finger gently over her lips. 'Pretend it's just the two of us in this house. There's nobody else here at all. Just us.' His lips replace his finger on her mouth, and she closes her eyes. When he kisses her, she can taste beer.

Afterwards, they lie together under her duvet, and her familiar self-consciousness at being naked returns. She pulls the sheet up to cover her breasts, and turns away from Christian's appraising eyes.

'She needs to be in a home or something,' he says.

'What? Who?'

'Your mum, of course. She needs help. Help you can't give her.'

'I'm trying. Really hard. But she managed to convince the GP there was nothing wrong with her, so what else can I do? I can't force her to do anything.'

'That's the problem, isn't it? But don't you see, Em? She's affecting our relationship. The more time you spend here, the more we drift apart. You can't juggle it all, can you? Nobody could.'

He sounds so reasonable, so convincing, that Emily has to remind herself this is her mother they're talking about.

'She's being selfish, Em, can't you see that?' Christian continues, his words slightly slurred. 'Controlling your life by refusing to get better. She's not even old! She should still be working. How can she even afford this house?'

Despite all her frustrations with her mother, Emily rushes to her defence. 'She hasn't been able to work since Dad left. She just couldn't cope mentally with it. And he let her have the house. The mortgage was already paid off.'

'I know, babe. I get all that, but she's a smart woman. She knows what she's doing.'

'No, she doesn't. That's the problem.'

'Open your eyes. Don't be naive. She's playing you like a piano. She doesn't want you to leave her so she's faking all this stuff.'

'You can't fake not eating,' she says, keeping calm. 'Becoming so thin that you're practically a skeleton. Can you? Do you know what Mum said to me earlier? The thought of death is comforting to her. Something like that.'

Christian stares at her. 'That's just it, isn't it, Emily? It would be better for Laura if she wasn't here at all.'

TWENTY

NOW

'What have you done?' I scream into the empty house, then I direct this rage to Christian.

What have you said to Jeremy's mum? Keep her out of it!

Pressing send, I throw my phone on the sofa, trying to ease the gut-wrenching pain in my stomach.

Take deep breaths, focus on something you can see. I repeat this mantra until eventually my panic subsides.

I've always had a good relationship with Pam – she's invited me into her family, made me feel as if I belong, and trusted me. And now Christian's destroyed that. Jeremy will never forgive me if he finds out that Christian and I used to be together.

When I've calmed down enough to focus, I grab my phone and call Christian, but his voicemail kicks in straight away. It's too risky to leave a message – it would only end up as something he could use against me – so I hang up and assess my options.

Calling the police is out of the question – how would I explain why Christian is doing this? And neither can I ask Tyler for his help; he can't know about Jeremy and Lexi, otherwise this all falls apart.

A reply comes through from Christian.

Remember this, Emily. How I can so easily plant bombs to explode in your life. This is just the beginning. A simple taste of what I can do.

Fighting my instinct to delete his words, to have any piece of him on my phone, I ignore it and put my phone on the coffee table. I need to think logically: Christian's had plenty of chances to tell Jeremy the truth about us; I'm sure he won't do it now. Not when he's barely got anything out of me. He's playing the long game.

But Christian is far from stable.

Doubt gnaws away at me, forcing me into action. He could be talking to Jeremy right at this moment. I need to find them.

I'm pulling on my coat when I hear voices outside. The sound of a key turning in the door stops me in my tracks, and when it opens, Jeremy and Lexi pile in, idle chatter innocently filling the air.

'Hi,' Jeremy says. 'You didn't want to come then? Shame. We had a good afternoon. Not the same without you, though.'

Relief surges through me, but under it fear still has a tight hold. 'That's good. How was the aquarium?'

'It was awesome!' Lexi says. 'You should have come, Emily. We had the best time, didn't we, Dad?'

I want to fire questions at Jeremy, to ask him every single word Christian spoke, everything he did. 'How was Christian?' I ask instead.

'He's so funny,' Lexi replies, before Jeremy can answer.

'Yeah,' Jeremy says, shooting me a look.

My face burns; maybe Christian hinted something to Jeremy, something he could easily dismiss if he was questioned further, but enough to plant doubt in my husband's mind. I grab Jeremy's arm and pull him towards me, kissing him. 'I'll definitely be there next time,' I say.

'Ugh!' Lexi says. 'I know you've just got married but that's a bit gross!' She notices her pink cardigan folded on the sideboard and picks it up, lifting it to her face. 'I thought I'd lost this,' she says. 'Where was it?'

'Your grandma dropped it back,' I explain. 'You left it at her house.'

Jeremy frowns and pulls away. 'She didn't have to bring it all this way. Lexi's always leaving things there. Funny, I spoke to her earlier and she didn't mention anything. I even told her we'd be out this evening.'

'I'm sure she just wanted to be helpful,' I offer.

Jeremy shrugs. 'I suppose.'

'Where were you going?' Lexi asks.

'Nowhere.'

She frowns. 'But you've got your coat on.'

I pull it off and hang it on the hook. 'Oh, I thought I'd left a shopping bag in the car. I was just about to check.'

Both of them stare at me, frowning. 'But actually, I don't think I did.'

Jeremy hugs me. 'Did the walk help?'

I nod. 'Yeah, it did.'

'Sorry you missed tonight. But don't worry, I've made sure that next week you'll have a day you'll never forget.'

It takes me a moment to catch up. My birthday. I've hardly given it any thought. I wonder if Christian remembers the date? We spent two of my birthdays together, and both times he went out of his way to surprise me. Is he planning to surprise me again this time?

'How old will you be?' Lexi enquires, pulling on her cardigan over her sweater.

'Thirty-five.'

'That's really old. And then you'll nearly be forty. Then fifty—'

'Yeah, okay, Lexi.' Jeremy says. 'No need to keep track.' He laughs and ruffles her hair.

'And you're even *older*, Dad!'

'Um, I think it's bed time, isn't it? Teeth first.'

Lexi bounds upstairs. 'I'm reading for a bit, too,' she calls as she disappears.

'It's still warm outside,' Jeremy says. 'Why don't we sit in the garden and have a glass of wine? It's been a while since we did that.'

For a brief moment his words transport me back to when we first started dating. We got into a routine on Friday evenings that summer, parking ourselves out there for hours until it got too cold. I picture us sitting under the pergola on the rattan sofa, each with a glass of wine in our hands. Talking until the early hours of the morning. It's how we spent the whole of last summer too. I had no idea that a year later my life would implode. I desperately wish we could go back. I've never felt at peace like that, and I want it again.

I study Jeremy's face; there is so much love in it that it brings tears to my eyes. And then it occurs to me that I'd never seen anything approaching that kind of look from Christian, not even at the beginning of our relationship.

Silently, I admonish myself for not picking up on the darkness beneath the surface that was spreading like cancer. And for holding on so tight to something that was broken from the beginning.

But it wasn't your fault. People can make you see what they want you to see.

Jeremy takes my hand. 'Don't worry about Lexi saying you're old. She probably thinks a twenty-year old is ancient.'

Inadvertently, he's given me an excuse for not being myself tonight. 'No one likes getting older, do they?'

'It's silly, when you think about it. It's happening to all of us constantly, yet we want to ignore it and pretend it isn't. Come on, let's have that wine.'

When I wake up the next day, Jeremy's side of the bed is empty. Slowly, things creep back to me, and I recall Pam's harsh warning. And the look of doubt that crossed Jeremy's face when Lexi insisted how funny Christian is.

Lexi's and Jeremy's voices drift upstairs – sounds of normality that clash with everything I'm silently struggling with.

I roll over and reach for my phone, where new messages vie for my attention: Tyler checking how I'm doing. Sue asking if I'll do an assembly on the first Friday back. And then there is one from Christian.

Dinner tonight at The Ivy in Tower Bridge. 8 p.m. There's someone I want you to meet. Bring your husband.

I read the message again, trying to infer the true meaning of his words. This isn't a cosy intimate dinner we're being invited to.

Lexi bounds into the room and springs onto the bed. 'You've been asleep ages!' she declares.

I check the time on my phone; it's only eight fifteen. For me, though, that's most of the morning squandered. But there was no way I could drag myself up at six thirty as I normally do, when I only fell asleep around four.

'I had trouble sleeping,' I explain.

'Why?' Lexi enquires. 'Is something wrong?'

'Sometimes, when you're an adult, you have a lot of things to think about, and often night time is the only chance to do that. But while your mind is busy thinking and thinking, it's not able to shut down and sleep.'

Lexi frowns. 'Okay. But what were you thinking about?'

'Just trying to get organised for school,' I say, forcing out the lie and wondering how much longer they are going to believe my excuses about school work. And Lexi is the person I hate deceiving the most.

'I never want to be a teacher she says. I'm going to be a ballet dancer.' She jumps off the bed and twirls around in a surprisingly graceful movement.

While I've been so caught up in the reappearance of Christian and everything he's doing to me, I've failed to observe the small changes in Lexi that before would never have gone unnoticed. She's always loved ballet, but until now she's never mentioned this dream.

When she twirls out of the room, I haul myself out of bed, preparing to tell Jeremy our plans for tonight. Because until I can build up enough evidence to convince Tyler that Christian needs psychiatric help, I have to go along with his demands.

My chance to speak to Jeremy comes soon enough when he comes upstairs after I've finished my shower. I'm still wrapped in a towel, my hair dripping water on the carpet.

'We don't have any plans tonight, do we?' I ask, towelling my hair.

'No, but I thought we could do with some time alone, and Lexi's been asking to see Mum, so I thought I'd take her over this morning. Maybe she can have a sleepover there. Mum's been desperate to have her more this holiday.'

The mention of Pam reminds me I also have to worry about what Christian said to her. The net is closing in on me.

I nod. 'Okay. Good idea. I just got a message from Christian, and he mentioned he'd like us to have dinner with him. Apparently there's someone he wants us to meet. At The Ivy.'

Jeremy's reluctant frown is replaced with a smile. 'The Ivy? Who does he want us to meet?'

I tell him I don't know.

'Intriguing. Yeah, let's do it. I've always wanted to go there. Remember I booked it for your birthday last year but then you got flu. Been meaning to rebook.' He looks at me and frowns. 'Christian's certainly making up for lost time, wanting to see you so much.'

There's a question behind his gaze, and I look away. 'Actually I think it's you he likes being around. You get on well, don't you?'

Slowly, Jeremy nods. 'Yeah, I guess we do. I'm surprised he's not sick of our company, though. Lexi and I only saw him yesterday.'

If Jeremy keeps probing, then surely I'll crack. 'He's a sociable person,' I lie. 'Anyway, how about I take Lexi over to your mum's?' I can't keep Jeremy away from Pam, but I can buy some time to find out what Christian said to her.

Pam answers the door, and Lexi gives her a hug before rushing through the house towards the gigantic trampoline in the garden.

'Slow down,' Pam calls, smiling.

Her smile vanishes when she looks at me. 'You don't look well,' she says. 'What's happened?'

'Nothing. I... Are we okay, Pam? I hate the thought of things not being right between us.'

She walks into the kitchen. 'That depends on whether you're being honest.'

Out in the garden, Lexi somersaults on the trampoline. 'I love Jeremy,' I say, praying my fervent words will be enough to assure her. 'Christian is just a good friend from years ago. There's nothing going on between us. There never would be.'

Pam folds herself into a chair and gestures for me to do the same. 'Does *he* see it that way? It didn't sound like it. Which makes me wonder why you're so close to him?'

I force myself to look at her. 'He's not interested in me. In fact, Jeremy and I are having dinner with him tonight. And a friend of his.'

Pam raises her eyebrows. 'Oh? Who?'

'He wants to surprise us. Don't you see, though, he wouldn't be inviting both of us out if there was something going on between us.'

'Nonsense. It's the perfect smokescreen.'

Lexi calls my name and asks me to watch her flipping over. I smile and wave, feeling Pam's stare on me.

'He told me you had a strong bond. Unbreakable. Who says stuff like that about another man's wife?'

'Christian likes to exaggerate. It doesn't mean anything. He doesn't have many other friends.'

Pam studies me for a moment before responding. 'Do you trust your instinct, Emily? I do. And mine is telling me that you're lying.'

TWENTY-ONE

NOW

We're running late. Jeremy had an online work meeting which overran, making him late getting ready. It's now nearly half past eight and the Uber we're in seems to move in slow motion. I turn to Jeremy, who smiles and squeezes my hand.

'Don't worry,' he says. 'Christian won't mind us being late. He's so laid-back, I can't imagine him stressing about anything. Are you sure he didn't give you any clue about who he wants us to meet? It's all a bit... strange.'

I tell Jeremy I have no idea who it is, and I clench my fists together so tightly that my nails dig into my skin. Is tonight what everything has been leading up to? What will I do if it's Ella he's brought to the restaurant.

It can't be. He's got as much to lose as I have.

Droplets of rain begin to spatter against the car windows, and I rest my shoulder on Jeremy's arm and close my eyes.

'I love you,' I whisper, so quietly that he doesn't hear. And I'm grateful that the darkness of the evening hides my tears.

When we step out of the Uber, I almost change my mind and tell him to get back in the car, that I'm feeling unwell and should probably go home. Jeremy and I are walking into a trap, I'm sure of it. 'Will you remember I love you, no matter what?' I say.

'Yeah, course. But, Em, you're being a bit weird. What's going on?'

My heart rate quickens as panic begins to consume me. I can't speak.

'What's the matter?' Jeremy asks.

Somehow his voice brings me back, and reminds me that I've got everything to fight for. I nod. 'I'm suddenly not feeling great. A bit of a headache.' I take hold of his arm. 'I'll be fine.'

Inside, the restaurant is busy, and the clanging of cutlery and plates blends into the heavy hum of voices. I scan the tables but can't see Christian. In the taxi, Jeremy was right beside me so I haven't checked my phone to see if there's any message from him, demanding to know why we're late.

'There he is,' Jeremy says, turning to a waiter who's approaching us. 'The rest of our party are already here.'

Sick to my stomach, I follow them both to the table in the corner, where Christian is deep in conversation with a woman. She has her back to us so I can't see her face.

Without warning, Jeremy stops, and I narrowly avoid bumping into him. He turns to me, his face ashen. 'Emily – look!'

I look more closely at the woman sitting with Christian. The neat, precision-cut bobbed hair. The expensive tailored black trouser suit I've seen her in before.

My husband's ex-wife.

'What the hell?' Jeremy says, reaching for my hand and clutching it tightly.

The waiter turns to us. 'Is everything okay, Sir?'

Before Jeremy has a chance to answer, Christian looks up and waves. 'I was starting to think you were a no-show,' he says, jumping up and holding out his hand to shake Jeremy's. He leans over and hugs me. I'm frozen. All I can do is stare at Tia.

'Guys, I realise this might be a bit awkward,' Christian begins. 'But I'm all for being open and honest. After I met Tia yesterday we... um, we got chatting and just hit it off. Her builders cancelled on her so we ended up spending the day together. It's early days of course but we wanted to be transparent about everything. For Lexi's sake.' He squeezes Tia's shoulder. 'Please join us. I'm sure we can all have a lovely dinner together.' Christian flashes a smile that only I know is laced with malice.

Tia also smiles. 'I've assured Christian that we're all adults here. There's no need for any of us to feel uncomfortable.' She looks at Jeremy. 'I'm sure we can get past, well, our past.' She chuckles, and I wonder if she's had a drink. I've never seen her this light-hearted. This relaxed.

While I remain frozen, unable to form a sentence, Jeremy quickly composes himself. 'Course,' he says. 'Let's enjoy the evening. Emily and I have been wanting to try this place for ages.'

Jeremy pulls out a chair for me, and once I've sat down I notice his shoulders are hunched. I briefly place my hand on his arm, hoping the gesture will comfort both of us.

'Good.' Tia pours some champagne for me and Jeremy, then lifts her own drink, which appears to be water. 'Cheers to being adults, then,' she says.

Despite what she did to Jeremy, I feel no animosity towards Tia. I would be a hypocrite to hold anything against her when the lies I've had to tell are so much more destructive. At least there are no secrets with Tia, not any longer. Still, I'm aware of how uncomfortable Jeremy must be sitting beside her. He's trying his best to be okay with this unusual and unexpected situation, and I love him even more for that.

What worries me is why Christian is doing this. It's no coincidence that he's somehow managed to get involved with Tia.

'I can highly recommend the steak tartare,' Christian says while we're studying our menus. The words are a mass of blurred marks, and I can't take any of it in. 'Not that I'm telling you all what to eat,' he continues, glancing at me. 'Everything's good, of course, but it's by far the best steak I've ever had.'

'I think I'll have risotto,' I say defiantly. There is no way I'll let Christian dictate what I'll eat.

But both Tia and Jeremy go along with his recommendation, and I catch Christian watching me when the others aren't looking.

While we wait for our food, Christian entertains us with tales of the people he met while living in America, and the things he saw. I have no idea how much of it's true, but it doesn't matter. All I need to know is why the four of us are here together.

'I'm intrigued,' I say to Tia, when Jeremy and Christian are deep in conversation about gun laws in America. 'So the two of you are... what exactly?'

Tia smiles, and there's a crimson glow on her cheeks. 'We've only just met. There's no need to put a label on it right now. But after what happened with Lexi in the park, we just hit it off. Connected somehow. I don't know if you'll understand this – if it's ever happened to you – but I felt as though he really *knew* me. As if we weren't strangers at all.' She glances at Jeremy and lowers her voice. 'I've never had that before.'

As she says this, it hits me that Tia might know everything. That somehow Christian has involved her in what he's doing to me. How else would the two of them have got so close so quickly? A bubble of panic begins to form.

If she knew, she wouldn't keep quiet. She would never let Lexi be in the same house as me, not even for a second.

Reason wins over, and I begin to calm down. 'Christian's definitely charming,' I say.

Under the table, Christian rams his foot into my shin. A warning for me to tread carefully. 'When you meet someone you click with there's no need for charm,' he says. 'It's all just natural.'

'And Lexi really likes him,' Tia explains, taking his hand. 'That's the number one thing for me. It would be a deal breaker if she didn't.'

'Course,' Christian says, smiling at Tia. 'That's how it should be.' He turns back to Jeremy and they resume their debate.

Tia lowers her voice again. 'It just helps that she already knows him, through you.' She smooths her already neat hair, massaging it with her hands. 'I want to thank you, actually.'

'Me? Why?'

'I find it hard to let men into my life. I just don't seem to ever get it right. So I haven't been interested in meeting anyone new for a long time. I've just thrown myself into work.' She chuckles. 'It's a great distraction. Anyway, if it wasn't for the fact that you've known Christian for so long then I wouldn't have even let it get this far.'

Tia's words stun me, and I struggle to make sense of them. I had no idea what's been going on in her life since her relationship broke down with the man she left Jeremy for. 'I, um, yeah, I can see how that helps.'

'Totally. I already know that I can trust him.'

I grab my glass and take a long sip of champagne. This is no celebration, but I need something to ease my anxiety.

'We should actually do this more often,' Tia says, addressing all of us. 'It's good to show Lexi that there are no hard feelings between us, isn't it, Jeremy? And who knows – soon we might all be in each other's lives on a more regular basis.' She glances at me. 'Given your close friendship with Christian.'

Beside me, Jeremy shuffles in his chair, twitching his fingers. It's something I haven't seen him do for a long time.

He looks up and nods. 'Well, Lexi's our priority, isn't she, Em?'

I nod.

'You know,' Tia says. 'The house is starting to feel really empty when she's not there. I miss seeing her in the week.'

Jeremy glances at me, and all I can do is offer a thin smile.

Thankfully, the waiter appears with our food before Jeremy can respond to Tia. The smell of steak turns my stomach.

'Bon appetit!' Christian says, lifting his glass.

I tune out the conversation as we eat our dinner. Surprisingly, Jeremy has started to relax, but I can't stop worrying about what Christian is up to.

While the others order dessert, I excuse myself. I have to get away from the suffocating atmosphere at the table.

I stare at my reflection in the bathroom mirror and try to pull myself together, forcing myself to take deep breaths.

The door opens and Tia walks in. 'Are you okay?' she asks, frowning.

'Yeah, fine thanks.' I wash my hands, watching as Tia reapplies her lipstick.

'I hope you're okay about me and Christian? I mean, it's early days so it's not like we're getting married or anything.' She laughs. 'Won't be making that mistake again in a hurry.'

'I'm happy for you,' I say. 'And it's none of my business what Christian does.'

She smiles. 'I'm curious,' she says. 'Are you sure nothing ever happened between you two? He says it didn't, but, well I'm just checking with you. Because I think I can trust you.'

I turn away and reach for some paper towels. 'No, we've always been just friends.'

'Good.' she says. 'This is messy enough already. If we allow it to be, I mean.'

She puts her lipstick back in her bag and heads towards the door.

'Tia? Can I ask you something?'

She turns back to me and raises her eyebrows. 'Go on.'

'When I dropped Lexi at your house after we got back from Kefalonia, you said that I should be careful. With Jeremy. What did you mean?'

Tia sighs. 'Oh. I just meant... well, Jeremy's a decent guy. Kind. But he never forgives. You could do the smallest thing, and if he takes it badly he'll write you out of his life without hesitation. I suppose it's a coping strategy.' She turns back to the mirror. 'That's what I meant. But you've got nothing to worry about. You're the perfect wife, aren't you?'

She leaves her question floating in the air and disappears. And it's another five minutes before I can bring myself to follow.

Christian is standing at the end of the corridor, leaning against the wall by the main door to the restaurant. He doesn't look up, but taps something into his phone before sliding it in his pocket.

'What the hell are you doing?' I demand, glancing behind me to make sure Jeremy or Tia aren't about to appear. 'You're doing this on purpose – you're not interested in Tia!'

'Rubbish,' he says. 'She's an intelligent, attractive woman. Why wouldn't I want to get to know her?'

'Because all you're interested in is destroying my life!'

'Relax. You really need to calm down a bit before everyone thinks there's something going on with us.'

'There is no *us*,' I insist.

'Stop being pedantic, Emily. You know exactly what I mean.'

'What are you trying to do? Just tell me!'

'I don't need to explain anything to you. But one thing I've learnt is to not judge people. Tia is not the person you've painted her as. I'm not saying I know her like I know you, but I like to think I'm now a good judge of character. She fell in love with someone else and didn't want to be with Jeremy any more. Big deal. Shit happens. Sometimes we choose the wrong person. Don't we?' He smiles, then glances through the window in the door.

'You just met her! You know nothing about her. Anyway, I don't judge her. But she did put everything before her daughter,' I say. 'Work. Alcohol. Herself. She was happy for Jeremy to have Lexi. She's not perfect. None of us are.'

'That's all in the past. She told me she doesn't touch the stuff now, and I believe her. Which reminds me. She misses her daughter, and it's causing her a lot of pain. She wants Lexi back.'

My legs buckle; it's an effort to keep myself standing. Of everything Christian's said since he reappeared, these are the most horrific words I could hear from his mouth. 'No. Lexi lives with us. That's what Tia agreed to. Lexi would never want to live with Tia. She loves her dad. She's been living with him for years.'

Christian moves closer. 'You don't understand, Emily. Tia wants her daughter back, and that's all that matters. I want to make that easier for her, and I'm perfectly placed to do that, aren't I? How ironic. And you're going to help me.'

'There's nothing I can do!'

'That's not my problem. I've told Tia that you and I are so close that I'll be able to talk to you about this. I've assured her that she'll get what she wants. So you need to find a way.' He smiles.

'You don't give a damn about Tia,' I insist. 'You're using her to get at me.'

He shrugs. 'Even if you're right, it doesn't make a difference. You're going to do what I want.'

'Jeremy would never—'

'He's like your little lap dog. I'm sure he'd do anything you suggested, if you approach it the right way.'

'No, he's not like that! He's just kind, that's all. You just can't understand that because that's not who you are! He would never put anyone or anything before his daughter.'

'As I remember, you're very resourceful, aren't you? You'll make this happen. Don't take too long, though. Tia's desperate to have Lexi back. She feels she was pushed into the custody arrangement. It's not her fault that she had an alcohol addiction that stopped her seeing things clearly. It's a disease, Emily. It was out of her control.'

'You're asking the impossible. I'm telling you now, there's no way Jeremy would give up main custody.'

Christian ignores me, only acknowledging what suits him. 'Think about it, Emily – all I'd have to do is tell Tia the truth about you. There's no way she'd want Lexi living with you if she found out. And as for Jeremy – I think it would crush him to know the kind of person he married. So, it all comes down to this – what choice do you have?'

He might be right, but there's always a way.

'She doesn't know anything, then?'

'Not yet. All I want right now is for her to have her daughter back in her life. She's made some decisions she regrets, and she wants to put it right for Lexi. It's breaking her apart. And I like Lexi. If Tia and I make a go of this, then I'll be Lexi's stepdad. Imagine that.'

Bile burns my throat. 'Stop pretending that you care about Tia,' I insist.

Christian ignores me. 'Anyway, you need to get to work on Jeremy. Start sowing the seed about Lexi. I want it sorted, Emily.' He turns away.

I grab his arm before he reaches the door. 'Wait! You don't have to do this. There has to be another way for you to have your peace or closure, or whatever you need. You don't have to involve Tia.'

'It must be tearing you apart,' Christian replies. 'Knowing that I can so easily damage every single person in your life. And poor Lexi – what ever would she do if something happened to her mum?'

TWENTY-TWO

BEFORE

Voices drift from the living room as Emily opens her front door. Kirsty and Erin. They're talking animatedly, but she can't determine the gist of their conversation. The voices stop when the front door clicks closed, and silence fills the flat.

Before she sees their faces, Emily senses that something is different. A seismic shift in the usual atmosphere of their home.

'Hi,' Erin says when Emily appears in the living room doorway. 'We were hoping you'd be home soon. You did tell Kirsty you'd be here this evening.'

Kirsty had asked her this morning whether she'd be home after lectures today, and Emily should have realised this was unusual. Neither of the girls have enquired about anything she does for months now. She can't blame them – she's with Christian most nights so they've probably got used to her absence, and almost forgotten she still lives here. Technically, at least.

Emily doesn't venture further in, and hovers by the door. 'What's going on?'

'Will you come and sit with us?' Erin pats the sofa. 'We just need to talk to you.' She watches Emily carefully.

This has to be about Kirsty and Christian. Her flatmates

must have found out what Christian accused her of. What's she supposed to do now? She still doesn't know what to believe.

Feeling as if she's about to face a firing squad, Emily contemplates refusing. They can't force her to listen. She's done nothing wrong in the flat. She never leaves a mess or gives the girls anything to complain about. What would they do if she told them she was busy and simply walked out of the room? She sighs and sits down.

'Emily, we've all lived together for a while now,' Erin begins. 'And we think of you as a good friend.' She glances at Kirsty. 'Which is why we have to talk to you about what's been going on. We haven't said anything before, but we can't stay silent any more.'

'I don't understand.' She is a child being chastised, and she feels her body retreating into herself, trying to shrink away.

'It's Christian,' Kirsty says. 'He's not good for you. We knew that pretty much straight away, but you seemed so happy. So we didn't say anything. People at uni talk, though. And say stuff about him. Did you know that?'

Emily tries to gather her thoughts. She's not prepared for this, and doesn't know how to respond. Of course she knows what Christian is like – she's just blocked it out, and shut it away so she doesn't have to deal with it. 'What stuff?'

A glance passes between her flatmates. 'He's got a rep,' Erin says. 'He's had a lot of... girlfriends at uni.'

'In other words, he sleeps around,' Kirsty blurts out. 'Is that the kind of guy you want to be with?'

Emily pictures fur-coat girl. How many others have there been? She can't look at Erin or Kirsty now. She's not used to confrontation; she's always chosen to go along with people, just to keep the peace. Her mother. Christian. 'Oh.' It's all she can think of to say.

'But even worse than that – we think he's controlling you,' Erin says. 'I'm sure there's a word for it but I can't think of it.

You're never here, and it's weird that he always has to meet you after work. It's like he doesn't want you to ever be on your own. That's not healthy.'

Of all the things they could have come out with, Emily hasn't expected this. 'But you're always with Andre,' Emily insists. 'It's the same thing.'

'No, it's not the same. Yes, we're together a lot, but Andre lets me do my own thing too. Remember when we were all going out for Kirsty's birthday? You said you couldn't go because you'd promised to spend the evening with Christian. Even though you'd been with him every day that week!'

'I... he—'

'Something just didn't feel right to me, so I've been writing stuff down.' Erin pulls out a small flowery notebook. She flicks through the pages. 'All the times you've spent here in the last few months. Two nights. And why doesn't he ever want to come here? It's like he has to keep you away from us.'

They're wrong. A lot of the time she's been with her mum. Emily has never spoken about her mum to her flatmates, which makes her wonder why they think of her as such a good friend when they know nothing about her.

She tries to think of a counter argument. Something she can say to defend Christian. 'We like spending—'

'It's not just that!' Kirsty raises her voice, stunning Emily.

'What, then? I don't know what you're trying to say!'

Erin sighs. 'This is exactly what we're worried about. You're so kind and...'

'Naive,' Kirsty interjects. 'Well, it's true,' she adds, when Erin scowls at her. 'Just tell her.'

Somehow Emily knows what she's about to hear. Her mother was right all along. 'What is it?' she asks. She's ready. She can face whatever she has to.

Erin lowers her voice. 'Does he do stuff like not replying to messages then telling you he did reply? Or turning up late to things and saying that he's right on time?'

'No,' Emily says, too quickly. This is making her uncomfortable.

'Does he claim you're treating him badly when you haven't even done anything?' Kirsty says. 'You know, make you feel like a terrible girlfriend?'

Emily stares at the floor. She can't bear to hear the words that fit her relationship like a hand in a glove.

'What about cutting you off from your family? Friends?' Erin moves closer to her on the sofa. 'It's abusive,' she says. 'And you need to get away from him. Kirsty noticed it because the same thing happened to her sister when she was seeing this guy. He seemed perfect. Really in love with her, but—'

'Stop!' Emily shouts. 'Please stop. You're wrong. Christian's not like that.' She turns to Kirsty. 'Are you doing this because you like him?'

Kirsty's eyes widen. 'What? No!'

'He told me all about you coming on to him,' Emily says. She's not sure how she can keep her voice so calm; perhaps it's because she doesn't feel like she's actually the one saying all of this. 'When he came looking for me and I wasn't here.'

Kirsty stands. 'That's rubbish! I would never do—'

Without another word, Emily leaps up and rushes to her bedroom, shutting the door behind her. She pulls out her weekend bag from under the bed and starts throwing clothes from her wardrobe into it.

There's no clear plan in her head, she only knows she needs to get away from this flat. Erin and Kirsty aren't her friends; they don't understand her like Christian does. Maybe their relationship isn't perfect, but he's always there for her.

While she's packing, she hears their muffled conversation coming from the living room. Something about how they haven't told her the worst of it. How there's no point now –

Emily will never hear a word against him. *She's too far under his spell.*

Emily clamps her hands to her ears; she can't listen to it any more.

Out in the hallway, Erin tries to stop her leaving. 'Please, Em, you don't have to do this. We were just trying to help. We care about you.'

Emily ignores her and opens the front door. 'I'll be back for the rest of my stuff when I can.' She fights back tears as she makes her way to her car, but if anyone asked her, she wouldn't be able to say exactly what's caused them.

Outside, she stares up at the window. This place no longer feels like hers. Like home. There's no going back now.

Pulling her mobile from her bag, she calls Christian. It rings for what feels like hours before his voicemail kicks in. She ends the call without leaving a message.

With the strap of her heavy bag digging into her shoulder, Emily trudges towards the Tube station. Her car isn't starting, and she doesn't want to risk driving it around London if it's going to conk out on her.

Even if Christian's not home, Emily can wait for him. For as long as she has to. Erin and Kirsty are wrong about everything. They don't understand her relationship with Christian. Nobody does. Yet as soon as this thought enters her head, it's quickly replaced. *She* knows he lies to her, but she doesn't want anyone else to know it.

'Hey, Emily!'

She instantly recognises the person walking towards her, waving. It's the student she met in the pizza place months ago. She's seen him in lectures, but there's never been a chance for them to talk, or acknowledge each other with anything other than a brief wave or a smile.

'You don't remember,' he says, smiling.

'Yeah, course I do. You go to my uni.'

He laughs. 'Er, yeah – I meant my name!'

Embarrassed, Emily apologises.

'It's Niko. Not that common a name so I'm not surprised you forgot it.' He gestures to her bag. 'Going to the gym?'

'Something like that,' she says, shifting the bag to her other arm.

'It looks heavy. Have you got a dead body in there or something?'

Emily doesn't laugh. 'Are you always this nosy?' she snaps, walking off.

Niko catches up with her. 'Wait, sorry. I didn't mean to pry. It's none of my business.' He holds up his hands. 'Geez, I'm an idiot sometimes.'

Shame floods through her. 'I shouldn't have snapped.'

'It's my fault,' Niko says. 'I'm always trying to be funny, but it never comes off right. I'm a bumbling fool. I definitely won't be making a career out of stand-up.'

'You are funny,' Emily assures him. 'Probably I'm just not in a great mood.'

He smiles. 'I'll take that compliment. Cheers.'

And despite the situation she's in, Emily smiles. 'Well, you're easily pleased.'

'Yep, that's me.' He points to the bag. 'But if there is a dead body in there, then full disclosure – I'd have to tell the police. As nice as you seem, I'm not covering up such a terrible crime.'

Emily laughs and punches his arm, surprising herself with how relaxed she feels around him.

'Hey!' Niko says, laughing. 'Just for that injury you've inflicted, how about you buy me a coffee?'

'What?'

'Okay, okay. I'll buy the coffee – deal?' He laughs. 'There's a place round the corner. Although I don't want to stop you going to the gym.'

There are a million reasons why Emily should politely

decline, but the pain in her shoulder from the bag reminds her that Christian isn't home, and she's got nowhere better to go for now. At least she'd have some company for a while.

'Deal,' she says. 'The gym can wait.'

Niko's eyes widen. 'Wait, what did you just say?'

'I said yes!'

'Okay, come on then, quick, before you change your mind and realise that actually, this Niko guy is not that funny after all. Not even interesting. Not worth having a coffee with. Not worth missing a workout for.'

'Talks too much,' Emily offers, as they head away from the station.

'Ha, you've got me there! Just one more thing. Let me carry that bag. You're walking funny under all that weight.' He stops. 'Wait, I do need some assurance that there's no dead body in there, though.'

Laughing, she's about to offer to prove it to him by opening the bag until she remembers it contains most of her belongings.

'You'll just have to trust me,' she says, handing him the bag.

TWENTY-THREE

NOW

The tinkling of the piano drifts in from the study. Hearing Lexi practising should lift my spirits, but today it only saddens me.

I stand at the kitchen sink, lost in my thoughts, washing the breakfast dishes instead of piling them into the dishwasher. A legacy passed on by Mum.

'You do realise we have something that will do that for you?' Jeremy appears, placing his mug in the dishwasher.

His sudden appearance startles me.

'It's only a few things. Thought I'd just do it myself.'

He kisses me.

'Are you okay after last night?' I ask. I pull him closer. 'I'm sorry I was too exhausted to talk last night. It must have been a huge shock seeing Tia there. You must have been even more uncomfortable than I was.'

He nods. 'I was, and I was angry with Christian for not warning us. But he sent me a message last night explaining. He said he wanted to tell us but Tia convinced him not to. She'd said we wouldn't turn up if we knew. I kind of get that. And anyway, I don't care who she gets involved with. At least we know him. And he's good to Lexi.' He smiles. 'Tia and Christian can do whatever they want together.'

I study his face, and I wonder if he's being honest.

Don't trust anyone.

'Are you sure you're okay with it?' I ask again.

He pulls me towards him. 'I made my peace with Tia leaving me long ago. Thanks to you.' He kisses me again. 'I don't feel anything for her. She'll always be in my life because she's Lexi's mum – we can't avoid that – but other than that she can do what she likes.' He strokes my cheek. 'Let's not tell Lexi yet, though. I want to make sure it's not just something that will fizzle out in a few weeks.'

I turn back to the dishes and focus on scrubbing away porridge to mask my anxiety. There is no way I will even try to convince Jeremy to let Lexi live with Tia permanently – not when I know she doesn't want to.

'Anyway, I'm sure Christian will see Tia's true colours. We can't hide who we really are, can we?'

I, too, have thought of this. But Christian doesn't care what Tia's like, as long as he can use her to disrupt my life.

'What are your plans for today?' I ask, finishing the last of the bowls.

'I'm taking Lexi and Mum to the ballet this afternoon, remember? Have you changed your mind about coming?'

This was arranged so long ago I'd forgotten all about it. With Christian's latest stunt, Pam confronting me has been pushed to the back of my thoughts. As much as I should go with them to make sure she doesn't say anything to Jeremy, I need to stay here to deal with Christian. And the clock is ticking.

'It would be too late to get me a ticket now,' I say. 'And I've got plenty to do, anyway. As always.'

'We shouldn't be too late back,' Jeremy says. 'Although knowing Mum, she'll insist we go for dinner afterwards.'

More time for talking, for her to reveal her concerns about me.

She has no evidence. Just focus on that.

'It's fine,' I say. 'You don't need to rush back. Lexi needs to spend time with your mum. And things like this will create amazing memories for her.' That's what matters. That we grow up having precious times we can recall at any moment.

Whatever it takes, I will make sure Lexi has that.

The minute they've set off, I get in the car and drive to Reading. Tyler is at his dad's, and he was happy for me to come over to see them both. Facing Anthony won't be easy. I need to be convincing, without exposing anything I can't let them know about.

Tyler had been surprised when I'd told him to tell Anthony after all. I hadn't wanted to yet, but Christian has forced my hand.

They both greet me at the door when I pull up outside Anthony's house. He seems to have aged, with lines creasing his head that I'm sure weren't there last time.

'Emily,' Anthony says. 'What's going on? Is Christian okay?'

Tyler pats his arm. 'Dad, let her in first, won't you?'

'When my son disappears for fifteen years, and you find out something's still not right with him, what am I supposed to think?' He stands aside to let me in then closes the door.

'I know,' I say, wiping my feet on the mat. 'This is hard for all of us. But please, you can't tell Christian I've come here today. If he thinks he can't trust me, he might disappear again – this time for good.'

'Come on then,' Anthony says. 'You'd better tell us everything.'

In the living room, I sit on the sofa, while Anthony and Tyler sit opposite me in armchairs. It's hard not to feel like I'm being interviewed for a job, and I keep reminding myself that Tyler has only ever shown me kindness. Anthony too, in his own way.

'I don't know how to start,' I begin, staring at the recently vacuumed carpet. 'I suppose I noticed things a while ago, but I just dismissed it. I didn't think any of it was important. But it's getting worse and I... I don't want to keep this from you. You're the closest people to him, other than me. You both have a right to know what's going on.'

'Please, just say it, Emily,' Anthony demands.

Tyler holds up his hand. 'Dad, give her a chance. We need to know everything.'

This is it. There's no going back now. 'I started to notice he was getting paranoid about things. First it was about... Tyler.'

'What?'

I turn to Tyler. 'I didn't say anything the other day – I was embarrassed. After that night he found us talking in the kitchen, he said that you were... after me.'

'That's insane!'

Anthony holds up his hand. 'Let's just hear Emily out.'

'But I would never do anything like that,' Tyler insists. 'Especially right under his nose! What does he take me for?'

'He's never been jealous or possessive,' I insist. 'It took me by surprise. That's why I know there's something else going on. The other day I caught him going through my phone. He didn't know I could see him. I've got nothing to hide so I just watched him do it. And then... I woke up the other night and he'd gone. But his car was still outside. I couldn't see him anywhere, so I drove around looking for him. I found him standing on the bridge over the motorway, leaning over the rail.' I look Christian's brother and father directly in the eyes. 'That's when I realised how serious this is.'

Anthony walks to the window, glancing outside for a

moment before turning back to us. 'What on earth was he doing?'

'I don't know. I think... maybe he was contemplating jumping, but I don't know for sure. It wasn't right, though, whatever he was doing.' I sigh. 'He denied it when I rushed up to him. He said his mind was jumbled and he needed to clear it.'

'And staring over the bridge helped?' Anthony shakes his head. 'He expects you to believe that?'

I shrug. 'I don't think he's thinking clearly.'

Frown lines crowd Anthony's brow. 'Are you trying to tell us this is some sort of mental breakdown?'

'It looks that way.'

'And are you sure he hasn't mentioned anything about the last fifteen years?' Anthony demands. 'Because now is the time to tell us.'

'No, he hasn't. Just that he was okay. But he has been saying weird things.'

'Like what?' Tyler asks.

With a heavy sigh, I picture Mum. 'Like, people are better off dead. And that there's peace when you're dead. Stuff like that. It's... it's scaring me.'

Anthony sits again, clasping his hands together. 'Are you sure he doesn't just want attention? Christian's always seemed to crave it.'

'Dad, we need to face facts,' Tyler says. 'Christian's not well. I knew we should have insisted he got help when he turned up like this with no explanation. And he was behaving so strangely at the funeral. He was jittery and couldn't sit still. Kept jumping up and going outside. Then coming back in again. No idea what he was doing. He didn't speak to anyone, even though all Mum's friends tried to offer their condolences.'

'It's not your fault,' I assure him. 'Christian is confident and persuasive. He can make anyone believe whatever he wants them to.' For once, every word I'm telling them is the truth.

'She's right,' Anthony says. 'From talking to him, you'd never think he was struggling with anything.'

Tyler nods. 'But something must have happened to make him leave like that. And he could have been doing anything all these years.'

'Please don't tell him I've come here and spoken to you about this,' I beg. 'It will just fuel his paranoia and he might disappear again. I couldn't bear losing him.'

'But he needs help, Emily,' Tyler insists. 'He needs to see a doctor.'

'I know, and I'll get him help. I just need... I need you to be aware. If it comes to it – I'm not his next of kin. That might mean one of you has to speak to the doctors. It would be against his will – Christian will never admit he has any kind of problem, and he won't speak to anyone.'

'Are you talking about having him sectioned?' Anthony asks, his eyes widening. 'Jesus. Can't they just give him some pills?'

'He won't take them. I know it seems extreme, but he's already threatening to hurt himself. Isn't it better that he's in a hospital rather than... dead?'

The word seems to echo around the room, silencing us all.

'What exactly is it you're proposing we do?' Anthony eventually asks.

'I'm going to start writing everything down. Keeping a log of Christian's behaviour and comments. That way, we'll have the evidence we need to get him help. And I'm sticking by his side. Day in, day out, so that I can make sure he doesn't follow through on any of his threats.'

'Where is he now?' Tyler asks.

Lexi told me earlier that her mum and Christian are spending the day together, shopping in the West End. It will be Christian's idea of hell, but he'll do whatever it takes. 'He's with a friend,' I say. 'So for the next few hours he's not alone.'

Anthony shakes his head. 'I don't like any of this. Not one bit.'

I stand up. 'We need to protect Christian. That's what we all want, isn't it?'

Anthony nods. 'He's my son, of course that's what I want.'

'Dad, Emily will look after him,' Tyler says.

'I suppose,' Anthony says eventually. 'But I really hate this. And all these lies and secrets. They never do any good. This would have destroyed Audrey if she was here to witness it.'

'No, it wouldn't, Dad,' Tyler says. 'Mum was strong. The strongest person I know. She would have dealt with it, just like she did everything else.'

I wish I could express my gratitude to Tyler, because if it was just me and Anthony in the room, I don't think it would have been so easy to convince him that Christian needs help.

With a promise to let them know what's happening, I tell them I have to get back before Christian gets home. I try to ignore the doubt that's so clearly written on Anthony's face.

At the door, Tyler thanks me for coming. 'It can't have been easy,' he says. 'Dad's a tough nut to crack. You did well to get through to him.'

'I just want Christian to be okay.'

'I know I've asked this before, but are you sure Christian's never hurt you? Or even threatened to?'

'Not physically, no. Apart from saying stuff about all of us being better off dead, he's never been violent towards me. That's what makes this even more worrying. How out of character it is.'

Tyler nods. 'Okay. Keep in touch. I know it can't have been easy saying all this to Dad after what Christian's already put him through, but I'm always here. Whatever happens.'

Thanking him, I hurry to the car before Tyler notices I've broken into tears.

.   .   .

Coming home to a silent house unnerves me, and I busy myself by tidying when there's nothing out of place. No mess anywhere. At this moment Christian is with Tia. His words last night at the restaurant were clearly a threat. What if he does something to her? Lexi might have a difficult relationship with her mum but she loves her, and if anything happened to Tia, it would rip her apart.

I can't let Christian do this.

It's not often that I message Tia, but I send her one now.

Hi Tia, can I pop over? I just need to talk to you about Lexi.

I have no idea what I'll say to her if she asks what it's about – all I want to know is that she's okay. I press send and wait, staring at my phone, willing a reply from Tia to come through.

Ten minutes later I'm still waiting – and my message remains unread. I convince myself that fear is causing me to overreact – surely Christian's threat is hollow and he wouldn't do anything to Tia?

It's a relief when Jeremy and Lexi get home, their voices filling up the silent void. For now, I have done what I can to ensure that soon Christian will be taken care of, even if only temporarily, and I can claim my life back.

We'll have to get away from here, of course, start over somewhere far from London. It might be a challenge to convince Jeremy, but I'll have to find a way. Once Christian is safely locked up, I can tell Jeremy that he's been stalking me, and we need to move far away from him. It would only be the truth. For once.

'The ballet was *so* good, Emily,' Lexi gushes as I meet them at the door. Her innocent words pull me back to the present, to what matters. 'I wish you could have been there. You would have loved it.'

I give her a hug. 'I'm sure I would have. And I'll definitely go with you next time.'

'How was your day?' Jeremy asks, heading into the kitchen. He pours us both a glass of wine. 'What did you get up to?'

'Tidied the house. Caught up with some reading. Did some more planning for next term.' *Set a plan in motion to get someone committed to a psychiatric ward.*

Jeremy opens his mouth but quickly closes it again. He doesn't believe me. The school work excuse is wearing thin.

'What were you about to say?' I ask.

He hesitates. 'Nothing. Just... well, there's no point telling you not to work so much, is there?'

'No. It keeps me sane.' I force a laugh.

He walks over to me but then seems to change his mind and asks Lexi what her favourite part of the ballet was.

Because of Christian, I am shutting my husband out, and there's only so much he'll take before he gives up on me.

While Jeremy watches a film downstairs, I climb into bed and check my phone. There are no messages, and the ominous silence makes me uneasy. I text Tia again, asking if she's okay, but my previous message remains unread. With our conversation the other day ringing in my head, I message Pam to ask if she enjoyed the ballet. She's usually up late, but she doesn't reply either.

It's nearly midnight, and it occurs to me that Christian might be spending the night with Tia, just to get at me. To prove that he can muscle in on every aspect of my life, and do what he likes. I can't let Tia be used like that.

I pull off my pyjamas and throw on joggers and a T-shirt, grabbing my phone before I rush downstairs.

Thankfully, Jeremy has fallen asleep, so I don't have to explain why I'm rushing out so late at night. He's a heavy sleeper, just like Christian; there have been many times I've found him on the sofa in the morning when I've come down for breakfast.

The lights aren't on at Tia's house when I get there, which shouldn't surprise me given the late hour. I scan the road as I pull into a parking space, and there's no sign of Christian's blue Audi.

I run down the short path to her front door, noticing that no curtains are drawn in the downstairs window, or the two upstairs. It's a large five-bedroom house, far too big for one person. I recall Christian's words about Tia wanting Lexi to live with her. I press hard on the doorbell, stepping back as it chimes into the silent night. I don't care how late it is, or how I will appear to anyone who sees me, I just need to warn Tia about Christian.

There's no answer, and no flicker of lights in any of the windows.

I rush to the window and peer through, into her living room. There's no sign of anyone, and nothing left out to suggest she's had a date night with someone. I try the side gate, but it's locked, and it's too high for me to climb over. Besides, if someone saw me and called the police, I would have no way to explain what I'm doing here in the middle of the night at my husband's ex-wife's house.

I call Tia's mobile again, and it goes straight to her voice-mail. 'It's Emily. Please call me as soon as you can. Lexi's fine, but it's urgent. I really need to talk to you. I'm at your house. If you're there, can you please open the door?'

I stare up at her windows, willing her face to appear, but there's only an eerie stillness.

Minutes pass before I give up and retreat to my car. Inside, I lock the doors and send another text, repeating how important it is that she calls me straight away.

Then I call Christian, and it rings for what seems like forever before his voicemail kicks in.

Ending the call, I drive home. I have no choice now but to wait until morning and try again.

Once again, I sleep restlessly. Jeremy didn't wake up when I got home so I left him downstairs, undisturbed. Each time I wake, I check my phone and find no new messages. It's hard to believe that Tia hasn't seen any of them – her phone is never out of her sight.

As soon as my alarm blares at six a.m., I'm immediately alert, calling Tia again, only to be once again greeted with her voicemail message.

Lexi pads into the bedroom, yawning. She flops onto the bed and tells me she can't get back to sleep. I tell her to cuddle up, and try to force out all other thoughts.

'Tell me about the ballet again,' I say, and she beams at me.

We talk for over an hour, and when Jeremy comes up, carrying the blanket I placed around him last night, I tell them I'll get dressed and make us all breakfast.

My mobile phone is set to vibrate in my pocket, just in case Tia calls while I'm scrambling eggs, and the kitchen door is open, ready for me to run out and take the call in private.

When there's still no word from her by ten a.m., I tell Jeremy I need to get some things from the high street.

'What?' he asks. 'Didn't you just go shopping yesterday?'

I make some excuse about forgetting a few bits, and pray he doesn't probe further. Thankfully, Lexi chooses that moment to announce in a panic that she can't find the book she's been reading. 'I need it,' she insists. 'Can someone help me?'

While Jeremy's distracted with the hunt for Lexi's book, I slip out of the house.

It's rained during the night, and my trainers squelch across the sodden ground as I rush to Tia's door. Fear of Tia being hurt in some way keeps me going, and makes me determined to do this, no matter the consequences.

Just as it was last night, her house is eerily still. I peer through the living room window again, and nothing has changed. The curtains remain closed. I ring the bell and wait, pacing her driveway.

Christian could be in there, although there's still no sign of his car.

I hammer on the door, attracting attention from a middle-aged man walking his dog on the other side of the road. Under his heavy glare, I walk back to my car and start the engine. But before setting off, I message Christian.

Where's Tia?

My phone rings, Christian's name appearing on the screen.

'Where is she?' I demand. 'What have you done?'

'I don't know what you're talking about. I'm not with Tia. I don't know where she is.'

'You were with Tia yesterday. Where is she? She's not replying to messages and she's not at home.'

Christian laughs. 'Imagine if something did happen to her? How on earth would you explain to Lexi that it's all your fault?'

TWENTY-FOUR

BEFORE

Emily walks with Niko, holding onto his arm as if they've been friends for years, instead of only the two hours they've spent having coffee this evening. She doesn't understand it, but they've definitely clicked. He's telling her about the time he stood at the front of his seminar group to do a presentation and his trousers – which were too large – fell down. Emily throws her head back and laughs. 'Hey, it was really embarrassing,' he says. 'My boxers had a hole in too! I hadn't got round to doing my washing.' This makes her laugh even more, and it feels good. Natural. Somehow, Niko has helped her forget about Christian, and about her mum's deteriorating mental health.

'So, what are your plans now?' he asks as they head towards the Tube station. 'I'm guessing it's too late to go to the gym now.' He taps her bag. He'd volunteered to carry it again, and she wasn't about to refuse. 'And just for the record, I'm still not convinced about what's in here,' he says, smiling.

Unease spreads over her, and she pulls her arm away. It's been so nice talking to Niko, she'd hate for it all to be ruined by having to explain why most of her belongings are in that bag.

'Yeah. Think I'll just go home,' Emily says. 'I need to do some reading for one of my lectures tomorrow. How about you?'

'Well, I live right over there.' He points across the road. 'And I'm about to rustle up a mean chicken arrabbiata.' He pauses. 'There'll be plenty of it if you're hungry?'

'Um, I—'

'It's okay,' he says. 'No worries. Another time. You've had a big enough dose of me already this evening. Totally understandable.'

'No, it's not that,' Emily assures him. 'I just...' Christian still hasn't texted and she's got nowhere else to go. What's she got to lose by having some food with Niko? 'Okay. Why not? But disclaimer: if you expect me to ever repay the favour then you'll have to put up with beans on toast. Just so you know.' She's joking of course; Emily taught herself to cook long ago, simply because her mother never wanted to.

He laughs. 'One of my favourites. You're on!' He grabs her hand. 'Come on, this bag's weighing me down now and I need this shoulder for basketball tomorrow.'

Unlike Christian's place, Niko's place feels lived in, as though he's put down some roots here and isn't just a temporary visitor. Photos of him with his friends on nights out in different places cover the fridge, and his shelves are full of DVDs and CDs. Emily's never noticed before how little of Christian's personality is reflected in his flat.

'You sit,' Niko suggests. 'Do that reading you were talking about if you want. Dinner will be served soon m'lady.' He bows, and it's such a ridiculous gesture that Emily can't help laughing.

She settles onto his sofa, which is adorned with scatter cushions, pulling out *Heart of Darkness* from her bag. She checks her phone again, but there's still nothing from her boyfriend. But somehow, being here with Niko, it's not bothering her as much as it was.

Niko is right – his chicken is the nicest she's ever tasted.

'I take it from your empty plate you liked it,' Niko says when they've finished eating.

His smile is nice, she thinks. Different to Christian's, but she can't explain how. 'Thanks,' she says. 'It was lovely.'

They stay seated at the table, and Niko tells her all about his family. His parents and younger sister live in Dubai.

'Don't you want to go out there?' she asks, hoping he won't ask about *her* family.

'No chance. I like to visit, but I'm a Londoner, through and through. What about you? Can you see yourself living anywhere else?'

Emily shrugs. 'It's different for me. I grew up in Surrey, so London is new to me. Maybe I'll end up somewhere else after uni - who knows what the future holds?'

'Indeed. I'll drink to that!' Niko lifts his glass of Coke. 'Cheers! To new friendships.'

She smiles and lifts her glass, but in that moment, guilt sets in. She shouldn't be sitting here with another man. It's Christian she wants to be with, no one else.

'I have to go,' she says, standing and taking her plate to the kitchen. 'I'm so sorry. There's something I need to do.'

Niko follows her to the door. 'I can't say I'm not disappointed, but thanks for having dinner with me.'

'I'll see you, then,' Emily says, reaching for her bag and hoisting it onto her shoulder.

'I'd give you a lift but I've just sold my car and I don't collect my new one till tomorrow,' Niko explains.

'Thanks for everything,' she says, rushing out.

He calls after her, but she doesn't turn around. She just wants to get to Christian.

People stare at her as she sits on Christian's doorstep, her large bag dumped in front of her. The temperature has dropped dramatically and Emily shivers, wrapping her thin cardigan tighter around her. She must have sent Christian at least ten messages, none of which he's replied to.

She's been sitting there for an hour when Christian finally shows up, his eyes widening when he sees Emily perched on his doorstep. 'What's going on?' he asks.

'Haven't you checked your phone? I've sent you a thousand messages.' Her voice is loud, fuelled with anger.

'My battery died hours ago. Sorry.' He pulls it from his pocket. 'See. It's off.'

A man walks past and stops to watch them.

'Can we just go inside?' Emily asks. 'Everyone's staring at us.'

'I can't deal with an argument tonight,' Christian says. His calmness worries her.

'Please, Christian,' she begs.

Without a word he unlocks the door, gesturing for her to go through.

As soon as she steps through the door, Christian turns on her. 'Why have you just turned up like this?'

'Where were you?' she asks, puzzled by his defensiveness. There's something off about him; it's as if he isn't quite here. 'Have you been drinking?' she asks.

'None of your business.' He walks into the living room, and she notices he's not steady. 'We didn't have any plans to meet this evening. I was out. Why are you having a go at me?' Christian pulls off his coat and slumps onto the sofa. 'I don't need this right now. I've had a bad enough day as it is.'

Emily sits beside him. 'I'm sorry. I've had a bad day too.' She tells him about the argument with her, Kirsty and Erin, how she had no choice but to pack up her things and get away from there. And all the time she speaks, it's as if he's not listening.

She studies his face, attempting to gauge his reaction. Christian should be pleased about this; he's been trying to get her to move in with him for over a year now. This is what he wants. But he just stares at her blankly.

'I think you should go back,' he says. 'Just sort things out with them. That place is your home too, isn't it?'

She's stunned into silence. She thought he would love that this has happened, especially after all the time he's spent trying to persuade her to move in with him.

'I... I was thinking I could move in here,' she says softly, as if speaking too loudly will make her comment unappealing. 'You did ask me to, remember?'

Christian sighs. 'I like living by myself.'

'But... this is what you wanted. I can do it now.'

'I went to see your mum this evening,' he says, ignoring her.

'*What?*'

'There is something going on with her and I had to know what it was. You never tell me anything.'

'What did you say to her? What have you done? She'll never be able to deal with this! That's why I haven't told her that we're more than friends.'

'Well, she knows now. I'm not some sordid secret, Emily. I'm worth more than that. And you've been lying, haven't you? Why would you lie to me?'

But Emily can't answer his question. All she can think about is her mum, and how vulnerable she is. How Christian could have tipped her over the edge. 'What did you say to her?' she demands. 'What have you done?'

He shakes his head and looks away from her. 'It doesn't matter now, does it? It's all too late.'

TWENTY-FIVE

NOW

Days pass and there's no sign of Tia. She doesn't reply to any of my messages, or return my calls. And her phone still goes straight to voicemail. I've been to her house every day since the night she spent with Christian, and there's been no sign of her.

I carefully broach the subject with Jeremy, asking if he's heard from her. He tells me he hasn't, that she's probably busy with work. 'It's not her turn to have Lexi for a while,' he'd reminded me.

'What have you done?' I demand, each time I call Christian, and when he bothers to answer, his response is always the same. He doesn't know what I'm talking about. He has no idea where Tia is.

'I think you're losing your mind,' Christian says this morning, when I'm locked in the bathroom with the shower on so I can't be heard from downstairs. I'm whispering, but my voice seems to echo around the room.

I won't take this bait. I know he's done something to Tia. 'I'll go to the police' I warn, in desperation. 'And whatever it is you've done, you'll go to prison for a long time. She didn't deserve to get mixed up with you.' I struggle to stop myself breaking down when I picture Tia's face. And Lexi's, when she realises her mother is missing.

'Like I said, you're crazy,' Christian responds. 'I have no idea what you're talking about. And we both know there's no way you'll go to the police.'

And then he hangs up, just as someone knocks on the bathroom door.

'I'll be out in a sec,' I call, turning off the shower. I glance in the mirror and it strikes me how ghostly I look. How I seem to have aged so rapidly. I don't even recognise myself.

I take a moment to pull myself together, and then I open the door to find Jeremy standing there, holding a tray of breakfast.

Lexi barges past him and hands me a present. 'Happy birthday, Emily! Open it, I know you'll love it.'

I give her a hug and turn to Jeremy, who places the tray on the bed. 'Happy birthday,' he says, kissing me. 'We were hoping you'd still be in bed so you could have this before you got up. Before you got any ideas about making breakfast for us.'

'You know me too well,' I say, forcing a smile. 'Thank you, though. This is lovely.'

'Were you talking to someone on the phone just now? It sounded a bit... heated.'

Overcome with panic, I say the first thing that comes to mind. 'Just someone from work. Having a go at me about leaving a folder on my desk with all the kids' photos and names in it. Bleating on about data protection.' I picture Tia's still and lifeless house, and it's a struggle to stop myself throwing up.

'Don't they know it's your birthday?' Jeremy asks.

I shrug. 'Probably not.'

'Bit early in the morning, isn't it?' His eyes narrow, and I know how far I'm pushing my luck expecting him to believe all of this.

'Thanks for all of this,' I repeat, reaching for Lexi's present.

Carefully, I unwrap it, wishing I could be fully here in this moment.

'It's mindfulness cards and a gratitude journal,' she says, before I've even taken it out. 'You're always saying you need one.'

'This is perfect, Lexi, thank you,' I say, leaning in to hug her.

'I chose it myself,' Lexi beams. 'And I saved up all my pocket money for ages.'

When I hug her again, my tears fall onto her T-shirt.

'That's not all you're getting,' Jeremy says. 'After breakfast, when you get dressed, we've got a surprise for you. It's been so hard keeping it a secret – glad I don't have to any more!'

While I know their surprise will be something pleasant, my body turns cold at the lack of control. Other people deciding things for me. Even if it is Jeremy. 'What is it? You know how I feel about surprises.'

He looks disappointed. 'Just enjoy your breakfast. You'll love it.' He points to the breakfast tray. 'And the eggs are over-done, just how you like them.'

'I burnt the toast a bit,' Lexi admits. 'Sorry.'

'It's all perfect,' I assure her, hugging her close.

'Hurry up, though,' Lexi says, jumping up. 'We're all packed and need to leave soon!'

I freeze. 'What?'

Jeremy sighs. 'Lexi! It's meant to be a surprise.'

'But she'll see her clothes are missing!' Lexi protests, folding her arms.

'What's going on?' I ask.

Jeremy perches on the bed. 'It was supposed to be a surprise, but I've booked a few nights away for us. You've always said you wanted to go to the Lake District, and Lexi's never been either. It will be the perfect break before you go back to school. Four days of peace and tranquillity. You work so hard, we just wanted to treat you. We've even packed your case. The plan was not to tell you until we got there.'

'And I need a break too,' Lexi insists. 'Year 5 is going to be super hard. That's what Elijah's been going around telling everyone.'

'You'll be fine,' Jeremy assures her. 'And isn't Elijah the boy who went round telling everyone the school was closing down and you'd all have to move to a different one?' He turns back to me. 'I've found a lovely cottage,' Jeremy continues. 'We can go walking every day. It's the perfect place to relax.' His eyes narrow. 'But you're not allowed to bring any work with you.'

Jeremy has put so much thought into this that it will crush him if I object.

'Thank you,' I say. 'It sounds lovely.' I'm already wondering how I can get to Tia's house to check on her again before we leave.

'Come on, Lexi,' Jeremy says. 'You can help me get everything ready while Emily finishes her breakfast.'

Jeremy turns back and glances at me. He pauses for a moment but then shuts the door.

How much time do I have before he realises something is terribly wrong?

I listen to make sure they've both gone downstairs, then take my breakfast into the bathroom and throw the food in the bin. I cringe at the waste, but the thought of food sickens me. I call Tia again. Something has happened to her – I'm convinced of it.

With shaking hands, I call the police. All I need to tell them is that I'm worried about a friend who hasn't returned my calls. I don't have to mention Christian.

After I make the call – with assurances from the police that they will look into it – some of the tension leaves my body. I turn on the shower and let the water cleanse my mind, hoping Jeremy won't hear it and question why I'm having another shower.

But the ritual doesn't clear my mind. Christian is still in my life, and if I'm going away for the next four days, it's going to take even longer to get him out of it.

A text arrives while I'm getting dressed.

Don't think I've forgotten about you. I hope you're working on Jeremy. Lexi shouldn't be living with you. Heard from Tia lately?

I send a message to Tyler, warning him Christian's getting worse, then I switch off my phone. It's something I never do, but it brings me some relief.

The Lake District is just as I've pictured it. Of course I've googled it over the years, and got an idea of it from websites, but it's Mum's vivid descriptions that have cemented this place in my mind.

It's a different world from London: sprawling hills and rocks, and long stretches of empty narrow roads. It's like stepping into a different time altogether.

Lexi is awestruck as she stares out of the window. She's travelled all over the world, but places other than London in her own country are alien to her.

'What do you think?' Jeremy asks, glancing in the rearview mirror. 'This is Ennerdale Valley.' He pats my leg. 'I thought you'd prefer to be away from the more touristy places. This is one of the most secluded parts. No one to bother us. Not much more than a pub and a café in Ennerdale Bridge.'

'It's perfect,' I say. And now I've set in motion the plan to stop Christian, all I need to do while we're here is work on Jeremy, and help him see that we can start a new life somewhere else.

'It's cool,' Lexi says. 'Can we go on our own nature trail? I bet there's loads of wildlife around here. Maybe red squirrels?'

'We can do anything you like,' Jeremy says.

'My parents had their honeymoon here,' I say to Jeremy, as we drive through narrow, deserted roads.

'I didn't know that,' he says, glancing at me before turning back to the road.

'It's okay,' I assure him. 'I'm fine talking about them.' This was my mother's happy place, the only time I'd ever seen her truly glow. 'Mum always said it was the best week of her life. Just the two of them and an idyllic landscape. They stayed in Windermere.'

'We can drive there tomorrow if you like. Might be nice for you to see the place.'

'No, it's fine. This trip is about new memories. Not the past.'

Jeremy takes my hand and squeezes it for a moment.

'I need the toilet!' Lexi shouts from the back.

'We're nearly there,' Jeremy says. 'The cottage should be right around here, on the left.'

My heart lifts when I see the property Jeremy's picked for us. It's a cedar-wood bungalow surrounded by woodland. It's completely secluded. And it's so far removed from our house in London that already I've almost convinced myself that Christian doesn't exist.

After lunch, Jeremy plays football with Lexi in the garden while I sit on a sunbed watching them. The tension of these last few weeks slips away, and for a moment I relax, hundreds of miles from London. From Christian. It's just the three of us again.

But it's only a brief escape, and my thoughts turn to Tia. It doesn't make sense that Christian would do something to her when he's trying to force me to give custody of Lexi to her. *What am I missing?*

I switch my phone on and check for messages. There's one from Tyler asking if Christian's okay and if anything's happened. I haven't heard back from the police, and it worries me.

'Come and play,' Lexi calls. 'Dad can be in goal.'

And I do, because that's what being a wife and mother means.

For the next half hour, it's just the three of us and I'm able to shut out the world, but as soon as Lexi says her legs are aching and she wants to rest, thoughts of Tia flood back.

'Do you mind if I go for a short walk?' I ask Jeremy.

He frowns. 'On your own?' And there it is again – the doubt scrawled on his face. 'Why don't we all go?'

'Dad, I can't!' Lexi protests. 'I'm injured.'

'Being tired isn't really an injury,' Jeremy explains.

'I won't be long,' I say, grabbing the key from the worktop. 'Just want to get my bearings a bit.'

I slip out of the cottage while Lexi keeps Jeremy talking; I can tell he wants to fire questions at me, and I'm not sure how much longer I can lie to him.

Walking the quiet country lanes alone would have made me nervous once. But now I'm emboldened. I won't live in fear any longer.

I pull out my phone and call the police again, finally getting through to someone who can help me. They're making enquiries, I'm told by an officer who sounds harried, as if he needs me to get off the phone as soon as possible.

They'll contact Jeremy soon, then. If they're taking this seriously, they'll work their way through everyone Tia knows.

I hang up and try to quell my panic. I know I've done all I can for now, but nothing feels right about this.

As I walk, I reply to Tyler's text, suggesting that it's time we got Christian to a doctor: *He's saying some worrying things about wanting to hurt someone.*

After twenty minutes, I turn around and make my way back to the cottage. A long absence will just give Jeremy something else to be concerned about.

Jeremy and Lexi are still in the garden when I get back, and the sound of their voices compels me to be present with them from this moment. The police are looking for Tia, and I've set things in motion with Tyler and Anthony.

'Hey! I'm back,' I call, making my way through the living room to the back door.

Lexi rushes in from the garden. 'Guess who's here?'

But I don't need to, because even before the words have left her mouth I see him outside in our garden, kicking Lexi's football to Jeremy.

Christian has come for me.

TWENTY-SIX
NOW

Seconds tick by and I can't move. I need to react quickly, otherwise Jeremy and Lexi will know something's wrong.

'Christian! What a surprise! What are you doing here?' I make my way outside, wondering if my words sound as fake to everyone else as they do to me. I turn to Jeremy. 'Did you plan this?'

Jeremy shakes his head. 'No. Um, Tia told Christian where we were going. He's heading back to America in a few days and didn't want to leave without saying goodbye.'

My throat constricts. Words evaporate before I can form them.

'We do have three bedrooms!' Lexi proclaims. 'Christian can stay.'

'I don't want to intrude,' Christian says. 'I can always stay somewhere else.'

'You'll never get anything now,' Jeremy tells him. 'I had to book this cottage months ago, and even then I could only get a three-bed one.' The irritation in his voice is unmistakable, but Christian doesn't seem fazed as he casually kicks Lexi's football between the sticks they've set up as goalposts.

'I didn't know you were going back,' I say. 'I thought you were putting down roots here.' I try to catch him out, but then realise he will already have an answer. He's told this lie to convince Jeremy to let him gatecrash our trip. There's no way Jeremy would agree to let him stay with us otherwise.

'Something's come up with work,' he says. 'I need to go back to help with a big project.' Christian kicks the football towards Lexi. Her aching limbs are quickly forgotten and she passes it back.

'How about this,' Christian continues. 'While I'm here, I can offer you my babysitting services so that the two of you can enjoy some time alone together. As it's your birthday.' He rests his foot on the ball, bringing it to a stop.

'You don't have to do that,' I insist. I will never leave Lexi alone with him, and he knows it.

Jeremy glances at me and frowns. 'Oh, yes he does. That's only fair. Right, Christian?'

'Right you are. You know what they say. It takes a village to raise a kid or something like that.'

'Don't I know it.' Jeremy laughs, thawing slightly.

'Hey!' Lexi moans. 'I know what you're talking about. I'm not five!'

'Come on, Lexi,' Christian calls. 'Penalty shoot-outs!'

I rush to the bathroom, making it just in time to lose the contents of my stomach. I sink to the floor, pulling my knees up to my chest, knowing all the while I'm doing it that I'm letting him win.

And I refuse to do that.

I rinse out my mouth and smooth my hair. Then I'm ready to go out there and face my opponent.

They're still playing football when I get to the back door, and Jeremy has joined them again. 'I'll cook something special for dinner,' I call from the back door. 'Christian, do you still like beef casserole? I remember your mum used to make it every time you went home from uni.' I smile. 'No promises I can make it as well as she used to, though.'

He stops running and stares at me, and it's the first time since he's reappeared in my life that I've seen him disturbed, the first time he's heard me genuinely say a pleasant word to him.

'Yeah,' he says, frowning. 'Sounds good.'

Lexi shoots the ball past him, straight into the net.

'Great. I'll head to the shop, Jeremy.'

After searching online, I realise that I'll have to drive further afield to get all I need, so I make my way to Cleator Moor. Not for the first time, I consider running. Driving until I get to an airport, and never looking back. But I will never leave Jeremy and Lexi with Christian. If I flee, who knows what he'll do to them?

I stroll around the supermarket, throwing everything I need into a basket. Whatever the cost, I will beat Christian at his own game.

When I return to the cottage, I'm horrified to find Christian alone with Lexi. They're playing a game of chess that's been left with some books on one of the shelves. It takes all my willpower not to rush to her and pull her away. 'Where's your dad, Lexi?' I ask, trying to keep my voice measured, despite the panic bubbling inside me.

'Went for a run. Christian said he'd stay with me. He's teaching me chess.'

Christian nods, smiling at me. 'Told you – just think of me as your babysitter.' He gestures to the board. 'Come on, Lex, your move. Watch your queen, though.'

His overfamiliarity sickens me. *Focus. This will all come together*.

'It's *Lexi*,' I say.

Christian shakes his head. 'Oops, sorry.'

'You and Dad call me Lex all the time,' Lexi insists.

'I'll get dinner started,' I say, before I say something I can't take back. I turn away, but not before I've caught Christian's wink.

My hands shake as I unpack the bags. I feel as though I'm only a witness to my actions, observing them from afar, not responsible for them. I wrestle with myself as I begin cooking, tears splattering onto the black granite worktop.

I'm relieved when I hear the front door open and Jeremy shouts a greeting. He is my reminder that I have no choice but to do this.

Christian has done something to Tia. Kidnapped her, or worse. He can't get away with that. And then what will he do to me? Or Jeremy and Lexi?

My whole body is tense as we sit down to eat, but still I manage to place food into my mouth as if I'm on autopilot.

'That was delicious,' Christian says, when he's finished eating.

I stand up to clear the plates. 'Not as good as your mum's though, is it?'

And there it is again – the flicker of pain in his face before he regains composure. It hurts him to talk about Audrey.

But my victory is short-lived when he catches up with me in the kitchen as I'm loading the dishwasher. 'Speaking of mums,' he says, 'what was it your mum used to love to cook? Oh yeah, I remember. Nothing! Such a shame, isn't it?' He glances at the door. 'Does Jeremy have any clue about what happened to her? I'm guessing he doesn't.'

It's a huge risk, but I ignore him. 'More wine?' I ask. He's already had three glasses. I'm keeping track. He was never dependent on alcohol – at least when I knew him – but if Christian's drinking socially, he can consume endless amounts.

'You're being particularly hospitable today, Emily,' he says

quietly. 'Not that I'm complaining. I like this side of you.
Compliant. Malleable.'

'I bet you do,' I say, turning away from him. 'We're not going
down this road.' I reach for my own glass and take a deep sip.
The wine is too dry for me, but it will help prepare me for what
I have to do.

'Now, now – you might want to slow it down a bit,' Christian warns. 'You wouldn't want to do or say anything you
regret.'

I ignore him and lift my glass. 'Cheers!' I say, taking another
long drink.

He watches me closely and looks like he's about to say
something when Lexi bursts in, begging me to play chess
with her.

'Maybe in the morning,' I say. 'It's time for bed.'

'Oh!' she protests. 'But we're on holiday!'

'I know, but we've got lots of walking to do tomorrow if you
want to go on a nature trail, so you need plenty of rest. Your
dad's running you a bath.'

'Okay,' she says, giving me a hug. 'Love you, Emily.'

When she's gone, Christian moves closer. 'Such a sweet girl.
And she really loves you, that's clear to see. Which makes everything just so much worse.'

I turn away, take another sip of wine.

Christian swipes the glass out of my hand, sending it
crashing to the floor. Red wine spills out like blood, and the
fragments of glass lie scattered across the floor, shining like
diamonds.

'What the hell?'

'I told you to slow down,' he says.

Jeremy appears in the doorway. 'Everything okay? What
was— oh.'

'I dropped my glass,' I say. 'I'll sort it.'

'Oh, Em. You always were a bit clumsy, weren't you?' Christian says, playfully nudging my arm. 'Here, let me do it.' He begins clearing up, but stops as soon as Jeremy's out of the room.

He stands by the kitchen worktop, watching as I scrub away at the pool that only seems to be spreading further.

'It's a bit like cleaning up a crime scene, isn't it?'

'Don't.'

He glances at the door then crouches down so that our eyes are level. 'Haven't you learnt by now that you don't call the shots here?' He leans in, so close that I can feel his breath, familiar but incongruous. Alcohol soaked. He pushes me backwards. 'Learn a lesson.'

Christian heads towards the door, turning back when he reaches it. 'Oh, Em, would you mind topping me up? I'll be outside talking to Jeremy. Nice to make the most of the warm weather.'

The second I'm alone, I know what I have to do. I pour his wine, then open the cupboard under the sink, reaching right to the back where there's a hole that lets the water pipes through.

'Looking for this?'

I jolt backwards. My body is frozen numb, yet feels like it's on fire at the same time.

I know before I see him what Christian is holding.

'Sleeping pills, Emily?' he says, walking towards me. 'Not very original, is it? Couldn't you think of a better way to do it?'

I could plead ignorance, but what's the point when we both know I'd be lying? I want to ask how he knew, but I don't. It doesn't matter. 'Where's Tia?' I ask instead, standing up so that he isn't towering over me.

He ignores me. 'You've upped the stakes now, Emily. Now I know what you're prepared to do. Again. Haven't you learnt anything from the last time you ended someone's life? Or perhaps when you've done it once, it gets easier?'

'No! It wasn't like that. It was—'

'An accident? Is that what you tell yourself so you can sleep at night?'

'I can't sleep at night,' I whisper. 'Ever.'

'So you do have some remorse, then?' He doesn't wait for an answer. 'You know what this means, don't you? Now I know you're capable of doing it again, I have no choice but to stop you. Protect myself at all costs. Self-defence.'

The sound of Jeremy's footsteps stops me responding. He rushes into the kitchen. 'I'm really sorry, I've just had a call from work,' Jeremy says, staring at his phone. 'They need me on a long-haul flight tomorrow evening. I'll need to get to Manchester Airport first thing in the morning.'

His words bounce off me, my brain struggling to compute. 'What?'

'I'll leave the car for you, though, if you don't mind driving home on Friday?'

I stare at him while I try to process this news. And what it means.

'That's a shame,' Christian says to Jeremy in the absence of my reply. 'But I can look after the girls. Take the car if you want – I can drive us all home. I was only meant to stay up here for a couple of days, but I'm happy to stay longer and help out. It won't affect my flight back to the US.'

'No,' I insist. I turn to Jeremy. 'Lexi and I can drive you to Manchester in the morning then we'll head home from there.'

'I can't let you do that,' Jeremy says. 'This is your birthday treat. We've still got three more days here. You should make the most of it. And Lexi will be devastated to leave early.'

I have no choice but to stay. Jeremy is already concerned I'm hiding something, so I can't make a huge fuss about staying here without him.

'I'll go and tell Lexi,' I say, leaving the kitchen as fast as I can without running.

When I get to Lexi's room, I try Tia's number again. Straight to voicemail. I end the call and send another message. Outside the room, I hear Christian telling Jeremy that he'll make sure we're okay.

And Jeremy's effusive thanks is too much to bear.

TWENTY-SEVEN

BEFORE

'What do you mean, it's too late?' Emily demands.

It feels as though the ground has been pulled from beneath her, and she's falling.

My mum. What has he done?

He avoids looking at her and stares at his hands. There's something different about him tonight. Normally, despite everything, she knows where she is with him. She has learnt what she can and can't say. But this new unknown scares her more than anything.

She doesn't wait for him to reply. She grabs Christian's car key from the coffee table and runs, picking up her bag from the hallway on her way out.

She expects him to call after her, to tell her that she's got it wrong – he hasn't been with her mum after all. But only silence follows her into the street.

Scanning the road, she rushes towards his red Golf, which he's parked across the road. She fumbles around trying to get the door open, even though she knows Christian isn't following. She has no idea what he'll be doing in there. But she doesn't care – she just needs to get to her mum.

In the car, Emily turns up the radio, as loud as she can stand it, to drown out her thoughts. Everything has changed, and her brain can't deal with it.

Shut it out. Just get to Mum.

Within an hour, she's reached their house, and now, walking inside, it finally hits her and she can barely make it through the house. Images of her mother lying silent and still assault her, and she wants to scream into the silence.

She switches on the living room light and her eyes are drawn to the body wrapped in a blanket on the sofa.

'Mum!' she cries, rushing over. Emily throws her arms around her mum's motionless body, and screams.

Beneath the blanket there is movement.

'Emily.' Her mum's voice is frail, devoid of life and energy.

'Mum! What happened? Are you okay?' Tears stream down her cheeks.

Her mother turns over and slowly pulls herself up. 'Why are you here? What time is it? Is he here?'

Emily's so relieved to find her mother alive that it takes her a moment to calm down. 'Do you mean Christian? No, he's not. It's just me, Mum.'

'Oh, thank goodness. He was here, though, just now. Saying all sorts of things.'

'It doesn't matter now, Mum. I'm here. And no one's going to hurt you. I've put the chain on the door too. We're safe.'

Her mother leans back. '*You're* not.'

Emily could question her about what she means, but she already knows.

'I warned you, Emily,' her mum continues. 'I told you that getting involved with him would only cause you pain.'

For once, Emily doesn't care if her mum's launching into one of her rants. She takes her bony hand and holds it tightly. She'll sit here all night listening to her if she has to. She's just glad her mum is okay. 'Let me make you tea,' Emily offers. 'And then you can tell me what Christian said. It's really important that you tell me every word.'

Her mother stares at her and nods as Emily makes her way to the kitchen.

'Just one thing, though,' her mum says. 'I've run out of tea bags. We'll have to have water.'

When she comes back, carrying two large glasses of water, her mother is staring at the wall. Emily needs her to be lucid, to recall everything that took place here today.

'Here you go,' Emily says, handing her a glass.

Her mother stares at it as if trying to work out what it is.

'Mum, can you tell me what exactly happened?' Emily holds her breath and waits.

'I don't know why he came here,' her mother begins. 'He was saying all this stuff. It didn't make sense. And he was talking really fast. Like in another language.'

Emily is losing her, and she wonders how much of what she's about to hear will be fact. Still, she needs to hear her mum speak. 'What kind of things was he saying?'

'About you. How no one knows who you really are. I mean, that doesn't make any sense does it?'

'No, it doesn't.'

'I kept asking him what he meant, but then he'd go on and on about things. And, oh... it's awful. The things he was saying. About me controlling your life, never letting you have any freedom. A prisoner, he said.'

Emily recalls it now: how Christian had accused her of lying. 'Mum, I need to know what you talked about. Everything.' She takes her mum's hand again. 'Just tell me what you said, Mum.'

Her mother turns to her. 'He asked me about your father. Said he was sorry that he left us and moved away.' Her dark, piercing eyes fill with pain. They never speak about her dad.

Emily's never spoken about the details to Christian, and he'll want to know why. 'And what did you say?'

'I told him the truth, of course. That he died.'

And now Emily knows there is no going back. 'But... but you never tell anyone that. You tell them that he left us. And you told me to always say that.'

'Because he doesn't deserve sympathy, Emily. If I told everyone he was dead then they'd just feel sorry for him, and it would erase all his dreadful acts, wouldn't it? He'd just be that poor man who died too young. That's why I've always told you it's better to say he left us.'

Emily nods. The narrative she's been fed since she was a kid is still part of her story, and she doesn't think she'll ever be able to change it. And now, she's numb with shock that her mum has told Christian the truth. She will have some explaining to do.

'I didn't want to tell him. He was so... he forced my hand,' her mother continues. 'You must know what he's like? I had to explain, didn't I? And tell him why I've tried so hard to protect you from making the mistakes I made.'

Still holding her mother's hand, Emily chews her lip. Perhaps there is a way she can make Christian understand why she's been holding on to her mother's lie for most of her life.

'I told him all about how while I was giving birth to you, your father was sleeping with that woman he'd just met at work. Phoebe. In our house. How he deliberately ignored the phone ringing, and then unplugged it. Even though he knew I was about to give birth. That's why I'd gone to your grandmother's house. I was feeling so ill and knew he wouldn't help me when the time came to get to hospital. He'd be too *busy*.' She scrunches her face, and for a second Emily believes she will cry, even though she rarely sheds any tears now.

Emily closes her eyes and squeezes her mother's hand tighter. She doesn't want to hear this, but it's better that her mother lets it out. 'What else?' she asks.

'I told him how I later found out that Phoebe had been only one of who knows how many women. Every time your dad was away on business, he'd end up finding some woman or other.' She speaks with such clarity now that Emily hopes this will be therapeutic for her. 'They'd call him an addict nowadays, surely.'

'But you were leaving him, Mum. Weren't you? Before he died? That's how strong you were. You were walking away.'

Her mother's eyes glaze over, any rational thought erased in an instant. 'It's all in the past, Emily. You need to stay away from Christian,' she says. 'I know you've been seeing him, and I'm telling you he's no good for you. I should know, shouldn't I?'

For a moment they both fall quiet, and Emily scrambles to work out how she will deal with Christian.

'Did Christian say anything else? Did you? Have you told me everything, Mum.'

'Of course I have,' her mum says, picking at her chipped nail polish.

Emily stands. 'How about I go to the petrol station and get some tea bags? If I'm staying the night, I'll need some caffeine in the morning.'

Her mother ignores her and starts humming.

She waits for her mum to warn her that it's too late to be driving around on her own. That it's not safe out there. That anything could happen.

But all she hears from her mum is a melancholic melody.

When she gets back, clutching a box of PG Tips, her mother is lying down, once again wrapped in her grey blanket.

'Come on, Mum, let's get you to bed. You'll be much more comfortable.'

Emily puts the teabags on the coffee table and gently pulls her mother up. She guides her upstairs, helping her dress and brush her teeth before she puts her to bed. It occurs to her how strange it is that she's helping her mother in this way when she has no physical disability.

It's what is unseen – that can do just as much damage as a physical affliction.

She tucks her mother into bed, like she would a child. Like her mother did when she was a child.

'Oh, Emily,' her mum moans, resting her head on her pillow. 'I don't want this pain any more. I just want it to stop.'

'What pain, Mum? What's hurting?'

Her mother doesn't answer. She doesn't need to. It's what's in her head that's causing her this pain.

'I'm calling the doctor,' Emily says, reaching for her phone.

Her mother leans forward and grabs her arm. 'No! No doctors.'

'But I don't know how to help!' Emily says. 'What can I do?'

'Please make it stop.' She rests her head back.

Emily can't hold back the tears as her mother reaches for a pillow and holds it out to her.

'I just want it to end.'

TWENTY-EIGHT

NOW

I watch helplessly as Jeremy packs his things. Morning birdsong drifts through the open window, incongruously cheerful when I'm sinking into despair.

He's quiet this morning, when normally he'd be apologising profusely for having to leave like this. Several times he glances at me, but doesn't speak, and I can't help but wonder what seeds Christian has planted in his mind while they've been chatting alone.

Several times I've been on the verge of telling him everything. He would never leave us alone with Christian if he knew the truth. But nor would he want to be anywhere near me.

'Are you okay?' I ask.

'Yeah.' He glances at me then turns back to his suitcase. He sighs and comes to sit with me on the bed. He hugs me, but doesn't say anything.

'I love you,' I say.

'Me too,' Jeremy says, but his words are barely a whisper.

Once he's packed, Lexi and I stand by the front door of the cottage, waving him off. As soon as his taxi is out of sight, nausea swirls around my stomach. Not for the first time since last night I wonder how I'll get through the next three days. Lexi doesn't know it, but we're both as good as prisoners here.

'I'll miss Dad,' Lexi says. 'But at least you're here.'

'And I'm not going anywhere,' I assure her.

'Can we go on a nature trail now?' Lexi asks, looping her arm through mine as we head back inside.

'You need to have some breakfast first.'

'But I'm too excited to eat,' she insists. 'If we leave now we might see creatures that won't come out later when it gets too hot.'

'Breakfast first,' I insist. There's no telling how this day will unfold.

Christian is already up, sitting in the garden under the shade of the tree. It's not even seven a.m., but the sun is already scorching.

'Not having any breakfast?' he calls from outside when I place a bowl in front of Lexi at the table.

'Already eaten,' I lie.

'She got up early with Dad,' Lexi explains, shrugging. 'Emily always likes to have time to herself in the morning. She says it helps her think.'

'Is that right?' Christian says, turning to me. 'I always thought you didn't like being alone. Some people just prefer not to be left with their own company.'

'Well, it's been a long time since you knew me, hasn't it? Anyway, you're up early. I seem to remember you were always a night owl. Didn't do mornings well.'

I'm taking a huge risk challenging Christian like this, but by now he must know I'll fight back. Besides, Lexi doesn't seem to be paying us much attention, as focused as she is on finishing her cornflakes as quickly as possible.

'I'm sorry I missed your dad,' Christian says. He springs up from his sun lounger and comes inside, sitting next to Lexi. 'I'm looking forward to this walk,' he says. 'I bet we'll find some really cool stuff out here.'

'You really don't have to come with us,' I insist. 'Lexi and I will be fine, won't we?'

Christian shakes his head. 'Oh no, I wouldn't dream of letting you two go wandering off on your own. You don't know this area. Best if we stick together hiking around here. A lot of those hills are very steep. And I've promised Jeremy I'll look out for you both.'

Lexi rolls her eyes. 'We're not stupid princesses who need saving like in some ancient Disney film. Girls don't need protecting!'

'That is so true,' Christian agrees. 'And I know for sure that Emily can take care of herself. But I promised your dad I'd look after you, and I never break a promise.' He looks up at me and smiles, before turning back to Lexi. 'Besides, I've got it all planned out. We'll drive to Wild Ennerdale – it's a nature reserve and is out of this world. There's definitely a chance we'll see red squirrels there.'

Lexi's smile stretches across her face. 'Really? What else?'

'All sorts. Woodpeckers. There's such a huge range of habitats there for all sorts of animals and birds.'

Lexi claps her hands. 'Yes! Can we go now?'

'I wanted to stay around here,' I tell Lexi. 'We don't know this area, do we? Best to stick close by. And there'll be plenty to see here.'

'Oh, Emily, please can we go to where Christian said? Please.'

I glance at Christian and his glare warns me I don't have a choice. 'How do you know so much about the place?' I ask. 'You've been in America for all these years.'

'Mum and Dad used to bring us here as kids. Every summer. Didn't I tell you that? I know Ennerdale as well as I know my own reflection in the mirror. Such a coincidence that it's the place Jeremy decided to bring you. Life's funny that way, isn't it?' He smiles, and I turn away, wondering how I could have known so little about him when we were together.

'I'll go and get dressed,' Lexi says, abandoning her cereal and rushing to her bedroom.

'Glad that's sorted, then,' Christian says, easing back his chair. 'I'll jump in the shower.' He rises from the table. 'It's funny, but this is all a bit like a game of chess – fighting to the end. Someone having to lose. Did you ever play chess?' He walks over to me and picks up a loose strand of hair that's fallen from my ponytail. 'I won't lose, Emily.'

As we walk around the nature reserve, I stick close to Lexi, keeping as far from Christian as he'll allow. Before we left, while Christian was showering, I warned Lexi to never let me out of her sight. Not for one second. But now we're out, I realise this won't be easy. She's constantly sprinting ahead whenever she thinks there might be wildlife hiding in the bushes.

Christian is right, though – being in this beautiful wilderness feels like we're in another country altogether. Another world. If it weren't for the dark and menacing shadow hanging over me, I would feel like I'm in paradise. A lake meanders through the forest, its unseen contents floating away. Is this what Christian has planned for me, if I don't beat him to it?

'Look, Lexi,' Christian shouts, sprinting ahead. 'A red squirrel!'

'Where?' Lexi rushes to catch up with him, ignoring my plea for her to wait.

Christian takes Lexi's hand and leads her off the path.

I rush after them, ready to get Lexi out of here – but then I spot the squirrel dashing up a tree.

'I've never seen one in real life,' Lexi says, aiming her

camera in the direction of the tree. 'Tons of greys, but never red!' She takes a photo.

Christian pats her arm. 'Well, now you have.'

'I'm writing it in my book,' Lexi says, pulling out her unicorn notepad from her backpack. 'This is the best nature trail ever!'

'Oh, we haven't even got started yet, Lexi,' Christian says. 'The best is yet to come.'

Fighting the urge to grab Lexi and run, I vow to put an end to this now. That was a clear threat, and I'll do whatever it takes to protect Lexi.

For hours we walk, until Christian tells us we need to stop for lunch. I'm about to protest – stopping will only prolong this agony – but I think better of it. Lexi needs to eat, and we've been walking for a long time.

'We can eat here by the lake,' he says.

'I'm not really hungry,' Lexi says.

'You need some fuel,' Christian tells her. 'We've got a lot more walking to do.'

'What are we having?' she asks.

'Cheese sandwiches. Emily and I made them together.' He winks at me. 'I couldn't let her do all the hard work.'

I barely touch my food, and Lexi's too excited to eat much of hers. Only Christian has an appetite, devouring most of the sandwiches.

'Let's head that way,' Christian says, as I pack up the food. 'Along the river. That way we can avoid most of the steep parts.'

'Maybe we should head back?' I suggest.

'Not yet. The day's still young,' Christian says.

I silently pray for Lexi to say she's too tired to carry on, and that she wants to go back to the cottage. But of course she doesn't, and sprints off again, pointing to a heron on the lake. 'Look!' she screeches, pulling out her camera.

Christian heads closer to the lake. This is my chance. Lexi's back is turned so she wouldn't see anything. All it would take is a gentle push. Christian once told me he can't swim, and even if he's learnt since we were together, it would give me and Lexi a head start. I'd explain it all to her later. How Christian isn't who we thought, and that he's done terrible things.

I walk up to him. He's pulling out his phone and messaging someone. Feeling a mixture of fear and nausea, I reach out my arms. But my fingers don't even touch his clothes before he spins round and grabs my wrists. 'What are you doing?' he says. 'Right here? In front of Lexi? You must be desperate.'

'I want this to stop,' I say. 'Please, Christian. You've terrified me enough. And I understand why, I really do. You want revenge – I get it. But you don't need to do this any more.' I glance at the lake. Then at Lexi, who is still engrossed in snapping photos. It's not too late for me to do this. 'I know I destroyed everything. I understand why you hate me. But look at Lexi. She doesn't deserve this.'

'Someone has to be collateral damage, Emily. You should know all about that.'

The muscles in my body are desperate to push my arms out. Or maybe it's my brain. Christian has blurred all of my boundaries.

I lean forward but it's too late – Lexi is running towards us, and I won't have her witnessing my mess.

'We're heading home now,' I say to Lexi. 'I'm not feeling very well.'

The smile fades from her face. 'Oh... okay.'

'Sorry, Lex,' Christian says. 'Sounds like Emily's made up her mind. Sometimes life just disappoints us, unfortunately.'

We trudge back towards the car, my eyes on Lexi the whole time. It worries me that Christian barely speaks. Twice now he's caught me desperately trying to end this, and I know he'll never let that go.

. . .

To my surprise, Christian doesn't join us for dinner. 'I have a few things to do,' he says, packing up his laptop. 'The Wi-Fi's terrible here. I'm heading into Cleator Moor to see if there's anywhere better.'

While I'm relieved to have some reprieve from his stifling presence, bizarrely, I feel safer with him here. Where I can see what he's doing. *What is he planning?* I'm prepared to wait up all night.

Just as he's leaving, he whispers to me that he's taking my car key and the cottage key. It's what I've expected.

He's still not back at nine p.m. when I tuck Lexi into bed, turning on the lamp for her. As much as she loves it here, being in the middle of this wooded area spooks her once darkness sets in. Especially now that Jeremy has gone. I don't tell her, but I feel the same.

'Where's Christian?' she asks, reaching across for her *Harry Potter* book. 'It's a bit scary without him or Dad.'

If only she knew that it's not the darkness we have to fear, but Christian himself. 'I know,' I say. 'But *I'm* here. We're safe.' I swallow the lump in my throat. I wish my mum had been able to say this to me, even just once. 'I'll be right next door.' I tap on the wall. 'If you get scared just knock like this and I'll come running, okay?'

Lexi hugs me. 'Thanks, Em. You always know what to say.'

'Not really. But I know I will always protect you, no matter what.'

I say goodnight and pull Lexi's door closed. I've already checked that her window is locked. But it was a futile act; Christian will be in the house tonight.

In the kitchen, I make myself a strong coffee and check my phone again. Of course there's nothing from Tia, and every one of my messages to her remains unread.

Remembering that I still haven't had a reply from Pam, I check to see if she's read it. She has. Minutes after it was sent.

It's nearly eleven when I hear his car pull up outside. I'm sitting on the sofa, an unread book in my hand, all my senses on overdrive. I want to demand to know where he's been for so long, but I keep my mouth shut. It doesn't matter. He's slowly taking away everything that's important to me, and I know that him coming here is the final act.

'Didn't think you'd still be up,' he says, pulling off his shoes and throwing them by the door. They land with a thud that I hope hasn't woken Lexi.

'I'm not tired,' I lie. I think of the caffeine pills I've taken to stay awake; my body is fighting them, and I pray I can make this work. 'Do you want a drink?' I ask.

He snorts. 'Do you think for one second I trust you to make me anything?'

'Is that why you didn't eat dinner with us? You could have stood over me like you did when I made the sandwiches.'

Christian ignores me. 'I'm going to bed. Don't be up too late, will you? You never know what tomorrow will bring.'

He leaves this threat hanging in the air and disappears into his bedroom.

When the light disappears from under his door, I rush to his coat and rummage through the pockets, holding my breath until I pull out my car key and the cottage key. An oversight on Christian's part.

Shoving the keys in my bag, I hang it back on the hook by the door. If Christian does happen to wake up, everything needs to be in its place. I make my way to my own bedroom, climbing into bed fully clothed. Everything is ready.

My eyes start to close and I force them open, grabbing my phone to check the time. It's nearly two a.m. I must have drifted off. I jump up and pull open the wardrobe – my bag is still there, filled with all my belongings. And next to it is Lexi's, packed with whatever she wouldn't notice was missing.

I grab the bags and creep into her room, closing the door

behind me. I kneel down by her bed and softly nudge her. 'Lexi, wake up.'

She stirs and mumbles something incoherent but doesn't open her eyes. I move her again. 'Lexi, wake up.'

My words seem to reach her this time and slowly she opens her eyes. 'Emily? What's happening?'

'Listen carefully. I don't want you to panic, but we need to drive home. Now.'

She pulls herself up and rubs her eyes. 'What? Why?'

'I had a message from our neighbour, Mrs Khan. There's been a flood at home. You know she was checking on the place for us? She went there earlier and a pipe must have burst. We need to get home straight away and find out what's happened.'

Lexi is so trusting that she doesn't stop to ask why the neighbour has only reported this to me at two a.m. For a moment I'm crippled with indecision – I need to tell her some of the truth. But it will have to wait until we're in the car, and far away from here.

'I packed our bags before I woke you. Can you just throw on your onesie over your pyjamas? You can sleep in the car. It's a long way home.'

She nods. 'Okay, I guess. Is Christian coming too?'

'No, he's going to stay here. No point this ruining his break too. He's asleep. I've left him a message.'

Still half asleep, Lexi climbs out of bed.

'We have to be quiet, though,' I whisper. 'I don't want to disturb Christian. He doesn't sleep well if he's woken up.'

In less than five minutes we're ready to leave. I grab the bags, and quietly we head into the living room, which is bathed in darkness.

I pull out my phone and switch on the torch, letting the light guide us to the door.

Lexi giggles. 'This is weird!' she says. 'It feels like we're sneaking around! Like burglars!'

At the door, I grab my bag and reach inside it for my keys. But they're not there.

'No!' I say, far too loudly.

'What's wrong?' Lexi asks.

Panic sets in and I tip the contents of my bag onto the floor, shining the light from my phone onto the pile. Tissues, my purse, phone charger, hand sanitiser. But no keys.

'Looking for these?'

Christian's voice booms into the room just as the light flicks on, enveloping us in its harsh yellow light.

I stare at him as he stands in the kitchen doorway dangling my keys in his hand.

Grabbing Lexi's arm, I rush to the front door and turn the handle. But as my instinct has already told me, it's locked.

I am too late to save us.

TWENTY-NINE
BEFORE

Emily gently lifts her mother's head and places the pillow beneath it. 'We'll get you better, Mum,' she whispers, as a tear splatters onto the duvet.

'I knew you couldn't do it,' her mum says, turning onto her side. 'It's not who you are.'

Emily lies down beside her mum and holds her, wishing she could extract all her pain. She'd take it all in herself if it would free her mum. 'But I'm here for you,' she says. She's not sure if that means anything, but she needs her mum to know she's not alone.

Her mother's eyes slowly flutter closed, and before long she's succumbed to sleep.

Emily shuts her eyes. The bedside lamp is still on, but if she moves now she might disturb her mum, and she wants her to have some peace.

Even if sleep won't come, she'll stay here all night. Because tomorrow everything will change.

. . .

At eight a.m., while her mum still sleeps, Emily creeps out of her mum's room. She's barely slept, but she is alert, ready for what today will bring.

Downstairs, she makes herself coffee and sits at the kitchen table, scrolling through the contacts on her phone to find the doctor's phone number. Her mum won't like this, but it needs to be done. She's not well and Emily doesn't want to turn up here one day to find her dead. Like she thought she'd find her last night.

The receptionist is kind and compassionate, and immediately puts her through to a doctor. Emily answers the doctor's questions and is told that her mum will get the help she needs, and that someone from the community mental health team will come and assess her.

'It's quite likely your mum will be taken to the Victoria Ward at Farnham Road hospital,' the doctor says. 'And I can assure you if that's the case, then she'll get all the care she needs. The staff are wonderful there.'

'Thank you,' Emily says, her voice cracking.

After she ends the call, with a plan of action now in place for her mum, Emily feels a heavy weight lifting from her.

Until she remembers Christian's words. And that she still has to explain her lie.

She sends him a message and waits. A simple *I'm sorry*. But her phone stays silent. She sends another. *I can explain*. And when half an hour passes with no reply, she knows she won't hear from him again.

It's for the best, that rational voice tells her. *He was no good for you. You know that, Emily. You've known it from the beginning. But you wouldn't heed your mum's warnings and now look what's happened.*

She switches off her phone and heads upstairs to help her mum get ready for the doctor's visit. Emily's got just a couple of hours to convince her that this will bring an end to the pain.

. . .

It's late evening by the time she drives Christian's car back to his flat. She has no idea if he's in – he's still not replying to her messages, and didn't answer when she tried to call. Driving down the motorway, it occurred to her that he might have reported his car stolen – just to hurt her – and that the police might be looking for it. And her.

She rings the bell, convincing herself that it will all be okay. She'll make Christian understand why she lied about her dad. All she was doing was protecting her mum. And surely, after the way he's loved her so intensely for almost two years, Christian won't give up on them so easily. *Walk away now. You've still got a chance.* But Emily doesn't listen to this voice in her head.

There's no answer. Emily steps back and peers up at his window. She gasps when she notices Christian standing there, watching her.

'Can you open the door?' she calls. 'I've got your car key.' She holds it up to prove she's giving it back.

He doesn't move, and instead watches her intently. 'Just post it through the letterbox.'

'No. Someone might take it. And I'm not leaving until you hear me out.' She plants herself down on his doorstep.

Seconds tick by until eventually the window opens and Christian leans out. 'Just give my key back and go, Emily. I don't want you here. I don't want to see you again.'

She stands and moves back so she can see him more clearly. 'I need to explain. Please, Christian.' She hates herself for begging, but she knows that this time she is the one at fault. 'I know I lied about my dad leaving us, and I'm sorry. Can you just let me in? I need to explain. We can't talk like this.'

He moves back from the window. 'It's over, Emily. It's all over. I don't even know you.'

The shock of his words renders her speechless. They've argued before – countless times, but he's never said anything like this.

'I'm sorry, Christian,' she says. 'I should have told you the truth about my dad. I understand why that's made you not trust me. It's just... it's what my mum's always told people.'

'You're sick, just get away from me.'

Emily ignores him. He's blowing this out of proportion. She has to make him see that. 'My mum just... she didn't want people to feel sorry for him. She wanted them to know what kind of man he really was.'

'I've heard enough,' Christian says. 'I don't need to listen to any more.'

'What does that mean?'

'It means you need to leave, Emily. Now. Or I'm calling the police.'

Once again, shock renders her silent. She can't comprehend what's happening, how everything has changed in an instant.

Walk away. Get as far away from him as you can, before he drags you under and you can't get out.

Acting on autopilot, as if she's outside of her body again, Emily posts his car key through the letterbox and turns away, heading towards the main road that will lead her home. She doesn't look up again, but somehow she knows he's still watching her.

'Well, this is a surprise. Didn't think we'd see you again.'

Kirsty stands at the door, making no move to let Emily in.

'Can I come in?' Emily looks past her, to the door of her room.

'You still live here, then?' Kirsty asks. 'I thought you'd packed up and gone for good.' She glances at Emily's bulging weekend bag and her eyes narrow. 'Didn't leave anything behind, did you?'

Walking over here, Emily had carefully planned what she'd say, yet getting the words out is harder than she's imagined. 'I'm sorry. You were both right. About Christian. I just didn't want to admit it.' Tears fall from her eyes, and she tries her best to stifle them.

The straight line of Kirsty's mouth curves slightly, softening her face. 'What's happened, then?'

Kirsty moves aside to let Emily in and closes the door.

'Is Erin here?' Emily asks.

'Yeah, in her room with Andre. I'll go and get her.'

Emily's about to call Kirsty back and explain that she doesn't want Andre listening to any of this, but quickly realises that she's not calling the shots right now.

While Kirsty fetches Erin, Emily goes to her room and dumps her bag inside. It feels cold in there. Unlived in. Even though she's only been gone for one night. *This is my home. It's all I've got now. It's not likely Mum will be able to live on her own any time soon.*

'I'm glad you're back,' Erin says, standing in the doorway, holding a mug. 'Come on then, what's happened? Has he hurt you?' Erin studies her closely.

'No. I'm okay. Where's Andre?'

'He says he's staying out of this,' Erin says.

Emily sits on her bed, her hands clasped together on her lap, while she waits for her roommates to settle on the floor.

The words she needs to set free are trapped in her throat, and it takes her a moment to begin. 'You were right about Christian,' she manages to say. 'I know that now.'

'Has he done something to you?' Erin asks. 'Because—'

'No, no, he hasn't hurt me or anything. It's just... after what you both said, it was like a wake-up call for me. I... began to realise that I'm in a toxic relationship.' Saying this aloud doesn't make her feel better. She feels hopeless, like it's her fault this happened. 'I know that makes me... weak or something.'

'No, it does not!' Kirsty says, too loudly. 'This is his fault, not yours.'

'But I let him do this to me.'

'No, you didn't,' Erin insists. 'People like Christian are clever. They're charming. Funny. They know how to make you feel like you're the most important thing in the world.'

'And then everything changes,' Emily adds. 'I see it so clearly now.'

For the next half hour, Emily tells them everything she's kept to herself over the past two years. How she was made to question her own sanity, and that she couldn't see the mind games that were being played.

'He made me feel like the worst girlfriend,' she explains, fighting back tears. 'Everything was always my fault. And he thought I was ashamed of him, but I just didn't want my mum to have to worry about me having a boyfriend. Things are... hard enough for her.'

Erin gets up and sits by her on the bed, putting her arm across Emily's shoulder. 'I really wish you'd talked to us about this before. Or to anyone. We *knew* something wasn't right. He's just so clingy and—'

'Controlling,' Kirsty adds.

'I know. I can see it now.'

'Please, Emily – you have to stay away from him,' Erin says. 'You'll find someone else. You're kind and intelligent – you can have your pick of anyone. Anyone decent. You don't have to settle for manipulators like Christian.'

'She's right,' Kirsty says.

'I won't go near him again,' Emily says. 'Besides, he wouldn't even let me in his flat just now, so I'm taking that as a sign from the universe.'

'It's part of his game,' Erin says. 'Later he'll be bombarding you with text messages. But you have to just ignore him.'

'It won't be easy,' Kirsty warns. 'Once people like that are under your skin, it's like a virus you have to fight until it goes away and finds some other body to infest.'

Despite the sharp jolt of pain in her stomach, Emily manages to smile. Friendship is all she needs.

Despite tiredness wreaking havoc on her body, Emily can't sleep for a second night. Fear and anger intermingle and clasp hold of her. If she didn't have an important lecture this morning, she wouldn't bother dragging herself out of bed. But she refuses to let Christian ruin her future.

She walks on autopilot down the corridors, heading to her lecture hall, wondering if she'll be able to concentrate. She can't fail now – she's worked hard to get through these two years. Forcing her eyes from the floor, Emily immediately notices fur-coat girl talking animatedly to another girl outside the library.

Even without that fur coat, Emily recognises her instantly by the beautiful spiral curls that float around her shoulders. How is it that she's never seen her at the university before? And now – when things with Christian have reached crisis point – there she is. She's wearing a deep red midi dress, and Emily feels a pang of envy at how effortlessly glamorous she looks.

Unbidden, her brain conjures up an image of Christian kissing this girl. She forces it away. She's not going to be a victim of that.

Emily gives no thought to what she does next; she simply acts on instinct, as if something is propelling her to speak. 'Excuse me? Can I talk to you a second?' Her tone is polite and respectful – whatever has happened between her and Christian, it's not this girl's fault.

Fur-coat girl turns and frowns, but continues chewing her gum as she stares at Emily, waiting for her to speak.

Emily glances at the other girl. 'Alone, please? If you don't mind? It's really important.'

The other girl shrugs, tells Fur Coat she'll see her later, and walks down the corridor.

'What's going on?' Fur Coat asks. 'Do I know you?'

The girl is even prettier close up, but Emily knows that doesn't mean anything. Not when she could have the personality of a slab of cheese. 'Not really,' Emily begins. 'But I think you know my boyfriend. Christian. I mean, he's actually my ex-boyfriend.'

Fur Coat rolls her eyes. 'Is that right? What's he done now?'

'I... um... can I ask your name?' Emily doesn't want to keep calling her fur-coat girl.

'Jada.' The sound of her chewing gum is beginning to irritate Emily. 'So what's this about?' Jada asks, glancing at her phone. 'I have a lecture to get to in a few minutes. Can't be late again.'

Emily's already late for her own, but this is too important to walk away from. Something has brought the two of them to this corridor at the same time this morning.

'Jada, I just need to know if he did to you what he's done to me.'

Jada stares at her, opening and closing her mouth several times before she finally speaks. 'I don't know exactly what you want me to say – but you should stay away from him.'

'I know. You're right. I just—'

'Look, I really have to go. But he's never going to change. You do get that, don't you? Do me a favour, won't you?'

Emily nods, even though she has no idea what she's agreeing to.

'Tell him he left his watch at my place last night. And I don't have time to track him down and give it back.'

Jada stalks off down the corridor, leaving her words, so casually delivered, to sink into Emily's head and explode like a bomb.

THIRTY

NOW

I stare at Christian – I'm not prepared for this day of reckoning. I had everything planned; we were getting away from him. Instinctively, I reach for Lexi's hand and pull her closer to me.

'What's going on?' she asks, looking from me to Christian. I'm not sure which one of us she's addressing. If it's me, I don't know how to answer, and if it's Christian, his response will end everything.

'We need to leave,' I say. 'There's been a flood at our house and we need to get home right now.'

Christian seems to ponder this, and just for a second I allow myself to believe this will be okay. That it's not time yet.

'And you expect me to believe that?' he says. 'It's just more lies, isn't it, Emily?'

Lexi looks up at me, frowning. 'What does he mean? Why is he saying that? What's going on? I don't like it.'

I grip her hand. 'You're frightening her,' I say to Christian. 'Just stop. We need to go. Like I said: the house—'

'It's too late for that, isn't it?' Christian steps towards us. 'Lexi and Jeremy deserve to know the truth. Enough of the lies. Don't you see how destructive they are?'

Lexi pulls at my hand. 'I'm scared. What's he talking about?'

I try to convince Lexi that it will be okay – that I will deal with this, but the fear remains in her eyes. 'You don't have to do this,' I say to Christian. 'Let me just take Lexi home and then we can deal with this on our own.'

Christian steps forward again. 'This isn't what I planned.' He leans down to Lexi. 'I'm sorry. This wasn't the way it was meant to be, but it's better you know the truth.'

Heavy sobs cause Lexi's body to jerk. 'I'm scared.' Her voice is a whimper.

Christian straightens and moves closer to me. 'Emily's been lying to you and your dad. The whole time you've known her. She isn't the person you think she is.'

'Stop it!' Lexi cries. 'You're lying!' She turns to me. 'Why is he doing this?'

I pull her away from him. 'He's not well, Lexi. Sometimes people's heads get sick and they... they don't know what they're saying or doing.' I want to tell her my concerns about Tia, but I can't do that to Lexi. It's not the right time.

'Like my grandad?' It takes me a moment to realise she's talking about Tia's father, who has Alzheimer's.

I nod. 'Yes. A bit like that.'

'Stop with the lies,' Christian says. 'I'm not sick, Lexi. In fact, if anyone in this place is disturbed, it's Emily.'

'She's not!' Lexi flies at him and rams her small fists into his chest. 'Stop talking about her!'

I pull her back, wrapping her in my arms as she continues sobbing. Lexi defending me like this makes me proud and sad all at once. It shouldn't have to be this way.

Christian reaches into his pocket, and for a second I imagine he has a knife. But when his hand emerges it's holding the bottle of sleeping pills I bought from the shop in Cleator Moor. 'You see these?' he says. 'Emily planned to put them in my drink last night. If I hadn't realised she'd do something like this I wouldn't be standing here right now.'

'No!' Lexi says. 'Emily wouldn't—'

'And at the river today. She was about to push me in but I stopped her. She knows I can't swim.'

Lexi turns to me, and for a fraction of a second I catch the glimmer of doubt in her eyes. She shakes her head but doesn't speak. 'No,' she repeats. But this time her words are tentative, softer. Loaded with uncertainty.

'Don't listen to him, Lexi. Don't believe a single word that comes from his mouth.'

But Christian will not give up until he's broken Lexi down.

'No one is leaving this house until the truth is out,' he says. 'And clearly Lexi is having trouble believing me. You need to tell her, Emily. Everything. Don't make it come from me.' He moves away from us, closer to the sofa.

'Do you remember what I told you?' he says to me. 'On your wedding day? I've got all the evidence I need to get the police investigating. So why don't you do the right thing for once and tell your daughter the truth?'

I remain silent. There will be a way out of this for me and Lexi – there has to be. I just need to buy more time.

'Okay, have it your way.' Christian reaches into his back pocket and pulls out a knife. Lexi screams and cowers against me.

Holding up the knife, he casually sits on the arm of the sofa. 'Don't be afraid, Lexi. This is just for my protection. I can't trust Emily. Right now, she'll be working out how she can get rid of me, and I can't take the chance she'll be successful this time.'

Lexi's sobs get louder, and I'm crippled with fear and panic. Even if we make it out of here alive, she will forever be scarred by this.

'Sit over there,' Christian commands, pointing the knife at

the other sofa. 'I need to see you. To make sure you don't try anything.'

'We'll be okay,' I lean into Lexi's ear and whisper. 'I promise.'

'Stop!' Christian shouts. 'If you've got anything to say then I need to hear it.' He stands and walks over to me. 'I need your phone.'

I back away from him. 'No!'

He points the knife millimetres from my neck, causing Lexi to shriek again. 'Hand it to me, now.' The cool blade of the knife presses against my skin.

'Okay.' I edge backwards and slide my phone from my pocket.

Christian snatches it and switches it off before slipping it in his own pocket. 'Just so you know, all the windows and doors are locked. There's no point even trying them. You've probably already gathered that.'

Lexi's sobs have turned to whimpers now, and I hold her close, trying my best to offer silent comfort.

I will get us out of this. It's my fault; I brought him into our lives so it's up to me to fix it.

'I'm thirsty,' she says. 'Please can I have some water?' It's me she's addressing – she refuses to look in Christian's direction.

I turn to him. 'Lexi needs water. And she's tired. She needs to go to bed. I can stay in here with you, but please let her rest.'

It takes him a moment to answer. 'You'll both stay in here. You can sleep on the sofa, Lexi. And when I need to leave the room, I've got these.' He reaches behind the sofa.

'What's he doing?' Lexi asks.

But before I can answer Christian lifts up some heavy, thick ropes. 'Just to make sure you can't go anywhere,' he says.

We both protest and struggle, but he flashes the knife and we acquiesce. He binds our hands and feet, and uttering an apology to Lexi, he goes into the kitchen.

'Lexi, listen to me,' I whisper. 'Please don't worry. I'm going to get us out of here, okay? I promise you. I'll stop him doing this to us.'

She stares at me but doesn't answer.

'You just have to trust me. Christian is very, very sick. He doesn't know what he's doing. But we'll get out of here. I just need time to work out what to do.'

'I thought he was your friend,' she says. 'Why would he do this to you?'

'I thought he was my friend too. But it turns out he's not after all. His illness has taken over so he doesn't even remember that we were friends.'

Lexi screws up her face. 'But what does he want you to tell me? Why does he keep going on about that?'

I swallow the huge lump in my throat. 'I don't know what he's talking about. It doesn't make any sense. But please don't worry about that. I just need you to rest now – try and sleep. He won't do anything to you. It's me he wants to hurt.' All I can do is hope this is true. But Christian will have learnt by now that losing Lexi would be the worst thing that could happen to me.

Lexi rests her head on my shoulder and lifts her feet. 'This hurts,' she cries, tugging at the rope. 'He's done it so tight.'

'It won't be for long, I promise.'

Christian comes back with a glass of water for Lexi. There's a straw sticking out of it; he's thought of everything. 'I've got you a biscuit too,' he says. 'Maybe you're hungry?'

Lexi snatches the biscuit and lets it fall to the floor.

'Have it your way,' he says, placing the glass on the coffee table. 'Drink up and then I need you both in Emily's room. I'll be locking the door, but there's a bed and bathroom in there so you'll be fine until morning. And hopefully by then Emily will have come to her senses.'

He ushers us off the sofa and we have no choice but to

comply. Even though my hands are bound, I reach for Lexi's hand and hope it's enough to reassure her that I'll keep my promise to get us out of here.

The bedroom door clicks shut behind us, and the turn of the key in the lock sounds as loud as thunder.

THIRTY-ONE

NOW

I feel as though I've slept with my eyes open, my bound arms placed protectively around Lexi as she drifts restlessly in and out of sleep. She called out for me in the night. Not for Jeremy, as she normally would, but for me.

Soft morning light floats through the windows, but without my phone I have no idea what time it is. All I know is that we're stuck in this room until Christian lets us out. I long for a shower, but Christian has our bags so without clean clothes there's little point.

Jeremy will be in the sky by now – uncontactable for at least eight more hours. That means it will be at least nine or ten hours before he'll realise something is wrong. Perhaps Christian is sending him messages from my phone. Pretending to be me so that Jeremy doesn't suspect anything. Or worse, telling him the truth about everything.

Regardless, it will be too late unless I act fast.

Slowly pulling my arms from Lexi without disturbing her, I slide off the bed and shuffle to the window. Just as Christian warned us – it's locked. So too is the bedroom door. I lean against it and listen for any sign of him; there's nothing but silence. He might not even be in the house. He's done this to me before – and disappeared for hours – so there's no telling what he'll do.

Smashing the window isn't an option – there's nothing in here that would break the glass, which appears to be double or triple glazed. This is a newly refurbished property, with no skimping on security. The window in the en suite is too small and high up for either of us to climb through. And even if we could open it, we'd never get up to it with our hands and feet tied.

I sit on the edge of the bed and try to stifle the panic that's threatening to overwhelm me.

Focus on what you can do.

There is something that might work, but I'll need Lexi's help to pull it off.

She begins to stir and slowly opens her eyes. 'Emily,' she says, almost cheerfully. And then her smile disappears when she tries to stretch and realises her hands are still bound. It all comes flooding back. 'Can't we go home yet?' There is already a fresh tear on her cheek.

'Soon, I promise. We need to get away from Christian, and I've had an idea.'

She pulls herself up and hugs her knees to her chest. 'But he's locked us in! We can't get out! And these ropes are hurting.'

I tell Lexi to listen carefully, and then I explain my plan. It takes some convincing, but eventually I persuade her that we have no choice.

When I'm sure she's ready, I bang on the bedroom door and shout for Christian. Lexi joins me, and we both pound on the door until he finally orders us to stop.

He opens the door, wearing clean clothes and looking refreshed; it's clear he's had a better night than us. 'Are you ready to talk?' he asks. 'Ready to tell Lexi the truth about who you are?'

'Can we just eat first? Please. Lexi's starving, and I barely ate a thing yesterday.'

'My heart bleeds,' Christian says. 'Come on, then. But I'm not untying you. You'll have to manage like that. Given the circumstances, though, I think that's the least of your worries.'

In the kitchen, Christian puts bowls and cereal out for us, while we sit helplessly waiting for him.

Just go with it. It's not for long.

With our shackles limiting our movements, breakfast is a slow affair. I don't want mine, but I force myself to eat to give my body fuel for what lies ahead. I greedily gulp water, as if my life depends on it. Lexi too. As young as she is, she fully understands the urgency of our situation, and what she must do.

Christian sits on the sofa and watches us, clutching the knife in his hand. His foot continuously taps the floor; he's nervous. Despite everything, he doesn't want to do this. He knows there will be no going back once he's done it. But that only terrifies me more: he's more likely to act even more irrationally when he's anxious.

'This is kidnapping,' I say. 'You'll go to prison for it. But if you let us go, we won't say anything, will we, Lexi?'

She shakes her head.

'I'll take my chances,' he says.

Lexi finishes her food and glances at me, and I give her the smallest nod. 'I need to use the toilet,' she says, standing. 'I'm desperate.'

'Sorry, but I'm not going to untie you,' Christian says. 'I'm sure you can manage.'

He leans forward to watch her as she heads through the living room, and I see her hesitate when she gets closer to the bathroom. I long to shout out that she can do this, to spur her on. I slowly move into the sitting room, hoping that being closer to her will give her the confidence she'll need to pull this off.

It happens quickly, almost taking me by surprise even

though I know what to expect. Lexi collapses on the floor, her body violently shaking and twitching.

Christian jumps up. 'What the?' He rushes over to her, but somehow I beat him to it.

'Don't touch her!' I shout. 'She's having a fit.'

'What?' There is panic in his voice, and this is just what we need.

'She has epilepsy,' I say, crouching down beside her and stroking her head. 'It's really bad for Lexi. We need to get her to a hospital now.' I hold my breath and pray that he has no experience of these kinds of seizures.

'No,' he says. 'It will pass. You don't have to go to hospital.'

'Usually, but not in Lexi's case. Whenever this happens she needs medical care.'

'You're lying. We're not calling an ambulance.'

'She'll die, Christian! We have to get her to a hospital now!' I'm taking a gamble here – I still don't know what he's planning to do about Lexi, but I'm hoping she's never been part of his plan to destroy my life.

He doesn't move, but keeps staring at Lexi, who's body has turned stiff, while her eyes stare blankly at the ceiling. She is playing her role to perfection.

'Christian!' I urge. 'If you won't call an ambulance, then please, I'm begging you – drive her to the hospital. I think the closest one is West Cumberland Hospital. You have to hurry! You can leave me here and lock me in. But please, get her to the hospital!'

He stares at me for so long that I'm convinced he won't agree. Then he springs into action. 'You're staying here,' he says.

'You need to untie her,' I plead with him. 'Quick!'

He hesitates, as if wrestling with himself. 'Get over there,' he demands, pointing to the sofa.

I do as he asks, and while he's preoccupied with untying

Lexi, I slide the knife from under my sleeve that he thinks still lies hidden behind the sofa cushion.

When Lexi's wrists and ankles are free, he unlocks the door before going back to pick her up.

Lexi jumps up and thrusts her foot into his groin with a force I wouldn't have thought possible from a ten-year-old. He doubles over, and she flies past him straight through the door.

I lunge at Christian with the knife, plunging the blade into his leg as deeply as my bound hands will allow. His scream is deafening. Recoiling in horror, I watch as he sinks to the floor, the bright red patch spreading across his jeans.

Aware that I only have a few seconds, I use the knife to saw through the ropes at my legs and run for the door, still clutching the knife.

Outside, I see Lexi up ahead, running in the same direction we drove yesterday. It's hard to gather speed when I can't use my arms to give me momentum, but I can't risk stopping to cut the ropes binding my wrists.

I look behind me, and as I've expected, Christian is coming for us, despite the injury I've inflicted on him. We've slowed him down at least – and now we have a chance.

Lexi turns around and runs towards me. 'Emily!' she screams.

'No, keep running. We have to keep going.' I'm struggling for breath, but there is no way I'll stop now that we have a head start.

'Which way?' Lexi asks. 'I don't know which way to go!'

'Over there!' I point to the right. 'Not the way we went yesterday. He might expect us to stick to the path we know. We need to head towards that cliff. He'll struggle to get up there.'

'But it's too rocky!' Lexi protests. And she's right; I don't even know how far up we'll be able to go.

I glance behind again, and somehow he's gaining on us. 'Quick,' I urge. 'Run faster.'

We hurtle along the unfamiliar path, fuelled by adrenalin and fear. The way ahead inclines steeply, and the gap between us and Christian lessens, but still we continue pushing forward. His injury *must* be taking its toll – I plunged the knife in deep.

But he's like a machine, and is only metres behind us now.

Our efforts are all in vain, and by the time we reach the top of the rocky hill, somehow Christian has caught up with us, and grabs Lexi under her arms, pulling her backwards.

'Emily!' she screams.

'Let her go!' I shout.

'I'm not the one she needs protecting from.' He pants, struggling for breath, even though I'm sure he is far fitter than I am. 'She's not going to tell you the truth, Lexi, so it's down to me.'

Once again, Christian has the upper hand.

The difference is that I am the one holding the knife.

THIRTY-TWO

BEFORE

The stalking has been going on for months now. It took Emily by surprise at first, even though the signs that things would escalate were clearly there. Abuse. She hates that word – so harsh. So black and white. despite everything that had already taken place. You never know what people are capable of. She hasn't breathed a word of it to Erin and Kirsty, and she's begun to shut herself off from them, even though they'd shown her such compassion when she opened up to them about Christian.

Her mum is in a home now, a safe place, and visiting her is the only respite Emily gets. Somewhere Christian can't touch. She'll have to think about selling the house soon. It doesn't look likely that her mum will be able to live on her own again. Not when she's a risk to herself.

'Are you okay? You seem... spaced out.'

Niko's voice brings Emily back to this moment, and she forces herself to smile. As much as she likes him, it's difficult being here with him. After Christian. 'I'm fine,' she assures him. 'Thanks for cooking for me.'

'I beg to differ.' Niko smiles. 'But it's okay if you don't want to talk about it. I'm here if you do, though.'

'I know,' she says, spearing pasta with her fork. And she does know this. Niko is the antithesis of Christian. Kind. Solid. Dependable.

'As long as it's not my food.' He laughs.

Emily looks at him. He always tries so hard; he wants her to like him. Maybe if she opened up to him, there would be a chance for them, and she wouldn't repeat the mistakes she made with Christian.

'I was in a... a difficult relationship,' she begins. Everything falls silent, and she stares at her hands. Why is she telling him this now? What could it possibly achieve?

'I'm sorry... that's awful. He sounds like a jerk you're well shot of.'

'I don't mean physically abusive,' Emily explains. 'But mentally.' She looks up at Niko, and isn't surprised to see a frown on his face. People easily understand physical abuse, but the complexity of emotional abuse is hard to get to grips with.

'It's nearly destroyed me. But here I am.' She forces a laugh.

'You don't have to talk about it if it's too difficult,' Niko assures her. 'I'm sorry if I've pushed.'

Emily wonders if he's saying this as a get-out clause – perhaps she is too much to deal with so he wants to brush it under the carpet. 'No, I want to tell you,' she says. 'The more people who know, the easier it is to talk about, and the less he can hurt me.' This should be how it goes in theory.

Niko stands up and gets a bottle of wine from the cupboard. 'I'm not really into wine,' he says. 'But people keep buying it for me so now I have a stash in the house. Don't tell my mum, but these are her Christmas and birthday presents for the next two years.' He laughs. 'Anyway, I think you could do with a glass.'

She doesn't know what exactly she needs, but she nods. 'Thank you.' She's hoping what she needs is simply to be here with Niko in his cosy home.

He hands her a glass. 'I get the feeling you need to talk,' he says. 'And I've been told I'm a good listener. Even though I never shut up.'

'A walking contradiction.' Emily laughs. 'Can we sit on the sofa?'

For hours they sit and talk, while Emily puts Niko's listening skills to the test. She tells him everything about her toxic relationship. All the harm it's caused. His eyes widen when she mentions the stalking.

'It doesn't make sense,' he says. 'He's the one who turned all cold on you, yet he won't leave you alone. It sounds like he just doesn't want anyone else to be with you.'

The wine is going to Emily's head, making everything swirl around, as if she's looking through a kaleidoscope. She's sure that if she stood up now she'd fall back down.

'Do *you* understand why I lied about my mum? All I was trying to do was protect her.'

'Course, I get it. It's family business, anyway – he should have respected that.' Niko pours more wine into their glasses. 'This wine stuff's not too bad after all,' he says. He takes her hand. 'I'm not like him,' he says. 'I hope you can see that.'

'What?' Her head feels fuzzy and his words float over her, drifting too far away to reach.

'That I'm different,' Niko explains. 'Not like other guys. You can trust me, Emily. What you see is what you get with me. I swear.'

Her head spins and she laughs.

Niko doesn't seem offended, and carries on talking. 'I really like you. *Really* like you.' He strokes her arm.

Emily laughs again. It feels quite nice, but all she can think about is Christian. She wonders what he's doing now. Where he is.

'Can I kiss you?' Niko asks. But he doesn't give her a chance to answer, and is moving towards her before she can work out what's happening.

His mouth presses against hers. And it feels just like Christian's. Confusion spreads around her. Who is this she's with? She wants to laugh and cry at the same time. And then darkness descends on her, filling her mind with a swirling fog. She can't breathe. She needs it to stop. It has to stop.

She pulls away, reaching for the bottle of wine on the table. Lifting it up, she smashes it into Niko's face. And then there is an explosion of wine, and blood, and other stuff she can't describe.

Then there is silence.

Recoiling in horror, Emily grabs her phone and calls the only person who can help her.

THIRTY-THREE

NOW

'Stop!' I shout at Christian. 'Keep Lexi out of this. This is between you and me.'

Ignoring me, he keeps hold of her. 'This has everything to do with you, Lexi,' he says. 'Because Emily isn't fit to be a parent to you. And if your dad knew... I should have told him when he was here. I made a mistake.'

Lexi wails and holds out her arms to me. But I don't dare move forward. Christian and Lexi are right near the edge, and there's at least a hundred-foot drop over the other side. 'Don't move, Lexi. Just stay still.'

'She doesn't deserve to be any kind of mother to you,' Christian insists.

At these words, my legs start to buckle. Of everything I've done in my life, being a parent to Lexi is what I'm most proud of.

'Tia is a good person, Lexi,' he continues, edging backwards. 'She's your mum. Not that woman standing there.' He jabs his finger towards me. 'You need to live with Tia. Get as far away from Emily as possible. And when your dad comes back, that's what he'll want too. He's already getting a glimpse of the mountain of lies Emily is capable of telling.' He glares at me. 'Did you notice that, Emily? How mistrustful he is becoming?'

I ignore him, while my brain scrambles to find a way out of this. A way to get Lexi away from him.

Lexi's tears flow down her face, and I move towards Christian, brandishing the knife.

For a second I see the flicker of fear in his eyes. 'I wish I could say she wouldn't use that on me – but I know for a fact she would. Emily knows how it feels to end someone's life. To play God. Nothing would stop her doing the same to me. Clearly it's something she's comfortable with.' Although he's aiming his words at Lexi, he looks directly at me.

'Stop it!' Lexi shrieks. 'Stop saying stuff like that!' Her eyes plead with me to do something.

I turn to Christian. 'You need help, Christian. We can forget all of this if you'll just let us go. Please. Just let us go and walk away. You'll never hear from us, or the police. I promise you.'

'Nice try,' he says.

And now I have no choice. 'Where's Tia? You know, don't you? The police are looking for her.'

Lexi's eyes widen. 'What? Mum?'

I nod. I have no choice but to tell Lexi now. 'Christian was the last person to see her. And now she's missing. I think he's...' I can't bring myself to complete the thought. I look around, desperate to spot someone out on a hike. But we're alone up here.

Christian laughs, a sound so incongruous in the midst of our terror that for a second I question whether this is really happening. 'I didn't do anything to Tia,' he says. 'I'm not the one who hurts people. Lexi, I promise you.'

'Where is she?' I demand. 'What have you done with her?'

Lexi screams and tries to wriggle free, and he tightens his grip. 'Lexi, your mum is right now living it up on a holiday I treated her to. Gran Canaria. Her choice.' He shrugs. 'She works so hard, and all people can do is focus on her mistakes. She hasn't had things easy in life so I thought she deserved a break.' He stares at me. 'Especially when I explained that I could never have a relationship with her. Not with our history. It wouldn't be fair to her. Not when my past is so heavily entwined with yours.'

I let his words sink in. 'No. You're lying. I don't believe you. Tia would have told Lexi she was going away.'

'Usually, but this was all last-minute. She had to rush to get packed. And she'll be back before she's meant to see Lexi again. I told her I'd let Jeremy know.'

I shake my head. 'No. Stop lying!'

With one arm still holding Lexi, he reaches for his phone. 'Then this photo should be proof enough.' He holds out the phone and shows me Tia, wearing a turquoise bikini and sipping a fruit smoothie by a swimming pool.

I glance at Lexi. 'He's lying. It's an old photo she must have sent you.'

He shows it to Lexi. 'What does that date say?'

She takes a second to take it in. 'It's... today,' Lexi says, between her sobs.

'Then you need to listen to me,' Christian says. 'Emily is a murderer. She—'

'No!' Lexi screams again.

And in that moment, I see what's about to happen before it plays out. Lexi kicks back, her foot smashing into Christian's injured leg and sending him flying backwards. Instinctively, I reach out for him, grabbing hold of his T-shirt. The knife flies from my hand, and hurtles down the cliff.

Christian will be next if I don't help him.

But I struggle to maintain my grip on his T-shirt and he topples over the side. Screaming out, I grab hold of him again, yanking him up with every shred of strength I can muster. 'You need to help me!' I shout. 'I can't hold you for much longer. Try and pull yourself up.'

His eyes are wide with terror as he scrambles to get purchase with his legs. 'Don't let me fall!' he begs. 'Please don't let me fall.'

There is no hesitation in my answer; I know what I have to do. 'I won't,' I say, praying I can keep hold of him. 'I won't let you fall.'

Time seems to stand still as I manage to pull Christian up enough for him to haul himself over. We both lie on the ground, spent, while Lexi's uncontrollable sobbing is the soundtrack playing around us.

Christian stares at me, as if he can't quite believe what's happened. Minutes pass before he speaks. 'You could have let me fall,' he pants.

I can't answer for a moment – all my energy has been sucked away. Now I have nothing left to give. 'No,' I somehow manage to say. 'I couldn't have.'

Lexi flings her arms around me. Her whole body is shaking, and I know that today will have scarred her for the rest of her life.

She nearly killed someone. And it's all my fault.

Christian is the first to move, slowly rising and holding out his hands to Lexi and me. Lexi shrinks back, refusing to take it.

'It's okay, Lexi. It's all over.'

Her face crinkles. 'I don't understand.'

'We need to get back to the house, then get home,' I say. I glance at Christian, wondering if he will object, but all I see on his face is relief.

But I know for me, this is only the beginning.

I help Lexi up myself, and we trudge back to the house, following Christian as he limps slowly along the stony path, leaving a trail of blood behind him.

'What's happening?' Lexi asks. 'I don't understand.' She bursts into tears again.

'Neither do I,' I say, taking her hand. 'But I think... we might be okay now.'

At least Lexi will.

'But... but Christian is sick. He needs help.'

There are two figures standing outside the cottage. Strange silhouettes I can't place. At first I think one of them must be Jeremy, and still clutching Lexi's hand, I begin to sprint. But quickly I realise the shape of both of them is all wrong.

The police, then. Christian must have called them before he came after us. Perhaps he'd planned that all along. It's okay, though. I am ready to accept what I've done.

As we get closer, the man and a woman come into focus, both of them familiar.

'Grandma!' Lexi cries, and she lets go of my hand and runs towards Pam. As fast as she'd run from Christian earlier. And then I realise it's Tyler standing next to her. The combination of them, in a place neither of them should be, is so at odds with everything that fear grips hold of me.

'What's happening?' I call to Christian.

He turns around, his eyes widening. 'I have no idea. But this isn't good.'

'What the hell's going on?' Tyler demands, marching up to us.

It's not clear whether he's addressing me or Christian, but it no longer matters.

'Emily isn't your girlfriend! What the hell is this?'

'I can explain everything,' Christian says. 'But not here. Not in front of Lexi. She's been through enough already.'

This time I hold my tongue, and don't point out that he's the one who has put her through this trauma, because I am just as responsible as he is. And now, seeing how Lexi clings to Pam, everything comes to me with clarity. I know exactly what I have to do.

'Who are you?' Pam asks, turning to me. 'You married my son and you've been caring for my granddaughter! We don't even know who you really are!' She turns away from me, as if she can't bear to look at me.

Facing Christian, she demands to know what's going on, but he doesn't answer.

'How did you find us?' I ask.

'You need to answer questions, not ask them!' Tyler shouts.

Pam strokes Lexi's hair as she crumples in her arms. She glares at me. 'I didn't trust you for one second after Christian told me you had *an unbreakable* bond, so I started to follow you. Whenever I could. You drove all the way to Reading and I've never heard you or Jeremy mention knowing anyone who lives there. After you left, this young man came out and drove off. I thought you were having an affair. It took me a while to track him down but I managed to find him. It didn't take long for us to realise that you've been lying to us all. You need to start talking right now, or we'll call the police.'

'I forced Emily to lie,' Christian begins. 'It was all down to me.' He turns to Pam. 'Please can you take Lexi somewhere so I can speak to Tyler alone?'

Pam frowns, but when Lexi begins to cry again, she agrees. 'I'm taking my granddaughter home.' She turns to me. 'I'll sort it out with Jeremy when he gets back, but for now I'm not letting Lexi out of my sight. I don't know what's happened out here, but I know it's messed up. I've never seen Lexi like this.'

'I think that's for the best,' Christian agrees. 'Tyler and I have a lot of talking to do. And it's way overdue.' He glances at me, passing on a silent message I have no idea how to decipher.

We all watch as Pam drives Lexi away, neither of them

saying goodbye to any of us, and I try to numb the crushing pain in my chest.

Christian leads Tyler into the cottage, and I follow. I have no idea if I should stick around, but I know everything has changed. And I am becoming untethered from it all.

Inside, the two brothers sit at opposite ends of the sofa, while I hover by the door.

'Is someone going to start talking?' Tyler demands, his eyes darting between me and Christian.

My judgement day is finally here.

THIRTY-FOUR

BEFORE

Rain spatters down on Emily as she sits on the pavement outside Niko's flat. But she doesn't care. Doesn't even feel it on her skin. People saunter past and stare at her briefly – take in her dishevelled appearance – but then walk on by, faster, without a second thought. To them, she's someone to avoid. And this is London, where people try not to notice anything. She's wearing a black jumper – so the red wine and blood won't stand out. Only Emily knows it's there.

Time moves in slow motion as she waits to see if he'll come. She almost wishes he wouldn't, and that time would freeze so she won't have to face what she's done. It would be as if it never happened.

When she eventually hears footsteps and a shadow falls right by her feet, she's too afraid to look up. She stares at his clean white trainers that now have a layer of dirt around the edges.

'What the hell have you done?'

It's Christian's voice, familiar and comforting despite everything.

'You came.'

'I shouldn't have. I don't know why I have. This is nothing to do with me. What the hell have you done?' he repeats. He is angry. She can understand that. 'I don't know why I'm here,' he says, more to himself than to Emily. He's clearly in distress.

Because he loves me. Despite everything, that must be it.

Perhaps Christian's reason for being here doesn't matter. He has come when she's needed him the most, erasing everything he's ever done.

'Where?' he asks, nodding towards the block of flats, where the main door is still open. There's no security system here. It's a free-for-all.

'Flat seven,' she says quietly.

He grabs her and pulls her off the step. The smell of his Fahrenheit is overpowering this evening. 'Tell me what happened!' he yells.

Emily shivers. She's been asking herself this, and the truth is she doesn't know how to explain it. 'I don't know. I panicked. He was... he was... kissing me. And I... I wanted it to stop.'

'So he forced himself on you? It was self-defence?'

She shrugs. The truth is, she just lost it. Because he wasn't Christian? If that's the case, how is she supposed to explain that?

'Jesus, Emily.' Christian paces up and down the path, shaking his head. 'I can't do this. I'm out of here.'

'Please, Christian,' she begs, and her tears mingle with the rain that's falling faster now.

'Fuck!' Christian says, crushing his temples with his hands. 'Stay here. I'll go in and check.'

Emily's not about to argue. She can't set foot in that flat again. Niko is dead because of her – and he didn't do anything to deserve this. There will be no future for her now. She's still got another year of her degree left. And she has lied to Christian. Again. Niko wasn't forcing her – Emily just needed him to stop. Why?

Because he wasn't Christian.

When he disappears inside, Emily sits back down on the doorstep and rests her chin on her knees.

It feels like hours pass before Christian comes back. Time has stopped making sense. It's meaningless now.

'Is he...?' Emily asks, turning round and peering up at him.

Christian nods. 'You need to come inside and help me. Now.'

'No... I can't.'

'Emily, this is your mess to clear up. I shouldn't even be here. Come in now and deal with it.' He grabs her hand and yanks her inside. Not too roughly, though. Just with authority. And now, she has shrunk to the size of a pea.

He has to drag her right to the door of Niko's flat, and without warning, she throws up all over Niko's blue doormat.

Christian ignores it, pulling her inside and shutting the door. 'Come on!' he shouts. 'You need to see this, Emily. Face the consequences of your actions.'

Emily closes her eyes as he leads her into the living room, and when he stops and lets go of her hand, he pushes her back so she stumbles onto the sofa. 'Open your eyes and look!'

Slowly she does as he demands, because what choice does she have?

And when she takes in the image of Niko sitting on the sofa, holding a towel against his split head, Emily realises that this is the end of everything.

'You left me for dead!' Niko shouts, standing up and coming towards her. 'You bitch! What kind of a monster are you?'

Emily shrinks back and glances at Christian, who makes no move to stop Niko. She was right in thinking Christian had been taking too long in here.

'Christian's told me everything,' Niko says, his face too close to hers. 'You're one sick bitch. You didn't even call an ambulance.' He shoves her backwards, and she bangs her hip on the bookcase. Despite the thud, the pain doesn't register.

'I... I didn't mean to hurt you. I'm sorry. I panicked... because of everything *he's* done to me. He made me this way.' She gestures towards Christian. 'I told you all about it earlier,' Emily says, but she's no longer even sure it was today that she told Niko. Seconds, minutes and hours all blur into one, ceasing to mean anything.

Niko shakes his head. 'You're a liar. He's shown me the messages. I've seen the mountain of texts you send him every day. It's sick. He's kept them all. Evidence to use against you.'

Emily frowns. 'No. You've got it wrong. Christian—'

'It's not Christian who's the stalker – it's you!'

When she doesn't reply, Niko continues. 'He's told me everything. About how you control and manipulate him. He's got bruises from where you've thrown things at him. He's terrified of you! And with good reason too.'

Emily sinks to the floor. The last two years flash before her in a series of images: Christian cowering on the floor, begging her to stop. The pain on his face when she'd turn up unexpectedly whenever he was going out without her. And then more recently, when she'd follow him, silently watching him, keeping track of his every move – his eyes wild with fear.

'He... he's a liar.'

'You're a psychopath, Emily,' Niko says. 'You knew he would always be too ashamed to report you or talk about it to anyone. Just because he's a guy.'

'He... he cheated on me. Right at the beginning. He's not innocent.'

Christian speaks up. 'I'm not perfect, Emily. I have issues, and you used them against me. But you could have just walked away. You had a choice. You didn't need to break me.' He turns to Niko. 'I made a mistake and cheated on her once, with my ex.

We had a long history together – I'd known her since school. It was complicated.'

'And Kirsty? She's my flatmate. You—'

'That was a misunderstanding. I gave her a compliment and she took it the wrong way. She thought I was coming on to her, but I wasn't. And all those times you made me meet you after work. I was terrified of what you'd do if I didn't turn up. And then I started lying to myself – telling myself I wanted to be there. I couldn't admit that I was scared of you.' His voice crumbles.

Emily shakes her head. 'You turned up at my mum's all those times. Even though you knew I didn't want her to know about you. You came anyway.'

Christian hangs his head. 'Because I was trying to prove to you that I loved you. Turning up to surprise you. Isn't that what people do in relationships? They were gestures I forced myself to make because I was always terrified of what mood you'd be in. Nothing was ever enough to convince you that I loved you, was it? I used to think it was my fault. But tonight I realise it never was. You're the one who's incapable of loving anyone.'

Christian's face merges into her father's, and she hears her mum's wails as he confesses yet another infidelity.

And then she runs.

THIRTY-FIVE

BEFORE

Her feet pound the pavements, the thuds echoing into the night. It's funny how this bustling city can be so deserted at night, as if no one exists behind the façade of houses and flats.

Someone shouts, and she loses her rhythm as she spins around.

Christian and Niko are coming after her. Now that another person has been brought into their circle, one where only two of them have existed until now, Emily knows that nothing will be the same. It's all over.

She runs again. Faster than she thought she'd be capable of, fuelled by the fear of such high stakes. She won't let things change. Darting down side streets, she heads towards the park; she might have a chance of losing them there. It's dark and she'll be able to hide.

She makes it to the entrance, but the gate is locked. It always is at this time of night – something Emily hasn't factored in. There's no time to think, they're closing in on her. She grabs the rails and somehow manages to pull herself over. Searing pain shatters her knees as she jumps to the ground, but she carries on running.

It's too dark, and she can barely see where she's going, but she weaves between trees, praying that they'll lose sight of her. She's outnumbered, though, so how long before she's out of time?

Within seconds she hears heavy footsteps and loud breaths. Arms reach for her, forcefully pulling her in, and she can't tell whether it's Christian or Niko, or both of them working in tandem. Whichever the case, they become a tangled mess of limbs as she's wrestled to the floor.

'Call the police!' Niko shouts. 'I'll hold her.'

A large tree root digs into her back, and Emily stares up at Christian. He hovers a bit further away, as if he doesn't want to come too close to her.

'Please,' she begs, attempting to sit up. 'Don't call the police. I'll stay away from you, I swear. You'll never see me again.'

'No she won't.' Niko shoves her back down, and her back slams into the root. 'She just tried to kill me! What will she do to you if you don't stop her? Just call, or I will.'

As she squirms in his grasp, Christian pulls out his phone and stares at it. She can get through to him. She's always been able to. It's just a matter of finding the right words. 'I love you,' she says, feeble words that evaporate into the cool air.

'People like you make me sick!' Niko says, spitting in her face. 'My sister was abused by someone just like you. She even ended up in hospital.' He turns to Christian. 'Is that what you want for yourself?'

Christian begins tapping into his phone, his breath coming in sharp bursts.

'No!' she screams.

Niko leans forward, his grip tightening. But then his fingers peel away and he staggers back, wobbling on his feet for a moment like a puppet on strings.

Behind him, Christian's wide eyes are fixed on Niko, his phone call all but forgotten. 'Niko? What's wrong?'

Niko tries to turn to him but slowly topples, his body smashing to the floor with an explosive thud.

'What... what did you do?' Christian yells at Emily. He rushes over to Niko and lifts his head, but it flops back down, like a ragdoll's.

'I didn't do anything!' Emily cries. 'What's happened to him?' She can't move – she wants to go to him, to try and help, but her body won't allow her to move.

Christian kneels down and places his head against Niko's chest. 'There's no heartbeat. He's dead!' He vomits all over the ground, right by Niko's head.

He stands up and steps back, his eyes wild with fear. 'You did this.'

'But I didn't touch him!'

'Before! When you smashed his skull! It must be some sort of bleed on the brain or something that didn't kill him straight away!' He clutches his stomach.

'No,' she says softly. 'That can't be right. He... he was fine.' She drops to the ground. When she'd thought he was dead before, that feeling was numbed by her anger at him for trying to kiss her. Now, though, there is only horror.

'What... what do we do?'

'We?' Christian stares at her. 'This is nothing to do with me. *You* did this! I should never have come here,' He grabs at his hair, and Emily's sure he tears a chunk out. 'I'm calling the police.' He reaches for his phone.

She springs up and grabs his arm. 'No, you can't. We're both in this now. Your DNA is all over him. We're in this together, Christian.'

'I don't care – I'm calling the police,' he says. 'I'll take my chances. I haven't done anything wrong!'

Emily grabs his phone and darts back. 'Please, Christian! You're not thinking straight. We need to get out of here. It was an accident. A horrible accident. I didn't mean to hurt him like that.'

'You killed him!' Christian yells. 'That's not just hurting someone.'

'I know, you're right. But we need to get out of here. Our lives don't have to be over because of this... this mistake. There's nothing we can do for him now.' Tears fall from her eyes and blur her vision. 'Please don't call the police. I'll leave you alone – you'll never see me again. Please, Christian.'

When he shakes his head, Emily realises her pleas are futile. There's only one thing she can do now, and she despises herself for it, even before the words leave her mouth. 'If you don't help me, I'll make sure you'll never be free of me. Every time you close your blinds at night, you'll wonder if that shadow in your garden is me. Or those footsteps you hear behind you as you walk home.'

His face crumples, and with his agonising groan, Emily sees with clarity that she needs to change. That the destructive path she's been on has led her to this heinous moment.

'We need to go and check his flat,' she says. 'Make sure there's nothing there of ours. And take his phone and wallet.'

Christian stares at her, his eyes wide with horror and loathing.

'It needs to look like a mugging.'

It feels like an eternity before he responds, and then finally gives a slow, agonising nod. He's a broken man. 'We... we can't just leave him.'

Emily fights back nausea. 'There's no choice. The longer we stay here, the more chance we'll get caught.' She starts to walk away, willing Christian to come with her.

It feels like minutes pass before he finally moves, trudging behind her in invisible shackles.

THIRTY-SIX

NOW

I stand and watch as Christian confesses to Tyler, struggling to comprehend that this is finally happening.

'I forced Emily to make you all believe we were in a relationship,' he admits. 'I blackmailed her into it. Scared her. I told her I would destroy her life if she didn't do what I wanted.'

Tyler shakes his head. 'Why would you do that? And what did you blackmail her with?'

Christian pauses, and I wonder if he'll change his mind about telling his brother everything. Although it's far worse for me, the stakes are high for him too. I glance at the door, terrified of where this will end.

'Because of what she did to me,' he admits. He studies Tyler's face. 'You didn't know anything, did you?'

'About what? I have no idea what you're talking about. None of this makes any sense.' He glances at me briefly before turning back to his brother.

And now, as I listen to Christian revealing to his brother how I broke him down and controlled him, I see exactly why he wanted to destroy me. Why he needed to. We all bear the scars of our trauma.

Tyler's eyes widen. 'Are you saying she was gaslighting you?'

'I don't know what it was, but it went on for nearly two years. She'd force me to meet her at work after every shift. Just so she knew where I was. She made me feel guilty – told me all this stuff about how it wasn't safe for her to be walking home late on her own. How if anything happened to her, I'd feel guilty for the rest of my life.'

Stabs of pain blaze across my chest. I haven't been that person for years now. I banished that Emily. Made sure she could never come back.

'I just couldn't deal with it any more. So I ended things. But she wouldn't accept it. She'd be outside my flat every day. Sending me messages,' Christian says. 'I was... scared for my life. You hear all these stories, don't you? About people killing their exes because they don't want to be with them any more. I was terrified. She'd already thrown heavy objects at me and threatened me with a knife.' He buries his head in his hands. 'And worse than that – I was ashamed of being terrified. I was a grown man, in fear of this tiny woman. Look at her! Who would understand that?'

Tyler's mouth hangs open. He's having trouble digesting Christian's words. And this is exactly the problem Christian would have faced – even more so all those years ago – if he'd told anyone. He looks across at me. 'Is this true?'

My silence is the only answer he needs.

'This is messed up.' Tyler turns back to Christian. Another moment of silence hangs between us all. 'It wasn't your fault,' he says to his brother. 'Size and strength have nothing to do with it. If someone is deranged enough and they want to hurt you, they'll find a way.'

Neither of them understands that I never wanted to harm Christian. All I wanted was for him to love me as he'd promised. To not be like my dad. I see this with absolute lucidity now, and it fills my body with shame. Because I understand now what I didn't then.

The disgust on Tyler's face almost makes me flee. I don't have my car key – it must still be in Christian's pocket – but I can still run, despite my exhaustion.

'The stalking was ruining my life,' Christian continues. 'I couldn't eat or sleep, or study. My whole life was falling apart. So I legged it. I used the money Nana left us and went to Florida. I lucked out. I met some people who helped me get back on my feet. I went to university there and finished my business degree.'

Silence fills the room for a few moments as Tyler continues to take in this new information.

'You could have told Mum and Dad where you were. You should have at least let them know you were safe. They went through so much heartache because—'

'I did tell Mum,' Christian says. 'She knew all of this, but I made her promise not to tell anyone. I had to tell her what Emily had done to me. I needed to keep you all safe.'

And now it all makes sense – how his mother was never there when I called in the days and weeks following Christian's disappearance. How it was only ever Anthony or Tyler I spoke to.

'I was never a threat to your family,' I say, unable to look at either of them.

Christian shakes his head. 'How did I know that? After everything you'd done?'

'Now things are starting to make sense,' Tyler says. 'Mum went to visit you in America, didn't she? All those times she was visiting her old school friend in Florida. It was you?'

Christian nods. 'Yeah. She begged me to tell you and Dad, but I couldn't risk it. I knew Mum would never try to find Emily, to make her take responsibility for what she did – but Dad would have hunted her down.'

The weight of shame becomes almost unbearable, weakening my knees so they threaten to give way. My actions have caused so much pain to Christian. And his family. All these years I've blocked it out, proud to have become this new person who would never dream of doing the things the old Emily did. And I've thrown myself into being a loving wife and doting stepmum. I am not the person I was.

'But why did you come back?' Tyler asks. 'You must have built a life for yourself over there? Met people. And Emily had moved on. She was leaving you alone. She has a husband and stepdaughter. So why now?'

'I *did* move on. It took me a long time to get over it, but eventually I did. But I was always looking over my shoulder. In the end, not every day maybe. Of course there were times when I didn't think of Emily. But it was always there, like a constant shadow hanging over my head. I wondered if there'd be a day when she'd show up and finish what she started.' Christian glances at me.

'What changed then?'

Christian takes a deep breath. 'I got it into my head that I had to check up on her. See where she was, what she was doing. I needed to be sure she wasn't coming for me.'

The hunter became the hunted.

'It felt weird,' Christian continues. 'Doing what she'd been doing to me. Stalking. Infiltrating her life. But it made me feel safe. And then... I found out what kind of life she was living. She was about to get married. Had a ready-made family. And all of this right on the back of Mum's death. It made me insane. To think that she'd got away with...' He glances at me. 'She was a teacher. Doing what she'd always dreamed of. And my life was as fragile as a cobweb.'

I stare at him – speechless because he hasn't mentioned Niko.

Maybe we finally understand each other.

'I snapped,' he continues. 'Then when Mum died, it hit me that Emily had stolen all those years I could have had with her. Not just brief trips to see me. Quality time. Emily had robbed Mum of that, and that tipped me over the edge. I wanted to destroy her.'

I think of all the threats Christian made, how I've feared for my life these last few weeks. I know more than most what we're capable of when we're pushed to our limits.

Tyler moves to the other sofa and sits beside Christian. There's no contact between them but it's the first time I've seen them in solidarity. 'We need to call the police,' he says. 'She's sick in the head. She was trying to convince me and Dad to have you sectioned. She wanted us to believe you were having some kind of breakdown. It was all lies! You could have ended up locked away.'

I try to explain my reasons to Tyler: that Christian was a threat to my daughter, and I needed to protect her, no matter what. Right or wrong, a mothering instinct took over and over-shadowed all else.

'I wish I could believe that,' Christian says. 'But how do I know you weren't only protecting yourself?'

'I'm not the same person I was back then. I told you that, didn't I? When you turned up at my wedding. Couldn't you see that everything about me was different? You must have been able to tell. Nothing about me is the same.'

'My mum always said people don't change,' Christian says. He turns to his brother. 'Do you remember, Tyler?'

Tyler nods. 'I told Emily that. At Dad's house the night you found us talking in the kitchen.' He stands. 'This is so messed up. We need to get out of here. Get away from her.' He practically spits his words at me. 'You stay the hell away from us. D'you hear me?'

Christian stands too. 'Can you wait for me outside? I just need to speak to Emily alone for a second.'

'No way! I'm not leaving you alone with her. What if she—'

'I'll be fine,' Christian says. 'Emily could have let me fall off that cliff just now. But she didn't. She saved my life. I owe her a few minutes.'

For a moment Tyler doesn't move. 'Have it your way. But you owe her nothing.'

As soon as Tyler leaves, Christian stands by the door, blocking my way. 'I'm not letting you run again,' he explains.

I stare at him, and try to decipher his meaning.

'Not this time.'

'Why didn't you tell him? About Niko. And about—'

'Because I don't need to. After everything, I've got my way. You can see that, can't you? There is no way Tia will let Jeremy have custody of Lexi now. Not after all this. It's over, Emily.'

'But it could be over for you too, couldn't it?'

'That's a chance I'm willing to take now. If that's the only way to end this.'

'It's not.' I say.

'I was telling the truth, Emily. I know I wasn't perfect. I was a crap boyfriend. I... I made some stupid mistakes with women, but I never deserved what you did.'

I hang my head. 'I know. You could have just told the police.'

'I was too scared of you.' He looks away, and I see what I did to him all those years ago.

'I left you alone, Christian. After Niko. All these years. I promised you I would and I did. You could have just let things lie. You didn't have to come back.'

'We all have our breaking point. I reached mine. You'd made me an accessory to murder. I had to live with that every day, and I couldn't live with it any more. He was a decent person. He didn't deserve to die because of you. That ripped me apart. Every single day I've lived with his image in my head. I should never have helped you cover it up.'

'Everything changed after that. I became a different person.'

Christian shakes his head. 'But what responsibility did you take for your actions? Did you even wonder about the police investigation?'

I don't answer. How can I explain that the only way I could cope, and maintain any pretence of normality, was to block it all out?

'They assumed it was a mugging,' he says. 'Never caught who did it.' He searches my face. 'Did you even wonder about Niko's family? His parents. And sister. All that devastation you caused them.' He looks away. '*We* caused them.'

We sit with his statement floating around us. His truth.

'What now, then?' I ask. 'You've been threatening to go to the police. You said you have evidence. I'm assuming you mean something that doesn't implicate you too.'

'Maybe I believe in redemption. Perhaps my mum was wrong, and people *can* change. I have. When I came back here it was my pain and trauma driving me. But then I saw what you did for Lexi just now. And maybe partly for me. I'll never know for sure. But I do know that you didn't want that girl to be responsible for taking someone's life.'

He throws my car key and it lands by my feet. I leave it where it is.

'Because killing Niko might have been an accident, but before that you already knew how it felt to take someone's life.'

Some part of me knew I'd eventually hear him say these words, but it still shocks me to my core. 'I... I wanted to explain that to you. And why. You never gave me a chance.'

'Our whole relationship – whatever good parts there were – was based on a lie. I never knew you. And that's apart from all the stuff you did to *me*. I hated myself for so many years for letting you do it. For staying with you. I don't just mean hated myself. I *loathed* my whole being. I felt weak. Stupid. But when I started to look into it, I realised that victims of gaslighting aren't weak – only the perpetrators are. But when I found out the truth about you, that was it. It gave me the strength to walk away.'

'What happens now?' I ask, even though I already know the answer.

'You walk away and we never see each other again.'

'But you want me to pay for what I did. You said you had evidence.' And then I understand. 'You didn't mean evidence about Niko, did you?'

'No. I meant evidence straight from your mum. She told me everything that night I went to see her. I'd gone there to tell her everything you'd been doing to me. We had a good chat. She listened to me and seemed to understand. She told me to get away from you. And that's when everything made sense. Why you were so desperate to keep me away from her. It's not because she didn't want you to have a boyfriend – that may have been part of it, but it's not everything. It's because you didn't want her to talk. But she did. And she told me everything.' He pulls out his phone and flicks through his photos.

He holds the phone up in front of me, and I'm staring at photos of my mum's handwriting. Diary entries. She always kept one. 'I've got the originals,' Christian says. 'She gave them to me. Insisted I have them. I photographed them for extra security.' He watches for my reaction. 'This is the important date,' he says. 'The 21st July 2001. Does that ring any bells?'

My stomach cramps. I've never seen any of my mum's old diary entries – she always kept them hidden away. And when she committed suicide a couple of years after I finished uni, I assumed she must have got rid of them. They weren't in the house when I cleared it out.

'She told me you were sick, and that one day I might need it.' Christian says.

'She was the one who was sick,' I say.

'Yes! Because of you! Surely you see that now?'

He doesn't wait for a reply, but opens the door and steps outside. 'I'm not going to the police, Emily. Because I want to believe that you will finally do the right thing. Yourself. It's the only way you'll ever be free.'

He walks away, joining Tyler by his car.

From the window, I watch them drive off, leaving me alone to face my demons.

THIRTY-SEVEN

2001

She's in her room, with her headphones on and *Whole Again* by Atomic Kitten blaring, but it's still not enough to drown out the sound of her parents fighting in the living room. Again.

It's too hot today, and she can't get comfortable, even with the window wide open. She could do without this. Emily doesn't need to hear the words to know what this argument is about. She might only be thirteen, but she's old enough to know it's her dad's fault. It always is. He's done it again. Some other woman he just couldn't keep his hands off. It's disgusting. Especially when her mum does everything for him. She keeps this family together, and without her everything would fall apart. Why can't he see that?

It doesn't even matter who the woman is this time – names and faces all blur into one; he's not fussy about looks.

Funnily enough, it is her mum whose shouts are the loudest this time. Her high-pitched shrieks mingle with her dad's booms in an ear-piercing cacophony that could surely shatter glass.

Emily flops back on the bed and turns up her music. *Whole Again.* This is how her mum must feel – as if she isn't whole.

Because her dad is constantly ripping pieces of her heart out. Her soul and mind too.

Sometimes her parents can go for a few weeks without this drama, and then just when Emily starts to believe things might actually be better now, it will all start up again. Constant. Endless. Painful.

She feels sick. And she vows then and there that she will never get married. Never. All love does is destroy you. If her mum didn't love her dad then she wouldn't be in such pain now. Even Emily can see that. She switches off her MP3 player and yanks her earbuds from her ears.

Climbing off the bed, she opens her bedroom door and listens. Yes, she was right. Another woman at his office. Twenty-three. It's nauseating.

What Emily can't understand is why her mum lets him get away with it. Again and again. He'll never stop. She needs to leave, Emily's told her that, but all her mum ever says is that Emily's too young to understand. That it's complicated. That love isn't black and white.

Sod that. Surely love means not hurting someone over and over again?

Emily steps out onto the landing. The living room door is closed, as if they think that will stop her hearing. Her mother is no longer screeching. Instead, she howls like a banshee, and in that sound is over a decade's worth of pain.

'You're irrational,' her father is saying. 'You need to get a grip and calm down. I made a mistake, that's all. That girl didn't mean anything. You're the one who's checking my phone all the time, assuming I'm doing something, even when I'm not. How do you think that makes me feel? I might as well do it if you're going to think I am anyway.'

Jerk. He's twisting things to make it seem like it's her mum's fault. How can such a horrible man be her father? She should call him Jack from now on, instead of Dad. Jack the Jerk. Emily smiles to herself.

But it's quickly replaced with tears as her mother's wails grow louder.

'For heaven's sake, Laura – Emily's upstairs and I'm sure she's heard every word you've said. Every name you've called me.'

Emily is outraged. Once again he's turning things around so that it's her mum's fault. She hates him. She wishes he would just disappear.

'It's not her fault!' Emily screams. But maybe the scream is a silent one in her head because nobody responds.

'I'll give you some time to calm down,' her father says, opening the living room door. 'I'll be back later, when you've come to your senses.'

'You're going to *her*, aren't you?' her mum yells. 'More than just a screw is she?' The howling continues.

When she hears the front door of their flat slam, Emily flies past her mum, flinging it open. She needs to make her dad see that he has to stop doing this to her mum. She's got to make him understand.

'Emily, wait! What are you—'

But she doesn't stop to answer. She rushes along the corridor and spots her dad making his way to the communal staircase. He's on his phone, probably calling the woman they've just been arguing about, the one he insisted doesn't mean anything.

She's fuelled with rage; he doesn't deserve to be alive. Emily charges towards him. It's the speed of her moving that thrusts him down the concrete stairs, and Emily stands at the top, watching as he thuds down like an object of some kind, inhuman, his body contorting in ways she would never have imagined possible.

Eventually the noise stops, and he lies at the bottom, his neck twisted so much it almost looks separate from his body.

Then the silence is replaced by her mum's scream, as she appears beside Emily.

'What have you done?' she howls. 'What have you done?'

EPILOGUE

'Emily? You seem to have zoned out. Can you tell me what you're thinking about?'

I turn to Zita, and for a moment I consider telling her it was nothing. A blank moment. I have them sometimes, even though I'm not sure she believes me. Perhaps it's a coping mechanism. Something that will help convince me I have a reason to carry on.

I've promised myself no more lies now. Never again will I utter anything untrue. No matter the cost to me. And my therapist's office is a safe space. Somewhere I won't be judged.

A year ago, at the beginning of our first session, Zita told me she wants me to have no fear of her, or of anything I say to her. 'Just let it all out,' she'd said. 'Anything you want to offload.' Her smile, and her casual jumpers in lieu of expensive suits – which I'd find intimidating – have taught me to trust her.

'I was thinking about my father,' I admit. 'My mind just conjured him up.'

She crosses her legs and leans forward. I've learnt over our year together that this is a sign she's expecting me to spill something huge. Something that will be a breakthrough in my therapy. Words that might be my salvation. It must frustrate therapists when they just don't seem to be getting anywhere with a patient.

Zita doesn't prompt me, but sits and waits, as if she's got all day, her expression soft and compassionate.

I focus on the scent of the diffuser she always has replenished on the windowsill. Flowery. Summery. Bringing that hot, suffocating day back to me. 'I wish I could say it was an accident,' I begin. I can't meet her gaze so I stare out at the flawless sky. Blue. No hint of clouds. Just the same. 'I really wish, more than anything, that...' I pause to gather my thoughts. Although Zita knows what I did – everyone does now – I've never spoken of the details to her.

'But... it couldn't have been,' I continue. 'Not really. It was just something I had to do. To save my mum. That's all I could think about.' I pause again, and stare at my trainers. 'Ironically, what I did made her even worse. Made her who she became. It wasn't my dad who did that, it was me.'

I look at Zita, wanting her to say something, but of course she doesn't. She will just let me speak, and give me the space to figure it all out for myself. 'And I remember... just before I pushed him... I could already see him lying at the bottom of the steps. Not moving. It's as if my mind knew what I would do before my body did.'

'Just remember, you were a child. Barely thirteen.'

I nod. 'Yes, but I was old enough to know right from wrong. And Niko? I wasn't a child then.'

'No, but you thought he was forcing himself on you. Remember, you handed yourself in, Emily. Don't lose sight of that. You could have walked away after what happened at the Lake District and never looked back. But you didn't. You chose to do the right thing and take responsibility for your dad's death.'

I'm grateful that she doesn't say *murder*. I was sentenced on the grounds of diminished responsibility, for both my dad and Niko. Not that it lessens what I did in any way. My dad would still be alive if I hadn't followed him out of the flat that day. Perhaps Mum too.

'You've served your time, Emily,' Zita continues. 'More than that, actually, because you were never able to live normally afterwards, were you? Even when you met Jeremy, your whole relationship was affected by your past.'

On this we can agree.

'Have you ever lined up dominoes to make them fall?' I ask.

Zita frowns. Even though she must be used to my tangents by now, my avoidance of her questions. But this has never been more relevant.

'Once or twice as a child, I think. Why?'

I lean forward. 'Well, you know that first push? It starts off a chain reaction, doesn't it? Everything that happens to the other dominoes is because of what that first domino did.'

She nods. 'Okay. Yes.'

'When I pushed my father down the stairs, it messed my mum up more than is imaginable. She was already fragile – my father had piled years of emotional abuse and infidelity onto her – so she already felt worthless. Paranoid. She was on the brink of a mental disorder, but what I did tipped her over and she never recovered.'

'You were a child,' Zita says, her voice calm and melodic. 'Your brain wasn't even fully developed. Just try to remember that. It's not who you are now.'

'And the hardest part is that after everything I did, Mum still wanted to protect me. We never spoke about it again. Not once.' I spread my fingers out in front of me and stare at my empty ring finger. 'She just called the police and told them my dad had fallen down the stairs. I don't remember anyone ever questioning it.' My breath catches in my throat. 'It must have destroyed her. She loved him. Despite everything, I don't think she ever would have left him. She said afterwards that she would have, but it's doubtful. And then she spent the rest of her life worrying about me. About everything.'

I study Zita's face. I desperately want her to ask me how I got through it. How I lived with myself. But she just sits and waits, her silence urging me to carry on.

'I blocked it all out. That's how I dealt with it. I... pretended it never happened. I shut it down. My brain wouldn't allow me to even believe it. That's how I could keep going to school. Do well in my exams. Carry on.'

'A lot of victims of trauma do that. It's your mind and body's way of protecting you.'

'But then I met Christian. Who, although he wasn't like my dad, was young and a bit reckless. He cheated on me with his ex and I... it set me off.' I've had a lot of time to reflect on this in prison. 'But he didn't deserve what I did to him. It was really my dad I was angry with. Christian took the fall for what my dad did to my mum. He was a man. And all men had to pay. Just another life I ruined.'

'What you needed was help, Emily. And to give you credit where it's completely due, you forged a life for yourself after what happened with Christian. And you saved his life in the end, didn't you?' She removes her glasses and rubs the bridge of her nose before replacing them. 'You were a great parent to Lexi.'

'Don't. Please.' Lexi is someone I still can't talk about. Zita knows this, yet now and again she references Lexi's name, just to see if I'll open up. I understand; she's only trying to help me. But there's nothing to say. I have lost her.

'And a good wife to Jeremy.'

Hearing his name, I picture his neat handwriting in the letter he wrote to me when I was in prison. Christian had told him everything, and Jeremy wrote to me to thank me for protecting Lexi. Of course, he was adamant that I could no longer be in their lives, but the fact that he wrote this meant everything to me. He ended it by saying he would always love the person I should have been.

'The best thing I did for Jeremy was letting him go,' I say.

Zita frowns. 'But you do understand that wasn't your choice. He had to leave. He wanted to. It wouldn't have been right to try and stop him. You see that, don't you?'

'Of course I do.' I try not to be offended by her question. She is right to doubt me. I couldn't let Christian go, after all. Zita once told me that it was probably my dad I'd been trying to cling on to. Almost like a way of saving him, even though it was too late. She offered up the possibility that when Christian cheated on me right at the beginning of our relationship with fur-coat girl – Jada – it triggered a response in me that was really aimed at my father.

Who knows? But whatever the trauma behind my reasons, it doesn't make any of it right.

'And are you still in contact with Niko's sister? Ella?'

I smile. 'Yes. I'm hoping she'll meet up with me one day. I'm not pushing her, but she's hinted that it might be good for both of us.'

Ella is an incredible woman. I couldn't believe it when she replied to my letter, thanking me for finally giving her some closure, and allowing her to heal. It was the unanswered questions that caused even more pain, she'd said.

'That's all very promising,' Zita says. 'And if a meeting is ever on the cards, then I'm happy to help you prepare for it.'

'Thank you.'

I glance at the clock. 'Three minutes left,' I say. This is an arrangement we have: Zita will always let me announce when the session is about to end, rather than her saying it and making me feel that she is just watching the clock the whole time we're talking. It's kind of her to agree to my unusual request.

'Yes, you're right, Emily. That's flown by.' She pulls a tissue from the box on her desk and blows her nose. 'Do you have any plans this evening?' she asks, throwing the tissue in the bin under her desk.

'I have to finish an article this evening,' I say. 'It's for an online magazine.'

'How's that all going?'

I shrug. 'It's early days, but it's going well so far. It pays my rent.' I still can't believe I've been lucky enough to find freelance writing work. It can be anything from magazine articles to copy-editing. I'm able to use a different surname of course, and I chose my paternal grandmother's maiden name. Eden. Emily Eden. There is no more teaching for me now.

'I need to take Lolly for a walk when I get home.' I picture her expectant face as she stands panting at the door when she hears my key in the lock. Her shaggy golden hair shining, and her paws clicking back and forth across the wooden floor. When Mrs Jenkins next door died, her daughter was more than happy for me to give a home to Lolly.

Zita smiles. She has three dogs of her own, so she understands the power of their companionship. 'I'll see you next week,' she says.

'Unless you don't,' I say, standing up and wincing as pins and needles shoot through my legs.

This exchange is the way we always end our sessions; I like to believe that if I say I might not come back, then it will mean I am fully healed. Just another way Zita humours me.

Stepping outside, the sun envelops me in warmth as I begin my walk home, and I feel my mouth turn into a hint of a smile.

Because I have to believe in redemption.

A LETTER FROM KATHRYN

Thank you so much for choosing to read *The Wedding Guest*. This is my twelfth book, and I really hope I'm still managing to infuse my stories with shocks and twists that you really don't see coming. Who doesn't love a roller coaster ride? Once again, I really enjoyed writing it (I always try to write the books that I would love to read) and hopefully you've enjoyed reading it.

If you did enjoy the book, and would like to keep up to date with all my latest releases, please do sign up at the following link. Your email address will never be shared and you can unsubscribe at any time.

www.bookouture.com/kathryn-croft

The Wedding Guest was a story that took even me by surprise, as my characters often went in directions I hadn't initially planned! I hope, above all, that it entertained you, and offered some escapism. If you liked the book, it would be amazing if you could spare a couple of minutes to leave a review on Amazon, or wherever you bought the book. Reviews are so important to authors as your valuable feedback helps us to reach other readers who are yet to discover our books.

Please also feel free to connect with me via my website, Facebook, Instagram, or Twitter. I'd love to hear from you!

Kathryn x

KEEP IN TOUCH WITH KATHRYN

www.kathryncroft.com

facebook.com/authorkathryncroft
twitter.com/katcroft
instagram.com/authorkathryncroft

ACKNOWLEDGEMENTS

So... book twelve. I still can't believe that I'm lucky enough to do this as a job, and it's all thanks to my readers. So, first and foremost, thank you to every single person who spends their precious time reading my little old words – it really means everything.

Lydia Vassar-Smith – editor extraordinaire – your ideas and insights blow me away. And I love the extra comments you add to my line edits – especially the one where you let me know that something made you laugh out loud in this book! Always a pleasure and never a chore to get your edits back. Although, maybe you could stop working so quickly and efficiently so I have more time in between edits?!

Hannah Todd – thank you for everything, and for always being so kind, yet so ready to fight for your authors. You work tirelessly and always listen when I'm having a wobble – thank you, thank you, thank you!

I'm so grateful to have two fantastic teams behind me, so thank you to everyone at Bookouture, and all at the Madeleine Milburn Literary, Film and TV Agency. So much goes on behind the scenes to bring books to life.

Dr Andrew Welch – I owe you a debt of gratitude for answering all the mental health questions I needed to ask to bring authenticity to my characters. If there are any mistakes, they're entirely my own.

Dr Grace Mckee and Dr Phillip Mckee (AKA my parents!) – thank you for answering the horrible questions I'm too scared to google (in case the police turn up at my door asking why the heck I'm looking up how someone can die!)

Michelle Langford – thank you for always responding when I message you with police questions. You and Jo will be pleased that I didn't have too many for this book, so I didn't have to park myself on your sofa for five hours again!

And as always, thank you to all authors who spend hours on end staring at their screens and tapping away on keyboards to keep us all entertained. Reading is still my favourite thing, and books are the answer to all life's problems (for escapism, if nothing else!).

Made in United States
Troutdale, OR
11/15/2023

14601658R00192